Sara dutifully took ~~~~~ ~~~~~ Grissom lifted them.

"Mrs. Salfer?" Sara asked, nodding toward the prints.

Grissom said, "Probably. Do you notice anything about this scene?"

Sara looked around the room and thought back to what they had seen downstairs. "Very clean."

"Exactly," Grissom said. "It only stopped raining a couple of hours ago, rained since noon yesterday. Ground outside should be a mess, and there should be—"

"Water or wet footprints on the floor."

Grissom nodded. "With rigor present, that tells us she was killed last night, during the height of the storm."

"Yet the house is bone dry . . . and so is the body."

"The evidence never lies," Grissom said, "but someone may be trying to lie to us through the evidence."

Original novels in the CSI series:

by Max Allan Collins
CSI: Crime Scene Investigation
Double Dealer
Sin City
Cold Burn
Body of Evidence
Grave Matters
Binding Ties
Serial (graphic novel)

CSI: Miami
Florida Getaway
Heat Wave

by Stuart M. Kaminsky
CSI: New York
Dead of Winter

CSI:
CRIME SCENE INVESTIGATION™

KILLING GAME
a novel

Max Allan Collins

Based on the hit CBS series "CSI: Crime Scene Investigation" produced by CBS PRODUCTIONS, a business unit of CBS Broadcasting Inc., and ALLIANCE ATLANTIS PRODUCTIONS, INC. in association with Jerry Bruckheimer Television.

Executive Producers: Jerry Bruckheimer, Carol Mendelsohn, Anthony E. Zuiker, Ann Donahue, Naren Shankar, Cynthia Chvatal, William Petersen, Danny Cannon, Jonathan Littman

Series created by: Anthony E. Zuiker

POCKET STAR BOOKS
New York   London   Toronto   Sydney

An *Original* Publication of POCKET BOOKS

 A Pocket Star Book published by
POCKET BOOKS, a division of Simon & Schuster, Inc.
1230 Avenue of the Americas, New York, NY 10,20

ISBN-13: 978-0-7434-9664-3
ISBN-10:   0-7434-9664-7

First Pocket Books printing November 2005

10 9 8 7 6 5 4 3 2 1

Cover design by Patrick Kang; cover photos by Donovan Reese/Getty Images

Manufactured in the United States of America

For information about special discounts for bulk purchases, please contact Simon & Schuster Special Sales at 1-800-456-6798 or business@simonandschuster.com

For Lee Goldberg—
media man.

I would like to acknowledge my assistant on this work, forensics researcher/co-plotter **Matthew V. Clemens.**
Further acknowledgments appear at the conclusion of this novel.

"Man's dying is more
  the survivors' affair than his own."
                    —Thomas Mann

"Any man's death diminishes me,
  because I am involved in mankind."
                    —John Donne

"A detective who minds his own business
  would be a contradiction in terms."
                    —Rex Stout's ARCHIE GOODWIN

WINTER WEDGED ITSELF INTO THE *Vegas valley, temperatures turning cold—by Sin City standards, anyway—with a high in the mid-fifties predicted for the coming afternoon. The thermostat had risen sharply after Christmas, and stayed there through the New Year's celebration; but now, a week into another year, a stiff wind blew down off the mountains turning litter into projectiles, women's skirts into billowing parachutes, and walkers into bad mimes trudging forward against frigid mountain gusts.*

Just last night, a half-inch of rain had pelted the area, Mother Nature forcing the desert to acknowledge the change of seasons, if only for a couple of days. Though the temperatures would rise back into the nineties soon enough, the city was currently wrapped in a cold, damp shawl, an indignity this desert fun capital could barely endure. Overhead, dark clouds threatened yet more moisture, and—other than the pedestrians who seemed to constantly patrol the Strip, visitors whose vacations made no allowance for less-than-ideal weather—the city hunkered down, waiting for the arctic blast to slide off to the east, the valley huddling indoors to dream about spring.

Cold did not prevent the tourists from cramming the casinos, while the locals forlornly watched the newspapers and TV, as their chance of winning the major league base-ball franchise (that vacated Montreal at the end of the sea-son) slipped away to Washington, D.C. A groundswell of support in the nation's capital had made the dream of a Vegas major league ball club yet another waking disap-pointment; but there was still the possibility of expansion, and that meant hope.

That was the one thing never in short supply in Sin City: despair's idiot grinning twin—hope. The water table might be coming up snake eyes, the land available for con-struction would possibly be gone in the next couple of years, real estate prices were already climbing toward the top of the tower at the Sphere; but the residents of Vegas still had hope.

As long as the visitors kept coming—and they were, at the rate of nearly one-hundred thousand a day (McCarran Airport had, in fact, just reported a record forty-one-point-four million travelers through its doors last year)—things would be swell, great, terrific, every damn day New Year's Eve.

After all, hadn't this very town—which, in the living memory of some residents, had once been little more than a wide spot in the road—just hosted the second largest New Year's Eve celebration in the United States? Right behind New York's Times Square? More than a quarter million revelers had counted down the last ten seconds in Vegas this year, and—if trends held—even more would be here next year. What said "hope" better than tourists celebrating the *possibilities of the year to come by spending money in your town?*

With the election scant weeks behind him, Sheriff Rory Atwater wasted no time in celebrating the success of the LVPD, pointing to a mere ninety-five ringing-in-the-new-year arrests. Not one to let a good media opportunity slip by, Atwater also informed the reporters that—although crime was admittedly up nine percent in the last year—his department had overseen a major drop in violent crime. In the past twelve months, murders, rapes, robberies, and aggravated assaults were all down; and this year, under his leadership, the LVPD would continue on that road. Keeping violent crime down made the city fathers happy—such statistics ran in papers nationwide, read by countless potential tourists.

And that wasn't the only good news: In the last year alone, a record thirty-seven-point-four million of those tourists had added thirty-two billion dollars to the Vegas economy. With money like that rolling in, the locals told themselves, so what if they ran out of water? You could always drink something a little stronger. . . .

The hypnotic allure the city held over the American public had made several transformations over the course of the sixty years since Benjamin "Bugsy" Siegel had built the Flamingo; but the country's Sin City love affair had gone on, unabated. When the cool, sexy Rat Pack sixties ended, made anachronistic in a country ripped asunder by Vietnam, the casinos experienced a dip in attendance; so (always a back-up plan in Vegas) strategy shifted, eventually turning Sin City into Disney World with casinos.

The tourists had never stopped coming, but their numbers once again swelled. Then when the family atmosphere started to grow tired, the city morphed into a playground combining Sin City of yore with family fun and a large serving of Hollywood glitz, the latter a technique dating back to Bugsy himself.

And more than just tourists came—in recent years an average of five thousand per month took up residence in the Las Vegas valley. Whether drawn by the absence of state income tax, the gambling, job opportunities, or the weather, these new Las Vegans quickly became part of the fastest-growing town in America.

Some hit it big, most do not; but always the hope of something better glimmers just around the corner, and each visitor—whether tourist or new resident—has dollar-sign eyes, hungry with somehow getting a piece of that thirty-two-billion-dollar pie.

Some don't really care how they get it, either—hook, crook; steal, kill. Those who consider themselves above the law, and entitled to their taste of that ever-growing pie, will do whatever they have to, to whomever they have to, to get their "rightful" piece . . . to get what they think they deserve.

The investigators of the LVPD criminalistics bureau—representing one of the most renowned crime labs in the world—feel the same way.

That is, the crime scene investigators also want to see these individuals get what they deserve. . . .

1

Monday, January 24, 6:30 A.M.

Los Calina nestled in the foothills at the far west end of Summerlin. Packed in north of Far Hills Avenue, just west of Desert Foothills Drive, the gated community was a relatively new addition catering to upper-middle-class dwellers of a . . . certain age. Such words as "senior" or "elderly" were not spoken here; and when these folks ate at a restaurant at 4:30 P.M., the reason was preference, not the savings afforded by an "Early Bird Special."

Not as trendy, nor as full of star power, as Lake Las Vegas—its more opulent eastside counterpart—Los Calina ("The Hills" in less romantic English) catered to older money, clients who wished to remain very private while living in something resembling luxury. Residents were mostly well-to-do retirees still able to live independently. Gardening, garbage collection, and other rudimentary services were provided or overseen by the Los Calina Association, in essence overseen by the residents them-

selves. For a retirement community, this made other
local options—even pleasant facilities—seem like
nursing homes without staff, at best, and tenements,
at worst.

A slim but shapely woman in her early thirties,
Sara Sidle—dark hair dangling out under a black CSI
baseball cap, her attractive oval face somber—pulled
the black Tahoe into the Los Calina entrance to stop
at a guard shack that squatted between the IN and
OUT gates. The small, mostly glass structure (about
the size of a double-wide phone booth) was the ar-
chitectural equivalent of the guard who lumbered
out of it, sweat rings on his short-sleeve brown shirt
beneath meaty arms, despite the chill and the
shack's thrumming window air conditioner.

In the passenger seat next to her, Gil Grissom
stared straight ahead; he might have been catatonic,
but was merely absorbed in his own thoughts. Pushing fifty, his hair and trim beard touched with gray,
the CSI supervisor wore his customary loose-fitting
black shirt and slacks, and an identical ballcap to
Sara's. Grissom had never been talkative, but since
the Crime Lab's deputy director, Conrad Ecklie, had
unceremoniously broken up the graveyard-shift
team, Grissom had become ever more interior.

Still, Sara could tell her boss was keeping up the
appearance that everything was fine, as best he
could; but she was attuned enough to him to detect
differences out around the edges. In fact, Sara figured she knew Grissom better than anyone else in
the crime lab, with the possible exception of Catherine Willows (recently appointed swing shift supervisor, but for years, Grissom's right hand).

Sitting quietly behind Grissom was Greg Sanders, the former DNA lab rat who had just completed his final proficiency, his two-tone hair (dark brown, orangeish blond) looking more controlled these days. Slender, with a narrow, handsome face, Greg fixed his eyes on something outside the vehicle—Sara knew that he had long since learned not to make conversation with Grissom, who on occasion still made life hard for the twenty-something former lab tech.

Nonetheless, Sara felt the young scientist—who had taken the "new kid" mantle from her (thank God *somebody* finally had!)—had already turned a corner. The glib, flirty "kid" had receded into a more serious, committed criminalist—didn't take many nights on the streets for a CSI to develop that kind of detached, no-nonsense attitude.

In the seat behind her, the newest member of their *new* team—Sofia Curtis—also sat in silence. Studying the woman in the rearview mirror, Sara thought the attractive CSI with the long blond hair—today pulled back in a loose ponytail—had already shown herself to be a highly competent investigator.

But they should be getting to know one another better by now, only Sara couldn't bring herself to let down her guard. Sofia had been the acting day-shift supervisor, seen by many as the much-despised Ecklie's lap dog. When Curtis had sided with Grissom against the vitriolic Ecklie, the woman had been punished with banishment to the graveyard shift and the recently dressed-down Grissom team.

That should have endeared Curtis to Sara. And,

yet, try as she might, Sara couldn't help but wonder if they might not have a spy in their midst. . . .

Then, shaking her head at her own (probably ridiculous) paranoia, Sara turned toward the square-headed, blunt-featured guard, who awaited like a carhop at her window, which she powered down.

"Can I help you?" the guard asked, and somehow she managed not to request a milkshake.

Not that the fiftyish guard didn't look properly official, clipboard at the ready, EVERETT stenciled on the nameplate pinned to one side of his brown uniform shirt, the other bearing a silver badge with a pressed-in logo—HOME SURE SECURITY.

She lifted her laminated ID on its necklace for his inspection. "Crime lab."

"Oh." His face saddened. "You must be here for Mrs. Salfer. . . ."

She nodded.

"Pity. Nice lady."

Leaning over toward Sara, close enough for her to get a whiff of the scent of his soap, Grissom asked the guard, "Have you been here all night, Mr. Everett?"

"Nope," the guard said, shaking a concrete-block head that seemed to swivel on his shoulders without benefit of a neck. "Jack, the night guy, he called in sick—flu. Going around, cold weather maybe."

"When did you come in, Mr. Everett?"

"About five."

Sara checked her watch—six-thirty. Why all these cases seemed to fall toward the end of shift was a bigger mystery than most of the crimes themselves.

Grissom was asking, "And who was here over-night?"

The guard looked at the shack like the answer might lie inside.

Grissom frowned. "Don't you know, Mr. Everett?"

He shook the blocky head. "Place was empty when I got here; we been short-handed. Office called me to come in early, so I did—don't know what the problem was, if any. Could be nobody was out here from eleven last night till I come on."

"The 'office' called you?" Sara asked. "What office is that?"

He thumped his badge with a forefinger. "Home Sure. We have the contract for security here at Los Calina."

Grissom's smile was faint. "How long do you anticipate holding onto that contract?"

The guard sighed. "Yeah, I know. No one in the guard shack, and here we have a . . . a damn murder, or something. Hell of a thing."

"Isn't it?" Grissom said pleasantly. "Thank you, Mr. Everett."

And the CSI supervisor sat back, eyes forward, in a manner that told Sara it was time to move on.

Sara said to the guard, "Thank you, sir," and powered up the window.

Giving them a nod, the guard backed away, then returned to his shack; you could almost see the sweat rings growing, despite the "cold" that was giving everybody the flu.

After a moment, the gate slid open, and Sara eased the SUV through, rolling twenty feet to a stop sign at a T-intersection. Houses went off in each direction, side streets veining to God only knew where.

"Which way to Arroyo Court?" she asked Grissom.

Sofia leaned forward. "Left here, then take the first right; then, when you can, another left."

"You've been here before?" Grissom asked without looking back.

"Just a couple months ago," Sofia said. "I did a seminar on identity theft for the residents. That was at the main office building. Which is the other way, to the right; but they showed me around while I was here."

"You're good," Sara admitted with a smile.

Sofia said, "Call it a gift for street names."

The streets in question wound past lines of stucco houses, both one- and two-story, all looking new and fronted by a lush carpet of green grass—a real rarity in these drought-stricken days.

Sofia's directions, not surprisingly, turned out to be right on the money, and they were soon parked in front of a large, two-story tile-roof stucco, with a two-car garage attached on the left; and the lawn looked every bit as well-maintained and manicured as the others around it. This struck Sara as decadent, in an oddly mundane way.

Two cars had beat them here: an LVPD squad in front of the Tahoe, and Brass's familiar Taurus, parked in the wrong direction on the other side of the street. A blue-and-white golf cart—a clear plastic covering protecting it from the rain, and the Home Sure Security logo painted on the front—was nosed in at an angle, not quite pulled into the driveway, and an ambulance in the driveway itself. Right now the EMTs were packing up their gear and loading it back into the ambulance—obviously in no hurry.

Sara hated seeing the defeat on their faces. She'd talked to enough of these men and women, over the years, to know that they were well aware they couldn't save every one on each call; but that didn't stop them from trying . . . or from feeling like shit when death won another one.

Already in strictly-business mode, Grissom said, "Big house."

"Evidently," Sara said, " 'retired' doesn't mean you have to downsize."

"Not in Los Calina," Sofia said.

They looked at her.

She smiled and shrugged. "Residents here run the full gamut—from wealthy to *very* wealthy."

"What if you're wealthier than that?" Greg asked, his eyes full of the impressive home. "Say—*stinking* rich?"

"You live at Lake Las Vegas," the two women said simultaneously.

They laughed, and Sofia said, "Bread and butter," and Sara enjoyed the brief bonding, while Grissom looked at them like they were at least mildly mad.

Recovering her sanity, Sara asked, "What do we know about this?"

"Four-ninteen," Grissom said. "Probably a four-twenty, if the EMTs are right . . . "

Four-nineteen meant a dead body, four-twenty a homicide. If you were the victim, Sara thought, you were having a bad day, either way.

Grissom was saying, "According to Brass, the EMTs think she may have been strangled."

"She?" Sofia asked.

"Mrs. Grace Salfer," Grissom said without referring to his notebook. "Owner of the home."

Sara had a feeling Sofia was wondering why Grissom had waited until they'd got here to share this; but Sara was used to it—Grissom often did that, preferring background information to have the context of the crime scene itself.

As they climbed out of the Tahoe, Captain Jim Brass—his suit a cloudy-sky gray, his face a somber mask—exited the house and started down the driveway. A rather small woman in a Home Sure Security uniform trotted along in his wake like an eager puppy.

From the back of the SUV, Sara yanked her crime-scene kit, then came around to see Brass heading in their direction; when the detective abruptly stopped, the woman tailing him nearly crashed into his back.

Grissom and Sara approached Brass, Sofia just behind them.

"What do we know?" Grissom asked.

Eyebrows lifted in Brass's otherwise blank countenance. "Just what I told you on the phone—dead body in an upstairs bedroom. Grace Salfer, woman who lives here. Lived."

"Nothing else?" Grissom said.

Brass almost smiled; almost. "Gil—you think I haven't learned not to disturb your crime scene, after all this time?"

"Have you?"

Sara glimpsed Sofia trying to figure out whether

Grissom was kidding or not. Good luck to her on that.

The short female security guard was next to Brass now, like a high-school football player on the sidelines dogging the coach's heels, hoping to get in the game. Her eyes were green and ever-moving—though Sara couldn't quite characterize them: *nervous or searching?*—in a long, thin face that belonged on someone much taller. Straight nose, high cheekbones, very little makeup except for some not-too-red lipstick, blonde hair licking at her shoulders, the guard whose nameplate said GILLETTE was in her mid-twenties at most; and—though the brown and tan uniform fit her all right—the black webbed belt with a flashlight and pepper spray gave her the appearance of a child playing dress-up.

"Did the security service call it in?" Sara asked, referring to the woman but addressing Brass.

"No," the detective said.

Before he could say anything else, Gillette interrupted: "Alarm didn't trip, for some reason."

Grissom's head made a mechanical turn toward the guard. "And you are?"

Mild irritation digging a hole in one cheek, Brass answered for her: "Susan Gillette—guard patrolling the neighborhood overnight. She—"

"Never got even a *buzz* on the alarm," Gillette said, as if completing Brass's sentences was something she'd been doing for years. "That sucker should have gone off like a thousand screaming babies, if someone broke into the house."

Brass closed his eyes, and Grissom smiled mildly and said, "Colorfully put."

Gillette shrugged. "Well, Mrs. Salfer was hard of hearing . . . not that that's a rarity around here . . . but anyway, she had the XLR-5000."

The guard imparted this latter piece of information as if everyone on the planet, or at least in law enforcement, would know exactly what she was referring to.

"Did she now?" Grissom asked. "And what is the XLR-5000?"

"The loudest alarm Home Security stocks, for private homes. And trust me, I've heard *hers* go off enough."

"Really?" Grissom's eyes tightened and his lips moved, as if he were consuming this knowledge. "Then this isn't the first problem at Mrs. Salfer's house?"

"Well, it's the first *real* problem. Her alarm was always going off, and . . . Look, maybe Mrs. Salfer and I didn't get along so great, but I would *never* have ignored a call if the alarm went off."

Grissom arched an eyebrow. "Didn't get along?"

The guard looked sheepish. "She thought her XLR-5000 going off all the time was *my* fault."

Brass looked sideways at her. "The alarm went off 'all the time'?"

"When she first moved in it did," Gillette said, nodding vigorously. "The techs were out three times, and it's been fixed. Either that, or she turned it off."

From beside Sara came Sofia's voice: "You're the only one patrolling, Ms. Gillette? This is a pretty good-size community."

"Yes," Gillette said, "and no."

They all just looked at her.

"I mean yes, it's a pretty good size . . . and no, I'm not the only one that patrols at night."

"How many of you are there?" Sara asked.

Gillette held up three fingers and said redundantly, "Three during the day and evening . . ." Two fingers. ". . . two of us, overnight. Bobby Ranson, the other overnight guard, he left at end of shift. I rushed right over here as soon as I heard that something was wrong."

"If there was no alarm," Grissom said, "who called the police?"

They all turned to Brass, including Susan Gillette, who had lost (probably just momentarily) her ability to read the detective's mind.

"Next-door neighbor," Brass said. "Carmon Perez—she's an early riser. Looked out her kitchen window and saw a ladder leaned up against Mrs. Salfer's house and thought it looked suspicious . . . too early for repairmen. From her angle, Mrs. Perez couldn't see that the second-story window was open, but the ladder was enough to make her phone Mrs. Salfer. When there was no answer, Mrs. Perez got anxious and called nine-one-one."

Grissom's head was to one side. "A ladder?"

"Yeah," Brass said. "Looks like someone broke in. There's—"

"An aluminum ladder up against the house in the back," Gillette said, her psychic network connection with Brass reestablished. "And some footprints nearby. Whoever it was went in through the second-floor window."

Grissom's frown was barely perceptible. "Was the crime scene disturbed?"

"No! I walked around the house and saw the ladder. As soon as I did, I went back around front."

Tightly, Grissom asked, "Weren't there any officers at the house?"

This seemed as much addressed to Brass as the security guard.

Gillette nodded. "Yes, and Captain Brass here pulled up, right when I was coming back around the house. I let them all in with my key, and the alarm wasn't on."

"You mean, it wasn't ringing?"

"No. I mean, yes it wasn't ringing. No, it wasn't even *set*."

Grissom frowned. "And it should've been?"

Gillette nodded again. "All Los Calina residents are strongly advised to set their alarms at night."

Measuring his words, Grissom said, "Sofia, you and Greg take the exterior, starting with Security Guard Gillette's shoes."

"My *shoes?*" Gillette blurted.

Grissom continued as if she hadn't spoken. "Sara and I will take the interior."

Gillette, small but feisty, got right in Grissom's face. "What do you want with my shoes?"

"You walked through my crime scene," Grissom said, his smile small yet somehow enormously reproving, his tone as mild as if he were ordering coffee.

"Uh, with all due respect, what makes this *your* crime scene? We're all law-enforcement professionals here."

"I'm the lead crime-scene investigator. That makes it my crime scene . . . but I'm not greedy. I'm going to share it with these other crime-scene investigators. With all due respect, *you* are a security guard who trampled through my crime scene, and turned her shoes into evidence. Those shoes will be processed, in part as an effort to eliminate you as a suspect."

"*Suspect?*"

Grissom's voice remained soft, calm. "This is Greg Sanders—give the nice man your shoes and he'll give you a set of plastic slippers."

"I don't have to give you my shoes—do I?" Her volume was lower now, matching that of the serene Grissom, only with a pitiful edge.

"You do. Greg? Would you help Ms. Gillette?"

To Sara, the exchange had been like watching one of those old movies of the snake charmer hypnotizing a cobra with a flute.

After a few moments of stunned silence, Gillette followed Greg to the SUV for the shoe exchange.

While Sofia stayed outside to process the entry point, Sara and Grissom followed Brass through the front door. A few seconds were required for Sara's eyes to adjust to the darkness within, but soon she found herself in a wide foyer with a Mexican tile floor. To her right, a round dark three-legged table made a home for a smoked glass vase filled with fresh lilies; maybe fifteen inches in diameter, the black lacquer table stood about thirty inches high and was covered with gold flowers. A spindle ran down to a much smaller flowered circle that sat upon three carved legs, the feet of which also bore the gold flowers. The table, which was museum quality, seemed from a different time altogether.

"Golden Khokhloma table," Grissom said, as he watched her study it.

"Golden . . . what was that?"

"*Hok-lo-ma*. The process is very old . . . around the time of Peter the Great." Grissom was spellbound now, his eyes affectionately taking in the table. "The 'gold' is actually powdered aluminum, not covered by the black lacquer. Gilded wood, they called it. Very popular. Collectors would kill for a table like that—but not tonight, since it was left behind."

He moved off into the living room to the right. Sara stood there wondering if there was anything in the world the man did not know. To her left, a long staircase with a dark banister rose to a second-floor landing off of which were three doorways, one open; that would wait. For now she followed her boss into the living room.

It was larger than her own living room, dining room and kitchen combined—Sara couldn't imagine having this much space at her disposal. Windows consumed the wall to her right, morning sun already leaking in, taunting Sara as her shift ended but her work continued. A tan leather sofa faced a thirty-six inch TV on a far wall otherwise taken up by book-shelves, a single arm chair angled, a squat coffee table providing a place for a neat pile of mail, stacked magazines, a remote control for the TV, and a pair of eyeglasses.

At left stood a four-panel Chinese screen across which flew four cranes, hand-painted on silk—symbols of happiness and long life in Chinese mythology. (Did Grissom know *that*? Probably.) In any case, their meaning rang empty for Grace Salfer, right now anyway.

The only thing out of place in this immaculate room was a pair of slippers under the edge of the coffee table.

Next, she followed Grissom and Brass upstairs to the master suite where the victim lay in bed, blankets pulled back, probably by the paramedics. Brass positioned himself to stay out of the CSIs' way but to take everything in; Sara knew of no detective on the LVPD more sensitive to the needs of a crime scene—but, then, he had once been supervisor of the crime lab himself.

This chamber was elegant and simple, a Mediterranean dresser next to the door, a taller, matching chest beyond the foot of the bed. The bed itself had four spindle posts and a matching nightstand on the left with a paperback book, a plastic daily pillbox, and a wind-up alarm clock.

On her back, one leg drawn up and bent out, her arms spread, Grace Salfer resembled one of the cranes painted on the screen downstairs. She wore navy blue lounging pajamas and nylon anklets. Her top, open at the throat, revealed no ligature marks.

The woman had been beautiful once, her eyes closed now, her features at peace.

Sara noted the short-trimmed, well-groomed white hair; high cheeks with just a hint of sag to them; straight nose; sharp chin; lipsticked lips crinkling up at the corners, as if death had been welcomed with a smile.

"Blue tinge," Grissom said, gesturing to the victim's face.

"She didn't die on her back," Sara said. "Otherwise, I'd say Mrs. Salfer just went to bed and to sleep."

"But not perchance to dream," Grissom said.

Rigor had already started to settle in. That meant the victim had been dead for somewhere between six and twelve hours. Autopsy would give them a more exact time.

Bending over the corpse, Grissom carefully lifted the woman's left lid and revealed one large, lifeless green eye.

"Petechial hemorrhaging," Grissom said.

"Possibility she was strangled," Sara said. "No bruising or other apparent hand marks on the throat . . ."

Not having budged from his position, Brass glanced around the room. "Doesn't look like she put up much of a fight. Suprised her in bed?"

"Pillow maybe," Sara said.

"Here's a thought," Grissom said. "While we're building hypotheses, let's also look at the evidence."

This sort of prickliness was hardly unusual for Grissom, but Sara couldn't help wondering if his irritability quotient hadn't risen since his dressing down by Ecklie.

Why was she thinking about this, and not the job at hand?

Partly, she was tired, a trifle punchy; but more than that, all this political infighting was taking its toll on her—on *all* of them. Ecklie had them looking over their shoulders, instead of concentrating on the case. Though one day she intended to be a supervisor herself—and exposure to the political b.s. that went with the job was a good learning experience for her—she also knew that until Ecklie was out of the equation, a supervisor slot was not for her: he wouldn't offer it, and she wouldn't take it from that jerk even if he did.

"For one thing, there's lividity in the face," Grissom was saying, pulling Sara back to the scene. "Vic was on her stomach for some time before she was turned over. Or *moved*. . . ."

Brass finally came closer. "Moved?"

Grissom nodded. "She's in bed here, but her glasses and slippers are downstairs."

Sara said, "I noticed those—didn't put it together, though. Nice catch."

"Thank you."

Her eyes went to the doorway. But why would the assailant move Mrs. Salfer upstairs, after killing her? And if he or she waited long enough to move her, so that post-mortem lividity set in . . . what was he doing during the interval?

"Didn't you hear me?" Grissom asked.

Hear him what? Sara wondered. "Sorry," she said. "I was . . . thinking."

"Thinking is allowed. But we also need some photographs."

"On it," she said, happy to have evidence to concentrate on instead of supposition.

She withdrew the camera from her case and snapped away at the body, often following Grissom's lead—he pointed to some faint bruising on the woman's neck and Sara took close-ups. He also found carpet fibers in the victim's hair, which Sara recorded with the camera before he put the fibers in an evidence packet.

"Bedroom floor is hardwood," Sara said, lowering the camera for a moment. "Only carpeting's in the living room, downstairs."

"Which is where she was killed," Grissom said. He threw her a smile. "*Keep* thinking."

Slowly, they worked their way out of the bedroom, then back to the first floor and, finally, back up to the rest of the second.

The only thing they had to show for their efforts so far were smudged prints Grissom got off five keys of the alarm keypad, some footprints gleaned from the Mexican tile floor in the entranceway . . . and even those were piled on top of each other, all the people who'd been in and out of the house since the call came in: EMTs, uniformed officers, Brass and both CSIs. And those were just the ones Sara knew off the top of her head. The victim's footprints would probably be in there too, and buried in among all those would be the killer's.

They found the open window on the second floor in a back bedroom made up to be a guest room. Small and tidy, the room had a twin bed you could bounce a quarter off, a dresser and mirror next to the door, and a short chest of drawers opposite the bed. The room appeared perfectly clean, a guest room that seemed never to have housed a guest.

Sara photographed the window and Grissom dusted the sill and frame, as well as the mirror (frame and glass) and the tops of both the chest and the dresser. They found only two prints, on the top of the dresser. Sara dutifully took pictures before Grissom lifted them.

"Mrs. Salfer?" Sara asked, nodding toward the prints.

Grissom said, "Probably. Do you notice anything about this scene?"

Sara looked around the room and thought back to what they had seen downstairs. "Very clean."

"Exactly," Grissom said. "It only stopped raining a couple of hours ago, rained since noon yesterday. Ground outside should be a mess, and there should be—"

"Water or wet footprints on the floor."

Grissom nodded. "With rigor present, that tells us she was killed last night, during the height of the storm."

"Yet the house is bone dry . . . and so is the body."

"The evidence never lies," Grissom said, "but someone may be trying to lie to us, through the evidence."

Sara wasn't sure she followed that, but said, "Yeah," anyway.

Outside they found Greg and Sofia in the backyard. Greg had camera in hand while Sofia put down a scale-providing ruler next to a footprint in the flower bed. Beyond the footprint, an aluminum ladder leaned against the house under the open second-floor window.

Grissom told the pair what he and Sara had found inside. "What have we got?" he asked.

"Two footprints in the mud," Sofia said. "But there's something about them I don't like."

"What's not to like about a footprint?" Grissom asked innocently, but Sara thought she was finally following him.

Sofia was new, but she knew enough not to bite. "Take a look, Grissom—and *you* tell *me*."

Squatting at the edge of the flower bed, Grissom studied the footprints. Over his shoulder, Sara looked at them, too: prints were even, and surprisingly well defined, considering the inclement weather last night. The ladder leaned against the house, its feet flat on the wet dirt. Something wasn't sitting right with her, either; but Sara couldn't quite nail it . . .

"You know," Grissom said, pointing to the prints, "I don't like 'em, either."

Sofia nodded and Greg inched closer to get a better look.

"They're too well defined," Grissom said. "With last night's weather, these prints should be a mess."

Greg said, "You couldn't find more perfect prints outside Mann's Chinese in Hollywood."

Grissom glanced up, Greg flinched, but then the supervisor smiled and said, "Aptly put, Greg."

Greg grinned.

Sara wasn't grinning, but she was nodding herself.

"They should be deeper, too," Sofia said.

"Deeper?" Greg asked.

"Yes," Grissom said. "These prints belong to about a size-ten man's shoes. Judging from the depth of these impressions, he weighed, oh . . . a hundred pounds."

"Child, maybe?" Greg offered.

"In size tens?"

"Same with the ladder," Sara said, gesturing. "If a man of normal weight for the size of these prints had climbed this ladder, the feet would be buried in the mud. And they're not."

"And where's the mud on the rungs?" Grissom asked, standing. "Only, they're clean." Hands on hips, he surveyed the scene, shook his head, smiled slyly. "No. Somebody thinks he . . . or she . . . is cute. This is all staged. Inside and outside both. And I *hate* cute."

"Complete agreement here," Sofia said. "This is orchestrated, all right."

Sara felt a ball of anger forming in her stomach. "Somebody thinks we're stupid."

"Which is the killer's *second* mistake," Grissom said, and cast a beatific smile upon his crew. "The first was thinking we'd let anybody get away with what was done to Grace Salfer."

2

CATHERINE WILLOWS WAS RARELY GIVEN to interior conflict.

As an LVPD crime scene investigator, she met conflict—or its aftermath—on her every working day. She had always sought to keep her relationships with both her family and her coworkers straightforward, with no game playing. Though not exactly confrontational, neither was she one to brood. She could face a problem unblinkingly, whether it was a crime she was assigned to solve, or a fellow professional with an attitude, or, for that matter, her daughter Lindsey with a school-related issue.

Her feelings about Conrad Ecklie—and the change and even turmoil the deputy director had created by dividing up the nightshift team of CSIs— were decidedly mixed. As Gil Grissom's second-in-command on graveyard, Catherine had developed a dislike for Ecklie, tinged with disrespect, largely due to the man's political gamesmanship and his jealous attempts to sabotage Grissom, an exemplary crime scene investigator who had—without at all trying— commanded respect and attention not just in Vegas but on the national scene.

Right now, however, her loyalty for Grissom— who had gone from mentor to partner in a demanding field whose rewards and costs were equally high—had come crashing up against her own needs and goals. She had warned Grissom countless times, had approached him in every conceivable manner, to try to get him to . . . *just a little* . . . "play the game." To accept and grasp the reality of politics and personalities in a department the size of the Las Vegas Police.

She hadn't been alone. Jim Brass, himself a victim of political pressure—Grissom's supervisor's chair had once been filled by the homicide detective—had ca- joled and pleaded at every step between, trying to get Grissom to come to grips with not just office politics, but city politics. The system claimed casualties every day—Sheriff Brian Mobley, for years the most pow- erful figure in the department, was gone now—and Grissom's oblivious, even condescending approach to this personality-driven, hidden-agenda-riddled world had put him on a collision course with his arch-rival: Conrad Ecklie.

And Catherine found herself in the middle, torn by friendship and loyalty, lured by advancement and self-interest. Ecklie had been fair to her, and even good to her. Rising to shift supervisor meant more pay, more responsibility, and the achievement of a long-held goal. A woman—no matter how skilled and how deserving, despite the system's paying lip service to equal rights—did not get this kind of opportunity every day.

Not that the swing shift was ideal: She had seen Lindsey more while working graveyard than she did now. These days she often left for her job before Lindsey got home from school, and Catherine missed those precious evening dinners and helping with the young girl's homework.

But if Catherine was ever to achieve her ideal assignment—day-shift supervisor, which gave her both a home life *and* a great job—she would have to play the game herself; she would have to make "nice" with Ecklie. Unlike Grissom, she had the ability to be at least partly a political animal. But did that make her a traitor to her friend and mentor?

She told herself no—she had warned him time and again, and even Gil admitted that this was a bed he'd made himself. Still, the space between herself and her old night-shift teammates Warrick Brown and Nick Stokes—transferred with her to swing shift—had changed somehow; she was not just their colleague but their boss now, and she found herself wondering if either CSI secretly felt she'd sold out Grissom, who had mentored them as well.

And when Catherine ran into Sara Sidle, the ice in the air was noticeably brittle. Only Grissom himself—was that Zenlike quiet he projected real, or was he raging within?—had treated her with understanding.

And when Gil Grissom was the most compassionate person in her world, Catherine knew things had turned upside down. . . .

The sky hung purple and red-striped as night crept over the mountains like a sneak thief, the breeze carrying a chill warning of real cold to follow, when darkness came. The temperature hovered around fifty and would dip closer to freezing by morning.

Nick was driving the Tahoe toward North Las Vegas, Catherine in the passenger seat, Warrick in back. Though everything seemed normal enough, she noticed that no one had really spoken since the three had climbed into the SUV—strange, after all this time together, to have a new awkwardness set in.

Nick's eyes were glued to the road, headlights on for safety, the beams barely visible in the fading light. He also had the blue flasher on, but no siren, as he wove in and out of traffic heading west on Craig Road. He wore a navy CSI-logo windbreaker and navy slacks, his dark hair cropped close to his skull. As Catherine stole a sideways glance at him, she admired the strong jawline and square chin that, in profile, gave him an aura of strength.

"What's the vic's address?" she asked, as much to break the silence as to gain information.

Still keeping his dark eyes forward, Nick said, "North Las Vegas—apartment complex, Red Coach Avenue."

He blew through the Martin Luther King Boulevard intersection and continued west on Craig.

They lapsed back into silence and Catherine couldn't help but wonder, if only for a moment, how Grissom was getting along with his new team—newbie Greg, outsider Sofia and the sometimes troubled

Sara. She grabbed the safety handle as Nick made a right, then a quick left and they ended up going west on Red Coach Avenue.

Where cases in the more affluent areas of Las Vegas proper would draw a small army—three or four squad cars, two or three detectives, an ambulance, maybe even a fire truck or two—in this North Las Vegas neighborhood, only one lonely NLVPD squad car at the curb, its lights no longer flashing, sat sentinel.

Nick drew up behind it and a patrolman climbed out of the waiting squad car. Catherine recognized him—Nissen, an officer she'd seen at various North Las Vegas crime scenes over the last several years. On the job for maybe ten years, Nissen typically wore his dark hair short, kept his dark glasses on most of the time, and he had wide-set dark blue eyes when he chose to reveal them. He also normally had a ready smile, which seemed M.I.A., his square-chinned face a grave mask, eyes hooded, the dark glasses dangling from a shirt pocket.

The rundown three-story white stucco apartment building, with tile-shedding roof, was midblock on a street lined with similar structures, none particularly inviting. In this neighborhood an Extreme Home Makeover would begin with a can of gas and a match. Cars, mostly Rent-A-Wreck refugees, lined the street as if hoping to be stolen, and Catherine wondered who actually parked in the lots around back.

They were out of the Tahoe and unloading equipment from the rear by the time the uniformed officer strode over to them. Warrick, crime kit in hand, a smile creasing his coffee-colored face, was the first to greet the guy. "Hey, Nissen—what's up?"

"Murder," Nissen said, automatically reaching for the notebook in his pants pocket. "I think the vic's name is Angela Dearborn."

Nissen was a good cop and usually friendly; cutting straight to the crime—no small talk—meant something nasty awaited them inside that stucco shambles.

"No detective yet?" Nick asked, glancing around.

Nissen shook his head. "Supposed to be here by now; must be running late."

The detective would not be one of their usual LVPD mates, rather a North Las Vegas plainclothes, drawing from a decidedly spotty roster—could be someone young, or seasoned, or a bored old hand playing out his string. With a detective this late to the scene, Catherine's money was on one of the latter. Unfortunately.

"Where's the vic?" Nick asked.

"Third floor, in the back," Nissen said. "Apartment twelve. You won't need a key: door was unlocked when I got here—that's how I got in. No obvious signs of forced entry."

Catherine asked, "What did you say her name was?"

Without checking notes, Nissen said, "Apartment's rented to a woman named Angela Dearborn. My guess is that's her, upstairs."

"Who called it in?"

With a nod back to the building, the officer said, "Next-door neighbor—Nellie Pacquino. Said she heard yelling yesterday evening."

"Yesterday," Catherine said thoughtfully. "So why is she calling it in *today*?"

"Mrs. Pacquino said she saw the vic every day. She hadn't seen her neighbor stick her head out of the apartment since Sunday, so finally she got worried enough to make the call."

"Would have been nice to have her get concerned a little sooner." Catherine shook her head. "Were they close?"

"Not really. They sometimes had coffee together, before they went to work, but it was hit or miss. They left for their jobs about the same time every day, and neither rarely ever misses work. Plus, they got home at about the same time every afternoon, so they'd bump into each other on the stairs, in the hall."

"So no coffee, no hallway banter before or after work, and Mrs. Pacquino gets to wondering."

"Right. Knocked on her neighbor's door, got no answer; called over there, same thing. Looks out the window, sees Angie Dearborn's car is still in the lot back there. Thinks about the yelling, day before."

"And finally makes the call," Catherine said, and sighed. "It's hell when the cavalry comes, the day after."

"My gut?" Nissen asked.

"Please."

"Goddamn frustrating. What might've been just another domestic violence call that we coulda broke up turns into something really bad. . . . All 'cause the neighbor drags her feet, getting involved."

Warrick, behind Catherine, offered, "We can't show up *until* they call, can we?"

"No," Nissen said. "No we can't. But I don't have to like it."

"No you don't," Warrick said pleasantly. "But if we beat ourselves up for that every time it happens, who'll call nine-one-one to stop *us*?"

Finally Nissen flashed his nice smile—just for a moment—and, leaving the officer on the street, the trio walked single-file up the sidewalk, past the dirt yard, to the front door. They were just about to enter when a dark blue Taurus rolled up to the curb—the unmarked police car had a dented front left fender and a broken headlight. And, trained sleuth that she was, Catherine suddenly knew why the detective was running late. . . .

Climbing out of the car, the plainclothes man looked their way with an apologetic shrug and half-smirk. Catherine was relieved to see who they'd drawn from the NLVPD pool: lean, lanky Marty Larkin, his longish black hair swept back, was coming around the car, looking it over glumly like an insurance adjustor having a bad day.

Larkin flipped a wave to Nissen, who nodded. Likely the best detective on the North Las Vegas PD, Larkin—not yet forty—was smart, clean, experienced, and it didn't hurt that he had deep brown eyes and eyebrows that arched in fifty different ways, depending on whether he was being sarcastic, funny, or flirting, the latter something he did fairly often with Catherine, without crossing any professional border.

This evening, the handsome detective's mouth was etched in a line so straight it might have been drawn with a ruler. Wearing a black suit with a black shirt and matching tie, he would have looked characteristically sharp if he hadn't been rubbing at his left leg as he limped up the sidewalk to join them. Some felt Larkin dressed *too* sharp—that citizens might mistake him for a show-biz guy or even a mafioso; but Catherine liked the man—he did the job well and played by the rules.

"You look like you've had a swell day," Catherine said, with her own arch of an eyebrow.

Larkin flashed his boyish smile, his eyebrow arching back at her. "I think I just met my future ex-wife."

Catherine laughed lightly and said, "Is that right? Love and hate at first sight?"

The detective shrugged, and embarrassment colored his normally confident face. "Yeah, sometimes it just hits you—like, I was coming north on Allen. At Craig, she turned in front of me." He pointed back to the fender and headlight. "She said she didn't hear the siren or see the lights. Listening to her Michael Bublé CD, too loud."

Nick grinned, a hand on one hip, crime kit in the other. "Don't tell me—you let her off with a warning."

Larkin shook his head. "Dude, the chief would so *not* understand! Hell, I gave her the ticket she deserved!"

Nick's smile turned skeptical.

"Of course, I *am* going to let her buy me dinner tomorrow night . . . to make up for my pain and suffering. And I'll take care of the damages to my vehicle."

"Somehow," Catherine said, "I think the damages

are just about to begin. . . . Can you interrupt the fascinating story of your love life, to take a look at what promises to be a disturbing crime scene?"

"Let's do this thing. And I do apologize for my lateness."

Actually, Catherine—despite her businesslike demeanor—had appreciated the brief moment of levity. Based on Nissen's words and, even more, his manner, she knew that things were about to turn deadly serious.

Noting twelve metal mailboxes, Catherine figured the three floors meant four flats to a floor, two on each side, the first floor having garden apartments. The stairs from the entranceway to the second floor smelled like urine and wet dog. Curving around to the right, Catherine headed up to a landing, then another right turn and the last flight up to the third floor.

Cooking smells, something Asian maybe, replaced the foul stairwell, emanating from the apartment immediately to her left, number ten. Nine was across the hall, eleven beyond that, twelve would be the last door on the left. Catherine detected no smell coming from the latter. The door was shut but not locked (as Officer Nissen had indicated) and they let themselves in.

Finding usable, meaningful prints on the knob would mean winning the lottery. There was no telling how many people had touched it since the crime, and Nissen had used it to gain entry himself.

Catherine was first inside; she felt a wave of sadness roll through her. In early years, that wave would have been nausea: now, a miasma of melancholy.

This happened to her more often than she would like to admit; but she had seen this scenario far too many times. The apartment, little more than a shoebox with windows, had been trashed: cushions off the sofa, TV smashed on the floor, the victim's possessions pulverized, shattered and scattered.

A woman in her early thirties lay in the middle of the mess, an abandoned broken toy.

One leg bent up at an obscene angle, her arms spread crucifix-style, flesh covered with indigo welts, her auburn hair streaked black/scarlet, her face raw, blood-caked, and purple-bruised, crystalline blue eyes staring sightless at the ceiling. She wore only denim shorts and a white, maroon-spattered *Romanov Hotel & Casino* T-shirt. The victim's nose had been broken, her high cheekbones bashed in, her full lips split, blood caked like cheap lipstick, her teeth broken, some missing, others jagged shards, forming a macabre smile.

Whoever did this had not just wanted to kill the woman, rather to punish her—make her suffer. If the victim was beaten to death with fists, somebody's hands would be bruised and scraped, at the very least. If she was battered with a weapon, where *was* it?

Catherine quickly scouted the rest of the tiny apartment. The living-room curtains over a modest picture window were tight-drawn; an overhead light, already on, provided illumination. This room joined a tiny dining alcove where a table and two chairs lay tossed beneath a low hanging ceiling light, also burning. Beyond that, a tiny galley kitchen also had been thoroughly trashed, its light not on, casting the area in shadows.

Beyond the living room, to the rear of the apartment, a short hall led to a bedroom that might be generously described as petite, as well as a minuscule bathroom. Both rooms had also been ransacked.

The three CSIs spread out, the detective watching, staying out of their way; all wore latex gloves.

Nick took photos. Warrick started sifting through the bathroom debris, and—while she waited for someone from the coroner's office—Catherine had a closer look at the body, Detective Larkin looming nearby.

"Who called this in?" the latecomer asked.

"Next-door neighbor," Catherine said. She glanced up at him and gave him half a wry smile. "Because she heard yelling—last night."

Eyes rolling, hands on hips, Larkin said, "Looks like goddamned World War III in here, and all she heard was yelling? And didn't call it in till *when*?"

"Less than an hour ago," Catherine said.

"I'll get the background from Nissen," Larkin said tightly, "and have a talk with this good citizen."

The detective marched out of the apartment, his jaw set, his eyes ablaze. The neighbor was about to have an unpleasant conversation, which was fine with Catherine. Angela Dearborn had gotten a hell of a lot worse.

With Larkin gone, Catherine got to work processing the victim, starting with Angela's hands. The autopsy would reveal the extent of the wounds, give them some insight into the weapon used to cause those injuries, and other information; but any trace evidence—say the killer's DNA under the vic's fingernails—might get lost in transport . . . and Catherine wasn't about to let that happen.

The CSI started with the left hand of Angela's wide-spread arms, the one nearest her. The hand was a milky white, made more pale by death. Long, elegant fingers splayed wide, a gold ring with a line of inlaid colored stones encircled her middle finger. Clear polish covered the neatly trimmed nails.

This was a pretty hand—an artist's hand.

Catherine steeled herself, trying to keep the sadness rising within from transforming itself into rage. Her job required coolness, dispassion. Even now, when she was a supervisor herself, she could not stop the mental reflex: *What would Grissom do?*

A nasty blue bruise covered most of the back of Angie's hand, as if she had raised it just in time to receive the full impact of a blow. Judging by the shape of the bruise, and the way it crossed the entire back of the hand, the blow had been struck with a cylindrical object.

Looking around the room, Catherine sought possibilities: Her eyes noted beer bottles, round-based lamps, but already she was thinking that the killer might have used a weapon, a baseball bat, for example, that had been brought along, and taken with.

She returned to the hand, carefully scraping under the nails to be rewarded with a few skin cells. Most likely, in a battle this intense, Angela had gotten in a few blows of her own, including scratching the killer either on the face or an exposed hand or arm.

Good girl, Catherine thought. So often the victim provided the very evidence that meant the perpetrator's downfall.

After sealing the small evidence envelope housing her prize, Catherine moved on to the other hand, whose nails rewarded her with more skin cells. She also noted and photographed defensive wounds on that hand, as well.

They were nearly an hour into working the scene, and Catherine was just finishing processing the corpse, when the coroner's crew finally arrived to pick up the body.

David Phillips, Coroner Albert Robbins's chief assistant, led the way. Medium of build and height, David had thin brown hair and ever-questioning eyes behind dark-rimmed glasses. Behind him, a two-man team guided a gurney: the front one, tall and thin with sandy hair and glasses, the one on the back end shorter, dark-haired and just as skinny as his taller buddy. Catherine wondered idly how this slight pair would manage the gurney down three flights of stairs to the street.

"David," Catherine said, by way of greeting.

He gave her a tight smile in return. "Homicide, huh?"

"Homicide."

Part of her didn't want to surrender Angela Dearborn to the coroner's crew, even David, whom she trusted implicitly. All CSIs, all cops for that matter, had certain hot buttons among criminals; for example, they all despised child molesters. Some of them found a way to harden themselves against crimes committed against women; but Catherine had never managed.

Though she hardly considered herself a radical feminist, she did carry a core belief that a crime of violence against one woman was a crime of violence against all women.

She had admitted this to Grissom once, and he'd said, "I agree, but I would widen that."

"How so?"

"A crime of violence against one of us is a crime of violence against all of us."

Noble words, and correct; but Catherine still retained a special empathy for victims like Angela.

Every bruise, every scratch would be detailed for her report. She finished her search for hairs on Angela's clothes, found a few, gathered them, then finally—reluctantly, almost sorrowfully—she turned Angela Dearborn over to David and his assistants.

"Are you all right, Catherine?" David asked her, with genuine concern.

"What? Uh. Sure. Fine."

"Been wild lately, all these changes. Congratulations, by the way."

"Thanks. Thank you."

The two men were carefully loading the body onto the gurney, covering Angie with a sheet, strapping her down.

David swallowed, nodded toward the victim. "You'd think something like this wouldn't get to us, after a while."

She smiled a little. "Shame on us when it doesn't."

He smiled back, nodded. "We'll have something for you as soon as we can."

Then he was following the gurney and the body out.

Returning to her work, Catherine studied the floor beneath where the body had rested, if you could call that "resting." This cheap carpeting might be able to tell her almost as much as the body itself.

Nick and Warrick had both moved into the bedroom now. Catherine closed that door on them, and turned off the overhead lights. She was down on her hands and knees—going over the dirt-gray carpeting with an Alternate Light Source—when Larkin came through the front door and hit the light switch.

Her head popped up and she decided not to swear at him, when she saw his doleful expression. At least he was still wearing his latex gloves.

"Find out anything?" she asked.

Larkin nodded. "Nellie Pacquino is a party animal. She heard the yelling around six last night, but being inclined to rowdy partying herself, didn't think all that much of it."

"Some party."

"Anyway, Nellie went out all night and got in just around sunup. She decided to stay up for her morning coffee klatch with the vic, but when she knocked on the door, she got no answer."

"The door was unlocked. Didn't she try the knob?"

"She says she didn't. She just went to work as usual, knocked on the door when she got home, and tried calling the Dearborn woman, too; and when she didn't get an answer again, she called us."

"If I hadn't wanted to preserve this crime scene, I'd've asked you to bring Nellie in to I.D. the body." Catherine gestured to where the victim had been. "We don't really have an official identification yet."

As Catherine was saying that, Nick was exiting the bedroom; he had something in his latex-gloved hand—a small blue wallet.

"I'm not often right on cue," he said, "but how's this for service?"

Nick held the wallet in one latexed hand and opened it with the other, to display Angela Dearborn's driver's license, along with a photo that— even with all the brutality the victim had suffered—was clearly a match.

"Thanks, Nick," Catherine said.

"I have my moments."

Nick briefly returned to the bedroom, to bag his find, and returned to move past the upturned dining table. Soon he was shining his flashlight into the shadowy depths of the kitchen. After a few seconds, Catherine saw the glow of an overhead light, once Nick found the switch.

Turning back to Larkin, Catherine asked, "Did the neighbor have anything else to say?"

"She was pretty broken up, seemed real enough; but said that Angie had an ex-husband that gave her some trouble from time to time."

Back of her neck prickling, Catherine asked, "What *kind* of trouble?"

A knock at the door headed off Larkin's answer.

Catherine and the detective traded a glance before

Larkin answered the door, where Officer Nissen handed the detective a piece of paper, then disappeared back down the hall.

Grinning as he shut the door, Larkin said, *"Everybody's* on cue this evening," then he read the sheet and made a click in his cheek.

"What?" Catherine asked.

Larkin waved the sheet of paper. "You wanted to know what kind of trouble Angie Dearborn had with her ex? Well, before I came back in here, I got Nissen to run him through the computer, just to see what crops up. Name's Taylor Dearborn. Guy's a career lowlife . . . and the victim had a *restraining* order against him."

"Well, that seems to have worked out well," Catherine said dryly. "Who says the system doesn't work?"

Larkin, apparently channeling Grissom for a moment, said, "Catherine, we don't know that yet. Just 'cause he's a wife beater that doesn't mean he's our guy. Just that he's, like I said, a lowlife."

"Point well taken. . . . What kind of lowlife?"

Larkin grunted a non-laugh. "Drugs, breaking and entering, assault on Angie—quite a laundry list, plus a lot of petty stuff."

Nick came out from the kitchen. "Could it be we have a slam dunk, for a change?"

Larkin said, "Wouldn't that be nice, for once?"

Catherine said, "Yeah, well, I can't tell you when we *ever* had a slam dunk. You got to work to win in this town." She dropped back down to study the carpet some more. "And that means, collect the evidence. . . . Marty, could you get that light?"

The detective flipped the switch, the room going almost black, the only remaining illumination from the kitchen's overhead light. Turning on her ALS, Catherine bent down and resumed combing the carpeting with the UV light.

"I'm going to canvass the rest of the building," Larkin said. "Maybe we'll get lucky and find a witness who saw Taylor leaving this apartment."

She looked up at Larkin, and quoted him: " 'Just 'cause he's a wife beater that doesn't mean he's our guy.' "

They exchanged grins, and Larkin was gone.

She could hear Warrick moving around in the bedroom and Nick clicking photos in the kitchen. Blowing out a long, deep breath, she looked through the orange filter attached to the pen-sized ALS.

The carpeting was light blue with hints of sea green and purple in an indiscriminate pattern designed to hide both wear and dirt. Though a fair amount of the former was evident, little, if any, of the latter showed up. Angela Dearborn had been a meticulous housekeeper. That much was clear, even among the detritus of what must have been a horrible struggle.

Spots darker than the purple in the carpet presented themselves—spots that fluoresced nicely under the glow of the UV light, blood droplets that raised up in several places, small scarlet periods punctuating the violence that had occurred here. Marking each one with a small plastic, numbered A-frame, Catherine documented the site. At one point, she found a single, long, dark hair, definitely not the same color as Angie's. After carefully photographing it, Catherine used tweezers to pick up the hair, then—studying it for a second—deposited it in a cellophane evidence bag, which she sealed.

At some crime scenes the team would scour for hours, seeking a solitary scrap of evidence. In the Dearborn apartment, everywhere Catherine looked she saw another piece of potential proof. Maybe Larkin was right; maybe they did finally have their slam-dunk case. The lab results would tell. In the meantime, she would follow the evidence wherever it led; but if it pointed to Taylor Dearborn, with his history of violence against his ex-wife, she would allow herself a sense of satisfaction for removing him from society.

The brutal clash had carried through the entire apartment, and the trio spent the better part of four hours sifting through everything. Catherine offered a silent *thank you* that the apartment wasn't any larger, or they would have been on overtime; and now that she was a supervisor, she had a budget to deal with.

You needed patience for this job, she knew that; and she had plenty—what single mother could survive without it? Still, in a city the size of Las Vegas, even as she was working one crime scene diligently, between one and six more would be turning up. This ugly fact she could not dare forget—not in her new position.

Once they had finished, packed up, lugged their gear down the three flights back to the SUV, and loaded, Larkin came over to join them behind the open back door of the vehicle.

"Any good news?" he asked.

"Well, Nissen was right," Catherine said. "No signs of forced entry. She probably let the killer in."

"Probably *knew* the killer, then," Larkin said. "Anything else?"

Catherine looked at Nick, but it was Warrick who spoke. "More like *everything* . . . except maybe the kitchen sink."

"Kitchen sink, too," Nick said with wry frustration. "I found blood drops there, and more in the trap underneath. Almost *too* much evidence. . . ."

Warrick withdrew an evidence bag from the rear of the Tahoe. Inside the clear bag, on a light-blue men's dress shirt, spatters of blood were plainly visible. "This was in the bedroom, tossed in a corner."

"All this blood the *victim's*?" Larkin asked.

Catherine gave him a look. "Marty, you've been doing this long enough to know we can't tell you that till we get back to the lab and test it."

Bouncing from one foot to the other, like a boxer warming up before a big fight, Larkin said, "I know, I know, I'm just getting antsy to pay our new pal Taylor Dearborn a visit."

"You have an address for him?" Catherine asked.

Larkin waved his notebook. "Right here."

Looking at Nick, she said, "You guys take everything back to the lab—I'll go with Larkin to inform Dearborn of his ex-wife's death."

Nick nodded, Warrick remained silent and put the evidence bag back into the SUV.

"I'm sure he'll be stunned and surprised and saddened," Larkin added sarcastically.

Catherine arched an eyebrow. "Aren't you the same guy who was warning me about jumping to that conclusion?"

"Hey—even if he's innocent, he's a prick who beat up his wife and got a restraining order slapped on his ass."

Warrick laughed. "How do you guys out here in North Las Vegas manage to stay so objective?"

"Go to hell, Warrick," Larkin said, but he was smiling.

Catherine's cell phone rang; she yanked it off her belt and hit the button. "Willows."

"Catherine," said a cheerful, even charming voice. Conrad Ecklie.

"Conrad. We're just wrapping at a crime scene."

Ecklie's voice remained sweet, but artificially so— he was the NutraSweet of CSIs. "Hope you didn't forget our meeting tonight—about the swing-shift budget?"

Shit.

She had.

"No, of course not," she said. "But I always remember what you say—the crime scene should take precedence."

Conrad Ecklie had never said this to her. Gil Grissom had. But she knew how Ecklie would reply. . . .

"Absolutely," Ecklie said. "It's my mantra. How are Brown and Stokes making out there?"

He said this as if the two longtime, stellar CSIs were new recruits.

"Doing fine. The best."

"Well, they're both competent crime-scene analysts. And I admire your loyalty. . . . I'll wait for you here, but hurry, will you? We're already late."

Catherine considered screaming, then said, "Looking forward to it."

"Just a small piece of constructive criticism,, Catherine. Putting the crime scene first is commendable; but you yourself say Brown and Stokes are capable people."

"Right . . ."

"Now that you're a supervisor, you need to start thinking like one. When necessary, delegate. See you soon."

He clicked off.

Forcing herself not to show her irritation to her colleagues, she said, "I need to get back to the office—who wants to accompany Marty to see the ex-husband?"

Nick and Warrick looked at each other. Nick gave a little shrug. "Warrick's probably a little less likely to clock the guy."

Warrick said, "I'm in."

Larkin said, "Let's get going," and he and Warrick did.

Alone with Catherine now, Nick asked, "Mind my asking? The phone call?"

"Ecklie," she said. "Budget meeting."

Nick shook his head in sympathy. "Guy's more worried about the price of paper clips than catching a killer."

Catherine almost seconded that; then she remembered what Ecklie had said: *Now that you're a supervisor, you need to start thinking like one.*

"Ecklie's got a job to do," Catherine said. "Just like us."

"I suppose," Nick admitted.

"Nickie—you know me well enough to realize I'd never let bureaucratic b.s. come between this team and bringing that poor woman's murderer to justice."

And they set out to do that very thing.

3

Monday, January 24, 11:30 A.M.

EVIDENCE STOWED IN THE BACK of the Tahoe and otherwise packed up, CSI Supervisor Gil Grissom gathered his team—Sara Sidle, Greg Sanders, and Sofia Curtis—on the sidewalk in front of the Salfer house.

The morning sun was losing its struggle to break through the overcast clouds, the sky a tarnished silver, the wind whistling through the gated community. Even so, morning had clearly arrived, putting their nightshift designation to the test. Neighbors now peeked through curtains to get a better view of the commotion in front of Grace Salfer's place. Few watched for long, however—ambulances arriving in a rush, and leaving in no hurry, were a part of life in a community awaiting death.

Brass joined the CSIs. They watched as the ambulance pulled away, taking Grace Salfer from the comfort of her Los Calina residence to a waiting steel autopsy tray in the domain of Dr. Albert Robbins.

Grissom was well aware that some considered him a cold fish, a scientist whose emotions—if any—were buried deep; but the truth was he felt the loss of life of each murder victim with a profound melancholy that the alchemy of his will transformed into resolve—resolve to see that a woman whose long life had ended in pointless violence would at least find justice.

Greg Sanders, heels of his hands on his haunches, risked a nervous smile. "Meanwhile, back at the lab?"

Sara stood with arms folded tightly, shivering at the morning cold; so did Sofia, making unwitting twins of the pair.

Grissom did not respond to Greg. His eyes were searching the grounds for the Home Sure Security golf cart. "What became of our fellow 'law enforcement professional?' "

"Uh, Susan Gillette?" Greg suddenly looked worried; had he goofed? "Security guard left as soon as I took her shoes. Was I supposed to—"

"You did fine, Greg." Grissom granted his charge a brief smile, knowing how edgy Greg could be around him at a crime scene; but that would improve—actually already had. "No reason to hold her."

"Ah. Good. Excellent."

"I just wanted to know if a Home Sure technician had been here to examine the alarm in the last week or so."

"I didn't think to ask."

"Well, neither did I, till just now. I'll get the information from their office."

"Home Sure, you mean?"

"Yeah. Meantime, we need to get one of our own techs out here to go over that alarm, and determine if it's been tampered with."

Sara had taken her cell phone out halfway through that. "How about Hendricks?"

"Call him," Grissom said to her. "Perfect man for the job."

The CSI supervisor sent Greg, Sofia, and Sara back to the lab in the SUV with what little evidence they had gleaned. Along with Brass, he remained at the Salfer house and waited for the electronics whiz.

Barely fifteen minutes after Sara's call, Hendricks drew up to the curb in an unsightly, battered gray van far older and closer to the bottom of the department-vehicle food chain than the Crime Lab's high-end SUVs. Next to the electronics van, Brass's standard-issue Taurus looked like a tricked-out ride. Misunderstood by much of the department—even among the more eccentric personalities in the lab—Duane Hendricks was a first-rate expert in his field. Even Grissom had to admit the guy was an odd duck, endlessly discussing such disparate obsessions as the Kennedy assassination, Shecky Greene, and Britney Spears.

Hendricks emerged from the van like a skeleton reassembling itself. Nearly six-five but likely weighing in at maybe one-fifty, with long, stringy, blond hair, and black glasses too big for his spade-shaped face, Hendricks wore torn jeans, and a black T-shirt with some undefinable skull logo. He might well have been a rock group roadie, lost and stopping for directions to the gig.

He ambled up to Grissom and offered a thin-lipped smile. "Hey, Gil." The tech gave only a noncommittal nod to Brass. "I just got to work and caught the call in the locker room—hope you don't mind the street clothes."

"Duane," Grissom said, "glad you were available. Ready to get to work?"

"Always. Electronics never lie—drive you crazy, but they never lie. . . . Sara says you guys have an alarm you want me to have a gander at. In there?"

"In there."

They began toward the house, and the electronics whiz said, "What's new with the bugs? Win a race lately?"

Grissom smiled sideways at the tall tech. "Actually, yes. My new star's named Strip Search."

"Ha! Cool connotations—mucho meaningful depth."

Brass had a glazed look and was making no effort to join the conversation.

But the exchange between tech and CSI revealed another reason why Grissom liked this so-called oddball. Hendricks never thought it weird that Grissom trained and raced roaches, and he always asked about them, sincerely interested, accepting the creatures as Grissom's pets and even close friends (some days, they were).

On the front stoop, the whiz asked, "What would you like this alarm to tell you?"

"If it's been tampered with—when, how; and could it have simply been shut off at the security-company office? And if so, can you be sure enough to call it evidence, and not opinion?"

"Electronics don't lie. Show me the baby and I'll teach it to talk."

Brass finally entered in. "That simple?"

The shaggy head nodded. "Once I know what I'm looking at . . . and get inside it."

"Well," Grissom said, opening the door, "keypad's around to the right."

They stepped inside and shut themselves in.

Hendricks regarded the keypad like a safe-cracker might a wallsafe, Grissom and Brass giving him breathing room.

Brass said, "Security guard unlocked the door when I got here—the alarm *not* turned on."

"But we found fresh fingerprint smudges on the keypad," Grissom added, "indicating it'd been used recently."

Hendricks nodded. "Meaning somebody turned it on or off . . . or both."

After the CSI instructed him to wear latex gloves and avoid surfaces within the device that might hold a fingerprint, the tech went right to work.

Then Grissom and Brass watched as the technician removed the keyboard's face plate, set the cover aside, and carefully freed the keyboard of its casing. Gesturing with his head, Hendricks called Grissom to his side and handed the CSI the guts of the alarm keypad.

"Hold still," Hendricks said.

The keypad lay face down, flat in Grissom's latex-gloved hands, a nest of wires curling up still attached to the wall, maybe eight inches away. Using a small Maglite and a tool that looked like a dental pick at one end and a screwdriver at the other, Hendricks poked and prodded at the wires and the connections.

Brass took a step closer. "Should you be able to open that so easily?"

Shrugging and half-smirking, Hendricks said, "Not much of an alarm—seven-digit key. Sends a signal to the Home Sure office—that's the phone line you see—and there's a siren to insure that the burglar gets plenty of warning to clear out before the guards show up. Also, probably gives the homeowners a heart attack, particularly in this neighborhood; and gets the neighbors in the act, too."

Brass winced. "And that's it?"

"That's about it," the tech said with another shrug. "Some alarms are state of the art—this one is bottom of the barrel."

"But it's a gated community," Brass said. "Big money, to live here . . ."

That got yet another shrug from the technician. "Home Sure provides security, but figures they'll never need anything but the most perfunctory gear."

Grissom said, "Gated community—security people patrol the grounds, and all the windows have Home Sure stickers—usually burglars avoid any house that might have any kind of security."

"Yeah," Hendricks said, "if they're never going to need it, why put in anything good? You know electronics—the current stuff is hugely expensive, but five year's ago's model goes for a song."

"True enough," Brass said again.

"Me, I'll stick with *my* security system, which with my JFK website I may damn well need."

"Boy," Brass said, "*you* must really have a state of the art system."

"I do," Hendricks said with a crooked grin. "A Rottweiler."

Grissom and Brass traded a look.

"Anyway," Hendricks went on, "from what I can see, this puppy hasn't been tampered with, phone line connection's intact, audible alarm hooked up— but there's no way to tell if it's still linked to the home office."

"If the electronic link to the master alarm system *has* been switched off," Grissom said, "can we tell where that happened? Here at the keypad, or at the home office?"

"Can't tell you just from eyeballin' it. You'll have to access Home Sure's records. They'll have 'em, even for cheap-jack crap like this."

"Why?" Brass asked.

"Insurance liability. If the homeowner requests it be turned off at the security office end, and then gets robbed, Home Sure will have a record to protect 'em from frivolous lawsuits."

Brass nodded. "Why would Mrs. Salfer have shut it off?"

"Maybe there's a short that caused the siren to keep going off, inadvertently," Hendricks said, "and the old gal got annoyed."

Grissom said, "According to the security guard we spoke to earlier, a Susan Gillette, Mrs. Salfer was in fact having problems with the device."

Hendricks grinned evilly. "Wanna see why she would?"

Then, without further warning, he used the

screwdriver end of his tool to undo a connection and pop loose the wire.

A siren screamed, filling the house.

Brass's mouth was wide open, making a sight gag—it was as if the detective were the source of the screech—but Grissom was too busy trying not to drop the keypad to be amused.

Hendricks reattached the wire and the sound ceased. "I rest my case."

Brass seemed to be contemplating how many years he'd get for strangling the stringy tech as Hendricks snugged down the screw again. When he finally spoke, he did so slowly. "Well, thank you, Duane," he said acidly, "for the generous demonstration."

"Hey, you're welcome," Hendricks said, oblivious to the detective's sarcasm. "This'll also let ya check out the response time of the golf cart patrol."

Grissom and Brass went out to stand on the front stoop while Hendricks put the keypad back together again.

Three minutes and a few seconds later, a Home Sure Security cart rolled up to an abrupt stop, and a big guy climbed down out from behind the wheel, calling from the driveway: "What's the *deal*, anyway?"

Brass crooked a come-here finger.

The big guy in the brown uniform sighed and trudged up the driveway.

The detective stepped down from the stoop and met the guard, who planted himself before the homicide captain with hands on hips.

This specimen of Home Sure's crack force stood at least six-five and weighed in the neighborhood of three hundred pounds, which stretched the limits of his uniform, not to mention the golf cart. The guard had light brown hair parted on the right, a mustacheless goatee that gave him the look of a bad guy wrestler on TV. The nameplate on the guard's shirt read: GOFF.

"Our technician was just doing a test on the alarm," Grissom said.

"Yeah, well we know you're working a crime scene here. But how 'bout a little professional courtesy?"

Grissom just looked at the man; Brass the same.

"I mean, if you guys think all I got to do is run around answering false—"

"I don't care what you have to do, Mr. Goff," Brass said, stepping up to the much bigger man. "This is a homicide investigation—a murder that happened on your company's watch, by the way— and we're going to do what *we* need to do."

The two men's eyes locked and held.

Grissom watched in fascination this wordless battle of wills. Just as the rabbit instinctively understands it shouldn't mess with the dog, this rabbit—although of Harveyesque proportions—somehow suddenly knew not to further bait the alpha canine, even one of Brass's pit bull dimensions.

The battle, therefore, was brief, the guard grinning awkwardly. "Well, of course, obviously, we wanna cooperate any way we can with you guys."

His dominance established, Brass asked not unpleasantly, "Were you responding because you heard the alarm go off, Mr. Goff?"

"No—I was a couple of blocks over." A thumb gestured over a shoulder. "The alarm tripped at the home office."

Grissom asked, "So this home alarm sends a signal directly to the Home Sure office?"

Goff nodded. "Then they radio the carts and the gate shack."

Frowning, Grissom said, "Still, it took you a good three minutes to get here."

Glancing at the cart with a wry smile, Goff said, "These things aren't exactly built for speed. Like I said, I was a couple of blocks over, and out of the cart—talking to a resident."

Grissom asked, "What's the response time when there's only one cart—like last night?"

The guard pondered that momentarily. "If the guard's on the other side of the compound? Could take five minutes, maybe six. No more than that, though. Why do you ask? My understanding was Mrs. Salfer's alarm didn't go off, last night—not the audible here *or* the silent downtown."

"That's right," Brass said. "We're just covering the bases. What's the procedure, when the alarm *is* tripped?"

"When the call comes, we roll to the house. Next, we ascertain *why* the alarm tripped . . . and call you people in, when appropriate."

"And it's not always appropriate."

"No. Actually, hardly ever is. See, sometimes these alarms, they just . . . go off."

"Really."

"Yeah, really. The equipment is, frankly, not the greatest—shorts out sometimes. Also, people might go on vacation, leave a door ajar or something, wind blows, door opens, alarm goes off. Or one of these old folks gets up in the middle of the night and wanders into an area with motion detectors. Tons of harmless ways they can go off. Hey, we try not to bring you guys out here for no reason."

"We appreciate that," Brass said. "What's the rest of the procedure, for a false alarm?"

"Not much to it. Guards have keys to all the residences, and the keypad codes—it's just a reset job."

"That happen often?"

Goff shrugged with one beefy shoulder. "Few times a week. These alarms weren't designed to protect Fort Knox, you know."

Hendricks came out on the stoop, saying, "He's got that right. . . . I'm done, by the way."

"Thank you for your help, Mr. Goff," Brass said. "Care to do me one more professional courtesy, and supply the address of Home Sure's main office?"

"Sure," Goff said.

Brass jotted the address in his notebook and Goff elaborated: "Down Charleston, over by the hospital."

"Thanks," Brass said. He turned to Grissom. "Finished here?"

"For now," Grissom said. "Mr. Goff can lock up the Salfer house."

"You want me to set the alarm?" Goff asked.

Brass frowned. "What? Why?"

"I mean, it's a crime scene, right? Wouldn't want anybody tampering with it."

Brass smiled, nodded, said, "With you people on patrol, we should be fine," then out of the guard's sight rolled his eyes at Grissom.

But before the man got very far, Grissom said, "Uh, Mr. Goff?"

The guard turned.

"What's to stop one of your Home Security force from using a key to enter a residence? Then, using the code, shut down the alarm before it went off?"

Thinking about it, Goff said, "Nothing."

Grissom nodded. "Thank you, Mr. Goff."

"Hey, but if you mean *Susan*, hell—she'd never do that. She's honest as the day is long. She wanted to be a cop, I mean *really* wanted to be a cop, but she was too short. You know they have these dumb rules and restrictions that keep a lot of good people off the LVPD."

"That wasn't an accusation, Mr. Goff," Grissom said with a gentle smile. "Just a hypothetical."

And Grissom thanked Goff who—satisfied with Grissom's response—nodded and returned to his golf cart, which (like its driver) was certainly not built for speed.

Turning his attention back to the tech, Grissom asked, "You get anything else, Duane?"

Hendricks shook his head. "Alarm looked fine. No internal tampering."

"Nothing else?" Brass asked.

"Like I said, electronics don't lie, Captain—but sometimes, unfortunately, they don't have much to say."

Brass had no reply for that.

When the lanky tech and his gray van had gone, Brass asked Grissom, "What about these fingerprints off the keypad you mentioned?"

"Hendricks says it's seven digits to key the alarm. There were smudges on five keys; other five were clean."

Brass frowned. "Only five keys? So, what . . . the other keys were wiped clean?"

"Probably not," Grissom said. "More likely, numbers repeat in the code. And the smudges were existing prints possibly made that way by gloves worn by whoever last accessed the keypad."

"You think Mrs. Salfer *did* set her alarm, then—and the killer turned it off?"

"It's a workable hypothesis."

"That's your way of saying 'hunch,' right?"

Grissom gave Brass a small grin. "No need to be insulting."

When Sara and Greg entered the autopsy room, Dr. Albert Robbins—the man they expected to find presiding over Grace Salfer's autopsy—was nowhere in sight. Across the room a body covered with a white sheet lay on one of several steel tables. The fluorescent lighting heightened the chamber's typically icy feel, which only seemed to warm in the presence of Robbins himself.

Enjoying the momentary solitude, Sara glanced over at Greg, who was shivering; and when the door at the far end of the room opened and Dr. Robbins came in supported by his metal crutch, Greg actually jumped a little. Robbins still wore his blue scrubs, but his plastic face shield and white paper breathing mask had been set aside.

Balding, his beard gone mostly to white, this was a man who had long since come to terms with a life filled with death; as properly serious as any coroner, he nonetheless had eyes that could laugh and was possessed of an impish smile, though neither were on display at the moment.

"Sorry I wasn't here when you came in," he said,

leaning his crutch in its familiar resting place in the corner. "I finished a few minutes ago and stepped out for some coffee. You haven't been waiting long?"

Sara shook her head. "We just got here."

He moved next to the body under the sheet. They stood on the opposite side, their eyes automatically going to the victim as Robbins pulled back the sheet to reveal her head and neck. Grace Salfer's short-trimmed white hair and lipstick still seemed almost perfect, as if death itself could not rob her of dignity. The smile she had worn in her bed was gone now, her mouth a narrow line.

"Your victim was strangled," the ME said. "A definite homicide. There's petechial hemorrhages in the conjunctivae."

Although a good sneeze might cause some clotting, the petechial hemorrhaging in the conjunctivae—the mucous membrane lining the inner surface of the eyelids—was considered a presumptive test for strangulation.

"Manual or ligature?" Sara asked.

Robbins said, "No marks of manual strangulation. No hand marks or bruising on the throat at all, however, so my guess is it was some kind of wide ligature . . . maybe even something like a bed sheet." He held the corner of the one that covered Grace Salfer as an example. "I found some cotton fibers in her throat and in her nose. I sent them to Trace."

"What about the lividity?" Sara asked.

"She was on her stomach when she died and remained in that position for some time," Robbins said.

"We found her on her back in bed."

"Posed," he said. "Greg told me earlier that the whole scene seemed 'off.' "

She glanced at Greg who shrugged.

"What are you telling us?" she asked.

"I'm saying that your killer had plenty of time to stage the scene once the victim was dead."

The Home Sure building sat on a side street, Desert Lane, just off Charleston. With a half-full thirty-car parking lot out front, the long and low-slung facility nestled in the shadow of I-15, a small discreet sign out front, the logo painted on double glass doors in the center of a stucco facade.

They got out of the Taurus, Brass circling around to join the CSI supervisor at the short sidewalk to the entrance. Grissom was stifling a yawn.

"Don't mean to bore you," Brass kidded gently, knowing that Grissom never seemed to run out of gas, but also aware that the graveyard-shift supervisor had been pushing himself particularly hard since Ecklie lowered the boom.

"No, you're still scintillating company," Grissom said with a tiny smile. "Just been a long week, Jim."

"Why not cut back from sixteen to your normal twelve-hour days?" Brass asked as they reached the entry. "And maybe take a day off once in a while? Surprise yourself and everybody else."

Shaking his head, Grissom said, "Too much on my plate."

Brass heaved a world-weary sigh. "You're a fine supervisor, Gil. I've watched you grow . . . in a job

that used to be mine, remember. Take it from somebody who's been there—don't let the politicians
throw you off your game."

Grissom's mouth tightened in a smile, and he
nodded. The quiet eloquence of this gesture meant
much more to Brass than a verbal "thank you"
would have.

The CSI opened a door and Brass led the way into
the building. Through a modest entryway they entered into a brightly lit chamber that looked more
like a showroom than the outer office of a security
company.

Lining the off-white walls and riding high, poster-
like framed color photos depicted uniformed Home
Sure guards checking locks, leading away handcuffed bad guys, helping school kids, and leaning
against Home Sure vehicles that looked a little too
much like police cars. Beneath the framed posters
were various products—alarms, keypads, automo-
bile antitheft systems and so on, on pedestals around
the perimeter and in small display cases placed at
odd angles across the floor. Chrome and faux-black-
leather furnishings, a couch and a few chairs, were
interspersed—this indeed was a waiting room of
sorts—with tables providing various Home Sure
leaflets; but no reception desk awaited.

Employees—some in the familiar brown uniform,
others in standard business apparel—wandered
through from doorways into office areas at left and
right, attention consumed by reports and printouts
they were studying. They moved through the dis-
plays without looking at them, like rats used to a

maze. The presence of the two LVPD personnel was noticed by no one but the security cameras in every corner, swivelling back and forth catching every movement.

A shapely young Hispanic woman, her long black hair in a bun, approached them with a pleasant if noncommital expression; she wore black slacks and a black Polo shirt with the Home Sure logo over one breast and a name plate saying TINA above the other. There was a phone bud in her right ear attached to a cord that ran to a cell on her belt, a tear-shaped microphone against her right shoulder. She had a practiced smile and dark brown, intelligent eyes.

"Law enforcement," she said cheerfully, noting the badge displayed on Brass's lapel and Grissom's necklace ID. "Always a pleasure to have the LVPD in the house. How can Home Sure be of help?"

Brass said, "I'm Captain Brass, this is Dr. Grissom with the Crime Lab. Are you in charge here, Tina?"

The woman's smile faded, if only for a moment, then in a lyrical voice, she said, "No, I'm sort of the welcoming committee—the person in charge is Mr. Templeton."

"We need to speak to him."

"He's very—"

"Busy, I'm sure," Brass said. "But I know you . . . and he . . . will understand that Dr. Grissom and I are investigating a homicide."

Grissom added, "The murder of Grace Salfer last night at Los Calina—she was one of your clients."

She nodded once. "Yes, we've heard. . . . I'll get him for you. Have a seat if you like, Captain. Doctor."

Grissom said, "We're fine."

Wandering a few feet away, Tina touched a button on the cell phone and it squawked. A walkie-talkie, Brass realized.

"Mr. Templeton," she said. "There are two police officers here to see you."

The thing squawked again and a voice said, *"See if you can arrange an appointment for this afternoon, Tina. I'm on a conference call."*

"I explained that you're busy, Mr. Templeton, but they're insistent. It's a homicide investigation. The Salfer matter."

Brass and Grissom exchanged glances—so murder was a "matter" around Home Sure.

"I'll be right there," the voice said gruffly.

They waited about a minute-and-a-half before a tall, handsome man in his early forties emerged from the warren of cubicles at right. He wore a black suit that was not off the rack, a gray shirt and a darker gray silk tie, his dark hair cut fairly short, sideburns barely visible, his face a sharp-featured oval. Wide-set brown eyes, slightly hooded, regarded them as the frowning man strode toward them, his gait confident, his posture erect.

As he neared, the one-woman welcome wagon said, "Captain Brass, Dr. Grissom, this is—"

"Todd Templeton," Grissom said coldly.

Brass had already sensed something awry between the CSI and their host, as the man had ignored the credentials the captain held up, his eyes immediately locking on Grissom, his frown deepening.

The young woman and Brass both took a step back, as the two men glared at each other. Brass wondered if Tina sensed the same thing he did: The temperature of the room seemed to get both hotter and colder in the same instant.

"Gil Grissom," Templeton said, his rich baritone voice as frigid as Grissom's. "I suppose this was inevitable."

Grissom arched an eyebrow so high it damn near touched his scalp. "*You* work here, Todd? I didn't even know you were in Vegas."

"You could *say* I 'work' here," Templeton replied, gesturing expansively with both hands. "This is *my* business."

"That's what's great about America," Grissom said lightly. "*Anyone* can get a second chance."

"How do you and Mr. Templeton know each other?" Brass asked Grissom.

But it was Templeton who answered, the frown having evolved into a glazed smile. "Oh, Gil and I go way back. How far, again? Funny, you'd think I'd remember. How long *has* it been since you destroyed my career?"

Looking from one man to the other, Brass said, "What the hell?"

"You've rebounded well, Todd." Grissom held Templeton's eyes, not backing down at all; he, too, was smiling. "And to answer your question, just under ten years. But let's not exaggerate—I didn't destroy your career. You managed that all by yourself. I can't take credit for anything but helping clean up the mess you made."

Templeton chuckled. "You haven't changed, Gil. Still the same world-class, arrogant, know-it-all prick."

Brass stepped between the two men, and Tina backed well away.

"Mr. Templeton," the detective said, "I'm sure there's some fascinating history between you two, but right now we are faced with the murder of a woman who, you might say, we were *both* paid to protect."

"I really don't know anything about the Los Calina matter," Templeton said with an uninterested shrug, still looking past the detective at Grissom, the glazed smile morphing into a sneer by now.

"Well," Brass said, "we need to talk it about it, just the same."

"What if I don't care to?"

Brass kept his voice low but his tone was serious. "We talk here, or at the station."

"Perhaps my attorney would disagree."

"Perhaps you'd like to call him. Maybe you feel not cooperating with police on a murder investigation sets a good example for Home Sure's staff."

Templeton said nothing, but he was thinking.

"Sir, we can talk right here, or somewhere more private—you make the call. But we *are* going to talk."

Templeton finally looked at Brass.

"Not with Grissom along," Templeton said. "No way."

Brass smiled. "Way. Where?"

The security man contemplated that for a moment, then sighed and said, "My office."

"Fine," Brass said.

The detective and Grissom followed Templeton; as they left the showroom, Brass glanced back at

Tina, standing alone now, surrounded by colorful security-guard posters, her expression confused. Apparently her boss had just shown a new side of himself.

They passed through a small workroom with an unattended desk, and shelves filled with alarms and other products lining two of the other three walls, some in boxes, others bare and tagged for repair. The fourth wall was home to a work bench, a solitary technician bent over an alarm box, paying no attention to these trespassers. Another security camera in the corner slowly turned on its arc, following their progress.

Then they were in a corridor with pale green walls, closed doors on either side, and security cameras at either end. The second door on the right stood ajar.

Their host strode into the office—the door nameplate read TODD TEMPLETON, PRESIDENT—and Brass and Grissom followed him into the spacious room with its window looking out on Desert Lane and the interstate beyond.

The large L-shaped desk was so clean it might have just been delivered, a single file folder on the blotter, a flat-screen computer monitor on the left. No pictures or other personal effects cluttered the desk, and only the large framed photos of golf holes on a side wall marked this as someone's office and not a generic model. The other side wall was a bank of monitors fed by the building's various security cameras; even this office had a security-cam high in one corner.

Home Sure sold paranoia—and lived it.

Templeton had plopped into an overstuffed leather chair behind the desk, and was saying, "Gil, get the door, would you?"

Grissom closed the door without comment.

Two ebony straight-back chairs were opposite Templeton. Brass and Grissom took them without waiting for an invitation.

"All I know, Captain," Templeton said, leaning forward, hands flat on the desk, "is what my people called in from Los Calina. A resident, Mrs. Grace Safler . . . *Sal*-fer . . . was killed. We'll do our own internal investigation, obviously, but I don't know a damn thing yet, and don't really understand why you're—"

"First," Brass said, his tone purposefully mild, nodding toward Grissom, "what's going on between you two?"

Temple grunted. "I'm sure you're just dying to tell your pal all about it, Gil—go ahead. I'd love to hear your version. I haven't had a good laugh in weeks."

"It's not relevant to why we're here," Grissom said, his face blandly blank.

For perhaps six seconds, a tennis match of silence sent Brass looking back and forth between their host and Grissom.

Finally, Templeton rocked back in his chair and let out a long sigh. "All right. Captain Brass, we might as well get this out of the way. . . . Ten years ago, I was a day shift crime lab supervisor in Reno."

Brass sat forward. "You were a CSI?"

"No—a detective captain assigned to the crime lab."

Brass glanced at Grissom, whose expression remained inscrutable.

Templeton was saying, "We had a case where it was claimed that I mishandled evidence. The powers-that-be brought in the renowned Gilbert Grissom to investigate—to provide 'a skilled, unbiased eye,' they said. Well, to make a long story short, your colleague got me fired . . . and I haven't been able to get a job in *real* law enforcement ever since."

"Looks to me you're doing well enough," Grissom said, no edge in his voice.

"Go to hell, Grissom," Templeton snarled.

"Whoa, whoa, whoa," Brass said. "Let's be civil here."

Templeton said, "For the sake of my business, Captain Brass, and to be a solid citizen, I am prepared to cooperate with you. But in future you would be wise to leave this . . . individual back in the lab with the other specimens."

"I'm the lead CSI on this case, Todd," Grissom said. "Our past history is irrelevant."

"*Fuck* you, Grissom!"

"Damn it!" the detective snapped. "Gentlemen— bottom line here is we have a homicide to solve." He turned to Templeton. "And you're the president of the security company that dropped the ball, protecting this woman."

Templeton ran a hand over his face, then sat forward, his eyes meeting Brass's. "How would you feel, Captain, if a guy who lost you your—"

"I'd feel like shit," Brass said. "But if I were a grown-up, I'd shut up and get past it and do my job."

"I resent the implication that our company was at fault when you don't have one shred of evidence to point to our being negligent."

Brass shrugged. "That may or may not be true. You admit you don't really know much about the 'matter' yet; but, hey—you go ahead and resent it, anyway, all you want. Free country."

Releasing another long sigh, Templeton said, "All right, all right. . . . Your point is well taken. This would definitely be a black eye for my company if it goes public. How about I help you, Captain . . . and you give Home Sure part of the credit, so we can all live happily ever after?"

Brass shook his head. "You'll help us because we're all supposed to be on the same side here."

"With Grissom a part of this thing, I need more than that—I need your personal assurance, Captain Brass, that you will make every effort not to embarrass my company."

Relenting a little, Brass said, "I'm sure when this case is solved, there'll be plenty of credit to go around."

Clapping once, as if he had just closed a big deal, Templeton leaned forward and smiled at Brass, suddenly friendly. "Okay! . . . Shall we get to work, then?"

"Good," Brass said. "Can you provide us with the name of Grace Salfer's next of kin . . . so we can make the notification?"

"No biggie," Templeton said. He already had the file on his desk. He opened it up, scanned it quickly, then said, "A nephew—David Arrington."

"Do you have contact information for Mr. Arrington?"

Templeton read off a phone number and address, and Brass wrote it in his notebook.

"What else?" The man's falsely cheerful tone reminded the detective of Conrad Ecklie. He wondered if Grissom was making the same connection; if so, it would be fingernails on a chalkboard . . .

"Well," Brass said, "obviously any specifics you might have, about Grace Salfer's situation. As you probably know, the alarm did not go off, and there's some question about whether Mrs. Salfer was even using the thing at all."

Templeton nodded. "I'll look into that in detail. But I have already made a preliminary check in that regard, and the only recent triggering of her alarm was this morning—when a technician was apparently testing it for you people."

Brass admitted as much. Then he sat forward. "How is it, last night of all nights, the gate booth at Los Calina was empty for maybe as much as several hours?"

He shrugged. "Just one of those unhappy coincidences. It's a longtime employee, Jack Rossi, who went home sick as a dog with this flu that's going around. You want his home address and other contact info, to check for yourself?"

"I would," Brass said. "With all due respect, your security people have access to every house at Los Calina—keys, security codes. So obviously—"

"No offense taken, Captain. I can see why you'll want to go down that road. We do thorough background checks on all our people, but bad apples do sneak through." The Home Sure president smiled helpfully at Brass, hands folded prayerfully on the desk. "Anything else?"

But it was the CSI supervisor who spoke this time,

saying, "We'd like you to gather all the Los Calina records for the last thirty days."

"*All* the records?" Templeton asked incredulously, the cheerfulness, true or false, dropping away.

Grissom nodded. "What alarms went off and when, whose alarms went off, any criminal activity that you're aware of. Which guards worked which shifts on which days, alarm repairs. Anything, everything."

Templeton glared at him. "You wouldn't be trying to make my life difficult again, would you, Gil?"

"Todd, you worked the crime lab. You know the drill."

The hatred in Templeton's eyes bore across the desk at Grissom like lasers. "Yeah. I know the drill."

Again feeling the temperature turn hot *and* cold, Brass rose. "I think that's enough for now, Mr. Templeton."

"No argument on that point," Templeton said.

Grissom got up and said, "We'll need *all* those records, Todd."

"I *said* I'd help. Good morning, gentlemen."

Once they were safely in the car, the detective turned to Grissom. "Are you sure you shouldn't recuse yourself from this case? You two do have a hell of a history."

"He got fired because he falsified evidence, Jim. I didn't get him fired, I merely verified what his department already suspected."

"Still," Brass said.

"Just drive, Jim—let me worry about Todd Templeton."

They stopped for a red light, waited in uneasy silence, and when the light turned green Brass eased the car forward, saying, "I don't doubt you, Gil. I would never doubt you. But we both know someone who's just *hungry* for ways to make you look bad."

"You talking about Conrad Ecklie, Jim? Or Todd Templeton?"

Brass said nothing. Then he grinned over at Grissom and said, "You make friends pretty much everywhere you go, don't you, Gil?"

Grissom shrugged and gave a small smile. "It's a gift."

4

WARRICK BROWN, SITTING IN THE passenger seat of North Las Vegas PD detective Marty Larkin's Taurus, stared out his window at the night, seeing nothing in particular. As they eased south on Decatur Boulevard, passing the lights of restaurants, gas stations, and various other small businesses along the busy thoroughfare, Warrick took in the neon parade without really focusing on it.

The world flashing by as an abstraction could be a comfort to an investigator whose work required close focus on details.

"You got anything down on the Super Bowl?" the dark-haired NLVPD detective asked, just making small talk.

Warrick and Larkin knew each other only in passing, so the latter could be forgiven not knowing about the former's gambling problem. The people who knew of that particular period in Warrick's life—which, thankfully, was well behind him now—

could be counted on one hand. Larkin wasn't one of them.

"Naw," Warrick said. "We don't even have an office pool at CSI."

"Yeah, but who do you like?"

Warrick shrugged. "I haven't really followed it much this year. Too busy."

"Too busy for football?" Larkin seemed astonished.

"Hey, Marty, I was on the night shift for years—I was either working when games were on, or sleeping through 'em."

Larkin grinned, shook his head. "Hey, man, no job's worth *that* much sacrifice."

Warrick grinned back, but offered no further comment.

This guy was obviously a hardcore fan, and maybe even an ex-player in high school and college, if the school had been small enough. Warrick didn't know how to break it to Larkin that the only jolt he'd ever got out of watching football was the one that sent him sprinting for the sportsbook.

That was one reason why, even on swing shift now, he spent so little time watching sports on the tube. When sports isn't about the game, or the skill of the players, just the point spread, well . . . time to pack it in.

And, anyway, Warrick really was too busy. Work took up most of his hours, and when he'd dug inside himself and pushed gambling the hell out of his life, he made room for something far more satisfying: his spare time was more likely spent now with sheet music, not tip sheets, with composing not wagering, playing tunes instead of paying debts.

Glancing at Larkin, Warrick knew the guy had only been trying to make conversation, to find some common bond that could give a little underpinning to the collaborative nature of investigative work.

Well, hell—why not talk about *that?*

"So, Marty," Warrick said, "what do we know about Taylor Dearborn?" The CSI had been in the bedroom earlier, when Larkin had talked to Catherine about Dearborn, and had only glommed a few words. He'd like to get the whole story before they pulled up at this guy's door.

Plus, he could size up where this detective he'd been partnered with was coming from.

In true Jack Webb fashion, the detective told him the facts, just the facts, which pleased Warrick, who'd learned at Grissom's side to focus on evidence, particularly at this early stage.

When he'd concluded, Larkin had finally editorialized a bit, saying, "Wanna see a mug shot of our ex-husband of the year?"

"Always nice to get a preview of who we're talking to."

The detective, at the wheel, glanced down to punch in some keys on the computer that rode the car's differential. A small monitor angled for Larkin's convenience was adjusted so they could both see the photo come up.

Any doubts Warrick might have harbored about Taylor Dearborn's position on the food chain evaporated when he saw the mug shot.

This guy was a poster child for lowlifes—stringy, greasy dark hair hung over his ears, past his shoulders, nearly covering his eyes. His scruffy beard seemed more like an act of negligence than an effort to grow facial hair. Puffy, dilated eyes squinted out, giving the impression of a lizard doing its best to avoid the sun, the pink tip of a tongue protruding through thin lips.

"Don't have to be a great detective," Warrick said, "to see whatever night this was taken, Taylor Dearborn was well and truly stoned."

"Isn't he a honey?" Larkin said with a laugh, as he swung the Ford left onto Concord Village.

They traveled a few more blocks before going right on Ridgefield, then left again onto Tabic Drive, a short street lined with one-story stucco homes. Dearborn had a house on the left side, about halfway down.

"With his troubles?" Warrick asked. "Where did our stoner score money for a house?"

"Rental," Larkin said.

"You know this because . . . ?"

"Made a few calls. Hey, no law against me getting a jump on it—I glanced into Taylor's life while you guys finished up at the apartment."

"I love a man who loves his work."

They exchanged smiles—bonding now—and Larkin parked on the wrong side of the street, but directly in front of Dearborn's address. They got out and paused for a quick appraisal.

Unlike most of the neighbors, Dearborn's house had no fence and no bars on the windows. Like all the neighbors, however, this residence had dirt for a front "lawn"; the local drought, into its twentieth year by some estimations, had killed whatever neglect hadn't got around to. Pale white stucco, with a driveway and a single-car garage, the bungalow hadn't been cared for by anyone who gave a damn for more than a decade. A beat-up green late-nineties Pontiac Grand AM resided in the driveway, a puddle of oil collecting beneath it. Living-room lights were on behind faded curtains; faintly, Warrick could hear a television.

He followed Larkin to the front door. On the stoop, the detective knocked and they waited. The detective rapped again. They waited some more.

"Guy's probably in there, blitzed out of his mind," Larkin said. This time he pounded on the door with considerable force.

Still no response, just canned laughter from a sit-com on the tube in there.

The detective's mouth tightened. "What do you think? Lights on, TV going, car in the drive . . . ?"

Warrick shrugged. "Right now this is just notification of the death of an ex-wife."

"Yeah." Larkin twitched a grimace. "Shit. Can't break down a door to talk to a potential suspect."

"Not without becoming one."

That made Larkin laugh, and they came off the stoop and walked down the driveway. At the curb, hearing a dog bark, Warrick glanced up the block, streetlights bathing everything in an unearthly yellow glow. Two shabby houses away, a man walked toward them, a basset hound on a leash trotting along next to him.

"That him?" Larkin said.

"Could be," Warrick said.

"Not sure . . ."

"Won't know till we ask."

They waited, and as the man got closer, Larkin held up his ID. "A moment, sir? Police."

Warrick could see the man better now, his face definitely resembling that of scruffy Taylor Dearborn, same nose, features; but this clean-shaven individual had short, neatly combed black hair, wide brown eyes, and walked in a relaxed manner.

His attire was wrong, too: khakis, a three-button golf shirt under a dark, waist-length jacket zipped halfway up, and what seemed to be brand-new sneakers—cheap sneakers, but new.

"Certainly, gentlemen," he said coming to a nearby stop. He shushed his dog, who was barking but in a friendly way. When the dog quieted, he said, "Sorry—what's up?"

Larkin made quick introductions as he put his badge away. "Are you Taylor Dearborn?"

He frowned in concern. "Why, yes—why?"

"We need to talk," Larkin said.

"Well . . . about what?"

"It might be better if we took it inside."

"Okay. You don't have a . . . warrant or anything?"

"No. Do we need one, Mr. Dearborn?"

"No! It's just . . . I was wondering if this was, you know, something serious."

Warrick said, "It's serious. Shall we go inside?" Dearborn looked down at the dog like *it* made the decisions; its tongue lolling, the animal seemed to nod. Perhaps that was why Dearborn consented, "Yeah, sure. Let's do this."

Inside, the clean-cut Taylor Dearborn had another surprise for them; if the shabby outside of the house reflected his mug shot, the interior represented the cleaned-up Dearborn. While everything—carpeting, curtains, furniture, TV—was low-end rent-to-own, this interior was clean, very clean in fact, in a minimalist way that Warrick rather liked.

Warrick wondered if the guy had learned a thing or two about housecleaning from his late ex-wife. Even in the aftermath of whatever upended her apartment, Angela Dearborn appeared to have been a neat freak, herself.

The only furniture in the living room was a nineteen-inch TV (playing an ancient *Seinfeld*) on a stand to the right of the front door, a sofa on the wall opposite that, a two-shelf plywood-and-cinderblock bookcase loaded with Stephen King and Dean Koontz paperbacks under the front window, a coffee table arrayed with the TV remote, an ashtray, pack of cigarettes, and a lighter.

In the corner next to the sofa, a guitar stand displayed a Fender San Luis Rey acoustic guitar, a model Warrick recognized—in fact, he had a similar guitar at home, same spruce top, rosewood sides and back, and the trademark Fender headstock with the keys on one side. Not an expensive guitar, but possessed of a good solid sound. Beyond the living room was a small dining alcove, with a door Warrick assumed went to the garage.

"You live alone, Mr. Dearborn?" Larkin asked, speaking up over loud laughter on the blaring TV.

Dearborn nodded and shut off the set. He released the dog from its leash, and the low-slung, tri-colored animal trotted off to the kitchen, its ears bouncing.

"Sorry about the TV," Dearborn said with a shrug.

"But this isn't the greatest neighborhood, and when I walk Coda, I turn it up, to make burglars think someone's inside."

Warrick nodded. "Not a bad idea."

The CSI was paying careful attention to the suspect's hands. If Taylor Dearborn had beaten his wife with his bare fists, no evidence of it showed on his knuckles, the backs of his hands, or on his fingers. Catherine had told Warrick that Angie had at least scratched her attacker, and Dearborn had no apparent scratches on his hands or face.

Larkin asked, "Any objection to my checking to see if anyone else is here?"

"Well . . . why would you want to do that?"

"Do you mind?"

"No. No, go ahead."

While the CSI stayed with Dearborn in the living room, Larkin took a quick stroll through the house.

"You say your dog's name is Coda?" Warrick asked with a smile.

"Yeah—it's a musical term."

"I know."

The suspect shrugged again. "Coda's my passage to the end—kind of the vehicle from my old life to my new one."

Coming back into the room, Larkin said to Warrick, "Clear," then asked their host, "*New* life, you say?"

"Yes. I'm sure you're aware I've had my share of . . . problems. No one to blame but myself." He motioned to the couch; when they didn't take him up on his offer, Dearborn sat on the sofa himself.

Larkin asked, "I take it that's why you weren't shocked to find cops on your doorstep."

With a dry, almost soundless chuckle, Dearborn said, "It's not exactly the first time."

"More like the fifth or sixth time," Larkin said.

Dearborn shrugged yet again; a guy who'd screwed up as often as he had did a lot of that. "Yeah . . . but this is the first time you fellas have come around since I got clean."

"Clean," Larkin repeated, as if the suspect had uttered a foreign word.

"Yes, sir. And it's been almost seven months now."

"Congratulations. You still see Angie?"

Dearborn fidgeted. "Not really. I guess you also know that . . . there's a restraining order against me."

"Yeah," Larkin said, eyes boring into his quarry. "We also know that."

His eyes pleaded with them. "Look, guys—we had some trouble, Angie and me. I got . . . rough with her. I don't make any excuses—when I wasn't doping, I was drinking, and when I drank, I got mean. So I don't blame her for getting that restraining order—she had to do what she thought was right."

"What *she* thought was right," Warrick said. "Does that mean *you* don't think it's right, Mr. Dearborn?"

Spreading his hands out wide, Dearborn said, "Hey, it's not up to me. Judge made that decision."

Larkin studied Dearborn for a long moment. "You still haven't really answered my question."

"Uh—what question is that?"

"Do . . . you . . . still . . . see . . . Angie?" The syllables bounced like dice across a craps table.

His eyes popped. "Is *that* why you're here?"

Just a little irritation was coming through, Warrick thought. Or . . . more like, frustration. . . .

Dearborn edged up on the couch. "Why—did Angie *call* you?"

"Did you give her reason to?" Larkin asked. "Have you violated that restraining order, Mr. Dearborn?"

The suspect ran a hand through his short hair. "Look . . . guys. Please. I didn't do shit."

"Did . . . you . . . violate—"

"Okay! Okay, I stopped over there . . . but just to ask her to go out to dinner with me. It was kind of a special occasion. See, she knows about me cleaning up. We've been talking on the phone—no law against that, she doesn't have to take my calls if she doesn't want to, right? I still love her. Haven't you ever loved anybody?"

"Yes," Larkin said. "I just never beat the hell out of them."

"Okay." He hung his head. "I guess I deserved that. . . ."

"Did she go out to dinner with you, Mr. Dearborn?"

"Well, you *know* she didn't, if you talked to her! . . . She said no, I begged her, but she said she was proud of me and everything, only Angie just . . . just couldn't trust me yet. So—I left."

"When was that?"

"Last night . . . Look, if Ange's sayin' I did something to her, she's lying! I don't know why she would, but . . . why would she lie like that? Damn it! It's not fair. . . ."

"Tell us what you did."

"Well, I left! What do you think? She turned me down, and I tucked my tail between my legs like anybody shot down by someone they love." He shifted on the sofa; his hands were clasped between wide-spread legs. "Guys . . . fellas . . . I know I wasn't supposed to go see her, but after the phone calls, I thought maybe, if we started slow, and she saw for herself just how *good* I was doing . . ."

Larkin nodded. "So you're saying you didn't kill her?"

Warrick would not have gone that way; if this man was innocent, the cruelty of Larkin's dropping this bomb was unforgivable.

Dearborn froze, his eyes suddenly going unfocused for a few seconds before he dropped his hand. He looked up first at Larkin, then at Warrick. Lower lip trembling, he said, "You guys . . . you . . . you wouldn't be screwing with me, would you?"

Warrick said, "She was murdered last night, Mr. Dearborn."

"She's . . . gone?"

Larkin said, "She's dead. Yes. And you're surprised?"

"You don't have any right . . . you don't have any right . . ."

Then he covered his face with a hand and began to cry.

The dog came loping in and jumped up on the couch and began to lick his weeping master's face; Dearborn hugged him, and moaned.

Then Dearborn petted the animal and shooed him back into the kitchen. Warrick sat on one side of their host, Larkin the other.

"What happened?" Dearborn asked, in a small voice. "Did she . . . suffer?"

Larkin said, "Yes."

"Oh, fuck . . ."

And he began to cry again.

Larkin's eyes remained cold, and fixed on his suspect; but Warrick could tell the detective was having to work at it, now. "Someone got into her apartment, Mr. Dearborn, and beat her to death."

"*Break* in? Hell, Angie didn't have anything worth stealing—"

"No," Warrick said, "it appears she let her killer in. Probably someone she knew."

As Warrick watched, he could see the exact moment that Taylor Dearborn realized he wasn't just the aggrieved ex-spouse, but the prime suspect. The guy should have known from the get-go, the way Larkin was behaving; still, the news appeared to have blindsided him.

If Dearborn was an actor, Warrick was impressed.

And to his further credit, Dearborn gathered his dignity and did not go around the bend and start proclaiming his innocence. Instead, his voice remained soft, a tear trickling down one cheek, as he said, "Well, I can see why you think I did it."

Larkin rose. He began to pace around the living room now. "I believe you're upset about Angie's death, Mr. Dearborn. You've convinced me of that. Now—convince us you didn't do it."

Dearborn shrugged. "How the hell can I do that?" He shook his head, laughed bitterly. "Karma's a bitch, ain't it?"

"Can be," Warrick admitted.

The detective continued to pace before the suspect. "To start with, Mr. Dearborn, tell us where you were last night."

"Having dinner."

"Where? Anyone see you?"

"A lot of people."

"Care to name one?"

He shrugged. "Mayor Harrison?"

The words stopped the detective as abruptly as a baseball bat to the chest. "Mayor Harrison . . . Mayor Darryl Harrison? Our mayor?"

"Yeah. Right. Our mayor, yes." Dearborn, his face slick with tears and snot, dug out a Kleenex.

Finally Larkin found the words. "Mr. Dearborn—your alibi for last night is you were having dinner with Mayor Harrison?"

Dearborn blew his nose. Nodded.

"Well, pardon me if I don't feel we need to check *that* one out, a little. *Why* were you dining with the mayor?"

"It was an Alcoholics Anonymous banquet. That was the special occasion I wanted to share with . . . with Angie. The mayor presented me with my six-month pin himself."

"An AA meeting? You were at an AA meeting with the mayor?"

Dearborn wiped away the tears. Finally some anger spiked in the suspect's voice. "Look, Detective, what is it . . . Larkin? Could we do this another time? You just told me my wife is dead—don't you have any goddamn decency?"

"Ex-wife, Mr. Dearborn. And I'm sorry, but we need to do this now. The early hours of a murder investigation are vital."

Warrick said, "If you really do care about Angie, you'll help us."

His head drooping, his eyes closing, Dearborn rubbed his forehead. "Yeah . . . yeah . . . I understand," he said, his voice barely above a whisper.

Warrick leaned in close to hear better, saying, "Tell us about how you cleaned up."

"AA turned my life around," Dearborn said with a bittersweet twitch of a smile. "In jail last time, I found the Lord—was born again. When I got out, I really saw the light. Started going to meetings. I got Coda—he gives me something to be responsible for besides my own sorry ass. And in return, he loves me. Funny, huh, a dog taught me that? Unconditional love? Then Jesus led me to a pawn shop window, and I got my guitar . . . I'd always loved music, but never learned to play. . . ." He nodded toward the Fender on the stand. "It gives me a way to channel my emotions."

Warrick, nodding, said, "Real deal, music. What about last night?"

Dearborn took a moment to get himself under control, then let out a long breath, as if blowing out a birthday cake. "I went over there around . . . five?"

"You tell us," Larkin said.

Warrick said, "Five's a little early for a dinner date, isn't it?"

"Actually, I was running late. The AA dinner's coffee half-hour began at six, I wanted to get to Angie's by four, plenty of time to, you know, make my case, convince her to come out with me, time for her to get ready . . . but I couldn't make it. I got off work late . . ."

"Where do you work?" Larkin asked.

"Fry cook. Over at Raw Shanks Diner?"

"At the Sphere," Warrick said with a nod. "Serve up a mean burger."

Larkin frowned at Warrick, maybe thinking the CSI was too soft on the suspect. But Warrick knew when one cop played bad, the other had to play good—not out of cynicism, but to try to make a real connection.

"Great place to work," Dearborn said. "Confidentially, the manager's AA, too—anyway, one of the afternoon cooks was late getting there, and I had to cover for him. By the time I got home, got changed, then drove to Angie's, it had to be pushing five."

Larkin asked, "Why did you go to see her? You knew she had a restraining order against you."

Warrick said, "You were talking on the phone, regularly. Why didn't you ask her first? Not just drop over?"

"You know the reason. I was afraid she'd say no. And I wanted to *show* her I'd changed. I figured . . . sounds like naive b.s. now, but . . . I thought if she even just *saw* me, how I look *now*, and heard about what the banquet was about, she'd . . . Oh well. Why did I go over there? Because I love her, always have."

"You beat her up," Larkin said.

He raised his chin, seeking dignity. "When we had our trouble, it was because the *drugs* and *booze* controlled my life . . . not me. It's been almost seven months, and I know damn well the mistakes I made. I'm not going back to that life. Never."

Warrick could only admire the resolve in the man's voice; on the other hand, Taylor Dearborn wouldn't be the first person AA failed to turn around. . . .

"I just wanted her to come to dinner with me, see that I really had changed," Dearborn was saying. "Thought if she knew that, that we might, you know . . . I thought she might give *us* a second chance."

"Only she didn't want to see you," Larkin said.

Dearborn shook his head. "No. She had a lot of residual anger against me—anger that hadn't come out on the phone, at least not the more recent conversations. But when she saw me standing there in front of her . . . " He shrugged. "Hard to blame her. I was a first-class dick in my day."

"Must've pissed you off, though," Larkin said, too casually.

Taking the pack of cigarettes off the table, Dearborn shook one out, then offered them around to Larkin and Warrick, who both declined. He dropped the pack on the table and picked up the lighter. Lighting the smoke, he inhaled deeply, held it, almost like he was smoking a joint, then finally let it out.

Apparently Taylor Dearborn hadn't dealt with *all* his addictions, just yet. . . .

"I'm not going to lie to you, guys. Yeah, damn straight it pissed me off, how hard I worked to change and then to be treated like I was the same old jerk . . . but I understand her thinking too." He laughed harshly. "You have any idea how many times I promised to change before? And changed for, what, a day or two, sometimes as long as a week . . . but the truth is I didn't *really* ever change until this last time. When Jesus got on my team."

"So," Larkin said, "she didn't buy it."

"No. She said—if I'd really changed, I wouldn't have disrespected her and just . . . showed up at her place like that."

Larkin's eyes burned into the suspect. "You tried to convince her that this time you really had gone straight."

"Yes," Dearborn said. He took a deep drag and let it out. "She couldn't see it, though—or didn't want to see it."

"You two had words."

"Yeah." He sighed smoke. "Yeah, you could say that."

"Did it turn into a screaming match?"

Dearborn shrugged. "No. I don't think so. We mighta raised our voices a little . . . you know, each just trying to make our point. Neither of us yelled or anything."

"I see. What if the next-door neighbor said she heard yelling from Angie's apartment?"

Dearborn took that in stride. "I'd say, either the walls are thinner than I thought . . . or she heard Angie and someone else yelling." He frowned. "When *was* this?"

Larkin said, "The neighbor said around six."

He waved that off. "Proves I didn't do it. Around six? I was driving to dinner. I got there about . . . ten after."

"Where was the dinner?"

"City Hall."

"Downtown?"

"Detective—don't you know where City Hall is?"

That was as close to smart-ass as Dearborn had got; but Warrick could hardly blame him.

Warrick asked, "When did you leave Angie's?"

"Five-thirty? I don't know, I wasn't paying that much attention. I was . . . was pretty upset."

"So it could have been later?" Larkin asked.

"Couple of minutes maybe, but let's face it—we all know I couldn't get from Angie's apartment in North Las Vegas all the way to City Hall . . . downtown? . . . in ten minutes at rush hour. Hell, it's probably at least fifteen minutes in the middle of the *night*, when there's *no* traffic."

The detective asked, "Mind if we look around?"

Dearborn's eyes tightened. "Didn't you already do that?"

"Humor us," Larkin said.

"I really oughta ask you guys to get a warrant. If you're gonna make a suspect outa me."

Larkin stared hard at the suspect.

Warrick said, "You said you wanted to help us."

"Screw it," Dearborn sighed. He waved, cigarette smoke making a jagged line. "Knock yourself out. Go for it. Just be nice to my dog, okay?"

Warrick pulled on a pair of latex gloves. Withdrawing a plastic-covered swab from a pocket, he said, "Mr. Dearborn, if you're telling the truth, what we find here will also help exonerate you."

"Well, I am telling the truth."

"Then, may I have a buccal swab?"

"What's that?"

"It'll provide me a DNA sample to compare with DNA from the crime scene. I just swab the inside of your mouth with this. Standard procedure."

With a weak shrug, Dearborn assented and Warrick swiped the swab into the suspect's mouth. After putting the plastic cover into place, the CSI stowed the evidence in his pocket and started his search of the house.

The small dining area beyond the living room held only a table with two rickety chairs under a two-bulb overhead light. The kitchen was about the size of a small bathroom. Down the hall were two bedrooms, one basically empty, the other room—Dearborn's—with a double bed, made, as well as a dresser and nightstand with a short stack of paperbacks, an alarm clock, and a small lamp.

Warrick performed a diligent search and came up empty. If Dearborn was guilty, something should turn up—bloody clothes, bloody shoes; but nothing. Maybe he'd ditched everything—they already had a blood-soaked man's shirt in the evidence locker; maybe Dearborn had gotten rid of the rest, too. Rejoining the other two men in the living room, Warrick gave Larkin a quick headshake.

Dearborn said, "Guys! Face it—you didn't find anything, 'cause there's nothing to find. I told you I didn't do this thing."

Warrick asked, "You mind if we have a look at your garage, Mr. Dearborn? And your car?"

"Come on, you guys! Enough is enough. How about a little grieving time, here!"

"Suit yourself," Larkin said with a nasty little

smile. "You and I will just sit here, while CSI Brown calls a judge for a search warrant. That'll *really* make you look innocent."

Warrick certainly didn't like the turn this conversation was taking, Larkin again stepping beyond the pale; but before the CSI could say anything, Dearborn caved.

"All right, all right! Door to the garage is unlocked. . . . Here are the car keys. Knock yourself out."

Warrick quietly took Larkin aside.

"Marty, why don't we get a warrant anyway—if we do find evidence, and this guy's lawyer claims coercion—"

"He gave the go-ahead, Warrick. It's righteous—just do it."

Larkin stayed with Dearborn while Warrick opened the door to the garage. He flicked the light switch, but nothing happened.

"Sorry about that," Dearborn called from the living room. "I never use the garage. Didn't even know the damn thing was burned out."

Using his flashlight, Warrick poked around the place. Wasn't much—a few tomato stakes in the corner, boxes (presumably from Taylor's move) against the far wall, some old oil cans in the corner near the overhead door.

Walking around, looking carefully, shining the flash into the deepest shadows, Warrick probed on. He moved the empty boxes, and—when he shifted the last stack—behind them, against a stud, leaned an aluminum baseball bat.

The CSI ran his flashlight up and down the length

of his find, his eyes relishing it, taking the thing in one inch at a time. Near the head of the bat, he saw some light almost white dust on it; and slightly farther up, in among the letters of the name painted on it, was what might have been a rust stain . . . or something more sinister.

He went out to the car and returned with his equipment. First he photographed the bat where he'd found it, then—after pulling on latex gloves—he gingerly picked it up and swabbed it with phenophaelin. In seconds, the swab turned pink—blood.

Warrick stowed the bat in a big plastic evidence bag and took it into the house. "This yours?" he asked Dearborn.

The suspect shrugged. "That? Yeah, I played ball when I was a kid."

"Used it lately?"

"To kill a couple of big honkin' rats I found in the garage when I moved in. . . .Why?"

Frowning, Larkin asked Warrick, "Blood on the bat?"

The CSI nodded.

The suspect sagged.

The detective asked, "Human or rat?"

"I won't know that," Warrick said, "until I get it to the lab." Turning back to Dearborn, he asked, "Do you remember where in the garage you killed these rats?"

Moving like a zombie, Dearborn got up, went to the garage door and pointed to two different spots on the floor. Warrick swabbed them both and found evidence of blood in both areas. Spraying the floor with luminol, then shining his alternative light source on the spots, Warrick revealed indications of blood dribble on the concrete floor. He took samples of the blood to take back to the lab.

The presence of blood on the cement gave a certain credibility to the ex-husband's story—it hardly seemed likely that Angela Dearborn was killed in this garage, then taken to her apartment and some elaborate hoax crime scene staged. . . .

But that still left the blood on the bat.

Gesturing with his index finger, Larkin indicated that Dearborn should turn around.

"Why?"

"Like it's the first time."

"I swear to you, I haven't done a thing. I'm clean."

Larkin's smile was cold. "You did admit to violating your restraining order."

"Oh, shit, come on, man," Dearborn said, dropping his smoke to the concrete floor and smashing it out with a sneaker toe in disgust.

Pulling out his cuffs, Larkin said, "Nothing I can do."

"This is chickenshit. I bend over backwards helping you guys, let you rummage through my stuff without a warrant, and you pull *this*? My wife was just murdered and you're going to do this?"

"Ex-wife," Larkin reminded him, "and you violated a valid court order."

"What about my dog?"

"You can get a neighbor to watch it."

Dearborn was practically shouting now. "In *this* fuckin' neighborhood?"

"Got any friends?" Warrick asked.

"Yeah. Of course I got friends! What, do you think I don't have friends!"

"Call one," Warrick said, looking toward Larkin who nodded that he would wait.

"But then," the detective said, "you're going with us."

After Dearborn made arrangements for the care of his basset hound, Warrick took a closer look at the suspect's hands as Larkin handcuffed him—no signs of bruises or scabbing.

Stepping in, Warrick pushed up one of Dearborn's sleeves.

"What now?" the suspect asked, exasperated. "Stick a needle in me and shoot me up with truth serum?"

"Looking for scratches," Warrick said examining first one forearm, then the other.

"Nothing to find, is there? Disappointed?"

Warrick said, "Mr. Dearborn, I'm fine with clearing you. But if you beat your ex-wife to death, you *will* go down for it."

Nick was camped out in front of the AFIS computer station when Warrick returned to the lab.

"Hey, 'Rick—how did it go with the ex-husband? Still look like a slam dunk?"

"More like a half-court last-second shot."

Cluttered with equipment, the trace/fingerprint lab contained the MP-4 camera near the glass wall to Nick's left, some old fingerprint cards in a massive file immediately to one side of the AFIS computer, and even more in a rotating tray system on the wall at right; behind Nick, an array of computer monitors, high-intensity lamps, racks of chemicals for the developing of prints and plenty of work-table space.

Shrugging, Warrick pulled up one of the wheeled stools scattered around the room and dropped onto it. He filled Nick in, finally saying, "If Dearborn's telling the truth—if he really is a changed man—what other candidates are there?"

Nick ducked the question, asking, "Where's that bat now?"

"Gave it to Hodges. You got anything?"

"So far, I've matched prints to the vic, one of the EMTs, and come up with two unknowns."

Just then the computer beeped, and both crime-scene analysts looked at the monitor.

"Make that *one* unknown," Nick said. "This print belongs to none other than your reformed doper friend, Taylor Dearborn."

A humorless smirk dug a dimple in Warrick's left cheek. "Well, he did admit to being there. . . ."

"Did he also admit to having a beer? Because the print was on a beer bottle."

"Really? And Dearborn says he's been clean for the last seven months. . . ."

Nick shrugged. "Maybe beer doesn't count, in his world view. Bottle was also used to inflict more than one of the wounds on the victim."

A frazzled Catherine came in, face creased with a frown, eyes hooded, body language tight.

"Ecklie?" Nick asked.

She just glared at a point between the two CSIs.

"Ecklie," Warrick affirmed.

"Take it easy, Cath," Nick said. "All you have to do is get comfortable with kissing—"

And Ecklie strode in, as Nick cut himself off.

"Progress on the Dearborn murder?" the slender, balding bureaucrat asked, unaware of—or ignoring—the sudden tension in the room.

Warrick coughed to cover a smile at the jam Nick had narrowly averted, then said, "We're still sorting through the evidence. Larkin has taken the ex-husband into custody."

"Murder charge already?"

"Not quite—guy violated a court restraining order. Gives us a chance to hold him while we work the evidence, which is stacking up against him, so far. We have blood on an aluminum bat from his garage—possible murder weapon."

"Fine work," Ecklie said. "Fine work, all of you." He nodded to each of them, Catherine last, then said, "Keep me apprised." And was gone.

Nick and Warrick exploded into laughter once they were sure Ecklie was out of earshot, but this didn't last long, as they noticed a distracted-looking Catherine not joining in.

"Okay," she said, her tone serious. "Do we have our killer in custody or not?"

Warrick shrugged. "Nick's got a beer bottle with Dearborn's fingerprint on it, used in the beating. Still . . . I suppose I don't 'think' anything yet, not till we have some sort of evidentiary foundation. What little evidence we have is offset by a very convincing performance out of Dearborn, reacting grief-stricken over the death of his wife."

"Operative word," Nick asked, arching an eyebrow, " 'performance?' "

Warrick didn't respond.

Catherine asked, "You took a buccal swab?"

"Mia has it," Warrick said, nodding.

Lovely African-American lab tech Mia Dickerson had taken Greg Sanders's place when the latter had turned CSI.

Catherine thought for a moment. Then she said to Warrick, "You're right—let's not get ahead of ourselves. If we *do* have the right man behind bars, we'll need a lot more to keep him there."

5

Monday, January 24, 12:30 P.M.

JIM BRASS LOVED HIS JOB but, like just about everyone who feels that way, he hated parts of it.

The duty he was about to perform—informing the next of kin of a murder victim—had to top that list. He'd dropped Grissom back at the lab and, technically, night shift was over, *way* over, with most of the city going to lunch; but Brass couldn't pass the buck on a thing like this. He steered the Taurus toward Boulder City, on the far southeast corner of the Vegas valley.

David Arrington, Grace Salfer's nephew, lived in a spacious one-story stucco on Coronado Drive, in an affluent but not ostentatious neighborhood. Arrington's home fit right in, at least in size, with a two-car garage and Xeriscaped front yard (an especially expensive touch); but the pastel-green paint job reminded Brass more of Miami than Vegas, a different color than any other house in the neighborhood, and only one of half a dozen or so on this street that had done away with their lush lawns.

Brass had just walked up to the front and reached out to push the doorbell when he heard the garage door swing open. Turning toward the noise, he waited a few seconds, then saw a red Miata backing out onto the driveway. Moving down the front walk and waving, Brass got the driver's attention. The vehicle stopped and Brass approached the car, holding out his badge in its wallet.

Remaining behind the wheel, the slender, thirtyish driver wore a dark gray suit over a blue denim shirt with a gold tie, tortoise-shell glasses shading small dark eyes, his hair dark and straight, neatly parted at the right, lending a conservative touch slightly at odds with his thin mustache and wispy goatee. Surprisingly, an easy smile crossed the guy's face when he saw the badge—not every citizen has a positive response, encountering a cop.

"Morning, Officer," he said, leaning out the window like a customer ordering at a drive-in. "Or I guess I should say, afternoon? How can I be of help?"

"I appreciate your attitude, sir," Brass said. "Are you David Arrington?"

But now the smile faded. "Why, yes—why?"

"Would you mind turning off the car, please?"

"Actually, I'm late for work as it is. If this is something we can take care of quickly, I'd rather—"

And this had started so well. . . .

"Please, sir," Brass said. "The engine?"

Reluctantly, Arrington turned off the car and Brass opened the door for him. Stepping out, Arrington revealed himself to be fairly short—about five-foot-five; he brought a pack of cigarettes out of his coat pocket and lit one, saying after the fact, "You don't mind if I smoke? Now, what's this about, Officer, uh . . . afraid I didn't get a close enough look at your I.D. to catch a name."

"Captain Brass."

Arrington stood there casually, smoking the cigarette, with a confidence that was starting to disconcert Brass. "What's this all about, Captain? We don't get much police activity in this neighborhood."

"Mr. Arrington, I'm not here on a pleasant task." Brass knew better than to try to sugarcoat such news. "This morning I was one of several officers dispatched to the home of your aunt, Grace Salfer."

"Is she all right? Is my aunt—"

"Sir, I'm sorry, but she's dead."

Cigarette-in-hand stopped halfway to Arrington's mouth, hesitated, then continued to his lips where he took a deep, solemn drag. "Please tell me she died quietly, in her sleep."

"I wish I could say that was the case. She was murdered."

"My God—how?"

"We don't have official confirmation yet."

"For Christ's sake, man—*un*officially, then?"

"The crime scene investigators say that evidence indicates she was suffocated."

Arrington took an involuntary step back—as if he'd been punched in the stomach. He dropped the cigarette to the cement of the drive, but absentmindedly did not stamp it out. He bumped back into his car.

"Are you all right, sir? Do you need—"

"Fine. Fine." He regained his footing. Swallowed. "Who did this to her? She was a sweet, gentle lady, with a great heart, generous heart—who *did* this?"

Brass shook his head. "We don't know yet, Mr. Arrington. I was hoping . . . if you're up to it . . . you might be able to help shed some light on that."

"Anything I can do, Captain Brass."

"I appreciate that, sir."

"But, uh . . . let's not continue this out here. Doesn't feel right, and . . . I could use something to drink. You mind?"

"By all means, let's go inside."

"I'll just put the car back in the garage. Meet you at the front door, in a moment."

"Certainly."

Arrington finally stubbed out his cigarette, got in his car, and soon was inside the house, opening the front door for Brass, who stepped inside.

On the way, Arrington had acquired a glass of clear liquid on ice that appeared to be a lemon-lime drink or perhaps sparkling water. He offered to get the captain something, but Brass declined.

Brass followed his host into a living room more wide than deep, carpeted a rich gray, French doors on the far side leading into a formal dining room. The walls were white, with white drapes on the front windows, sunshine streaming in.

This was a living room that got lived in: an entertainment center with a massive rear-projection widescreen television on the right wall and a white leather sofa slunk under the front window. Two leather arm chairs sat at angles to the sofa, a low square table in the center. Framed photos of Arrington with other people—national and local show business folk—rode the walls, striking Brass as more appropriate to an office.

Arrington waved for Brass to take one of the leather armchairs, which he did, the host perching in the other.

"How can I help?" Arrington asked, setting his glass on a coaster on a glass table.

"First, you can tell me about your aunt. It's important in a murder investigation to get a sense of who the victim was."

"I'll do my best. But why don't you take the lead, Captain."

Brass got out his notebook and a pen. "Did Mrs. Salfer have any enemies that you know of?"

Arrington frowned and smiled simultaneously. "Captain, please—she was an eighty-year-old woman."

Brass shrugged. "The longer we're alive, the more friends—and adversaries—we create, and collect. I'm sorry, Mr. Arrington, as predictable as this may seem, it's the first question I have to ask."

"I understand. No, she had no enemies."

"Your aunt wasn't a poor woman—"

"Calling her wealthy would be overstating, but no, she was certainly not poor."

Brass nodded. "Do you know how her estate will be settled?"

Arrington's expression lengthened. "That's a . . . sobering question, Captain." He thought for a moment. "We were friendly, my aunt and I, but we weren't what I'd call . . . close. We talked fairly frequently, but I haven't seen my aunt since Christmas

Eve, and haven't spoken to her, on the phone, since just after the first of the year. Her estate is something we . . . we never discussed. I wasn't her *son*, you know. Really strikes me in poor taste . . . not your question, I mean. But the issue of her 'estate' would have been an awkward, awful subject for me to bring up."

"And she never did."

"No."

"You may not be her son, Mr. Arrington, but as far as we're able to determine, you're her only living relative."

"As far as I know, I am. Certainly closest living."

"Then you would be in line to inherit, correct?"

Arrington considered that. "That's not something I've given much . . . hell, *any* thought to. I make a good living. I suppose I might get something, even everything, from her will, assuming she has one. But who's to say my aunt didn't leave everything to charity, or her old college or something?"

"What college would that be?"

"I don't know! I *think* she went to college. I just meant, she had a life of her own—a life for a lot of years before I was on the planet. So I would not be surprised either way."

Brass shifted in the chair and the leather squeaked. "No offense meant, Mr. Arrington, but coming into that kind of money—"

"*What* kind of money? Do you have any idea what her estate is worth? *I* certainly don't." He gestured around the living room with its entertainment center. "Does it look like I *need* my aunt's money?"

Actually, it didn't—but Brass also knew he himself could go out to Best Buy this afternoon and put that same big-screen TV on his credit card; that didn't mean Jim Brass could afford such a purchase. . . .

And *he* didn't have a rich aunt.

Moving on, Brass asked, "Any employees or former employees of your aunt who might have a grudge?"

With a quick head shake, Arrington said, "As far as I know, my aunt never had any employees. She probably hired out the housekeeping and yardwork and so on, but not an employee per se."

"Do you know who those people might be? Housekeeper? Yardman?"

"No."

Another tack. "Can you tell me where you were last night?"

Arrington sipped at the glass of sparkling liquid. Perhaps too casually, he asked, "Am I a suspect?"

"It's a routine question, Mr. Arrington."

"Do I need my attorney?"

"Do you?"

Arrington returned the drink to its coaster. "Why would *I* be a suspect? That's all I'd like to know."

"Not very many people had contact with your aunt," Brass said. "Those who did, I have to talk to—just to rule people out."

Arrington seemed to accept that. Then he said, "I had a business dinner that kept me out until nearly midnight."

"On a *Sunday* night?"

Leaning forward, Arrington offered a small grin.

"Is there such a thing as 'Sunday' night, in Vegas, Captain? You know how it is—no rest for the wicked. I book shows at the Platinum King Casino."

Perking, Brass said, "Then you must know Doug Clennon . . ."

"Of course. I work for him."

The detective could not help but be impressed, aging baby boomer that he was. Clennon had climbed to fame by hosting his after-school *Rock & Roll Dance Party* from the fifties into the mid-eighties. At first a syndicated show, *RRDP* had eventually won a network audience and became a fixture until it finally succumbed to MTV.

Still, Clennon had enough foresight to open the Platinum King Casino and Showroom, which in recent years had become a staple of the Vegas scene. Featuring mostly oldies acts—Bobby Rydell, Frankie Avalon, Fabian, the Association, the Grass Roots—the casino drew an upscale middle-aged crowd.

But Clennon still appealed to younger folks as well by hosting occasional pay-per-view live events, like his recent Tsunami Aid concert featuring everyone from Outkast to Metallica in an eight-hour extravaganza that also included the likes of Weezer and The Darkness. (Brass would just have to be forgiven for preferring Rydell and the Association.)

"Mr. Clennon and I met," Brass said, "on a case a while back."

"Well, I work closely with Mr. Clennon," Arrington said. "I'm surprised you and I didn't run into each other, Captain. What case was that?"

"The murder of Busta Kapp."

Arrington nodded. "Ah—I was in the Bahamas, at

the time. . . . But that was a tragic crime. And that's the kind of publicity we *don't* want at the Platinum King."

White punk-rapper Kapp had been a killer himself, one Brass had been on the verge of busting when Busta got capped and became a victim—fortunes change quickly in Vegas.

"Who were you having dinner with last night?"

"Alex Hunter. Rep for a show themed around Ray Charles and Bobby Darin, trying to take advantage of the movies that just came out on both those artists. Perfect for the Platinum King crowd."

Brass wrote Hunter's name into the notebook. "Is Mr. Hunter a Vegas resident?"

"No, he's a guest at the Platinum King . . . and probably will be for at least one more night."

Brass jotted that down, too. "Do you live here alone, Mr. Arrington?"

Arrington nodded. "Yes—I'm unencumbered at the moment."

"Then you were married at one time?"

"Engaged a couple of times, but no. Whether that's lucky or unlucky, who can say? And I guess I'm kind of a kid in a candy store, with so many beautiful women around me at work—makes it hard to commit." He shrugged. "Can't blame any woman for not putting up with that . . . *and* the kind of hours I work."

Brass smiled gently. "I know that last problem. . . .You seem to be handling this unfortunate news all right."

Arrington frowned. "Is that a . . . *suspect* question?"

"No, not at all. Just want to make sure you're okay." Brass shut his notebook. "I'll take my leave, then. You'll have things to do."

"I guess so." His eyes widened. "I guess I'm the one who'll have to deal with . . . funeral arrangements and so on."

"Yes, you will."

"You never think about these things, do you? And then suddenly, here they are."

"Actually," Brass said with his own grave smile, "I'm afraid I think about these things, every day."

Arrington showed Brass out.

The captain drove back to the station, mulling over how little they seemed to have to go on. He hoped Grissom was having better luck with the physical evidence. Seeing himself yawn in the rearview mirror, the detective determined from *that* evidence that the best thing for him to do right now was grab something to eat, and try to catch a few hours sleep.

Greg Sanders sat in the straight-back chair, the sharp edge of its seat digging into the backs of his thighs, as he looked at the mountains of paper spread out on the bronze-colored metal table.

He was in a gray concrete room, at the back of Home Sure Security, a chamber with all the charm of a mausoleum, going through the records Grissom had demanded the company manager produce. Exhaustion nagged at Greg. Grissom had called the CSI only a couple hours after he'd gotten home and gone to bed.

The boss had wanted Greg to meet him here at Home Sure, ASAP.

"I've got a project for you," Grissom said on the phone.

And Greg knew what the answer to any request Gil Grissom made of him: *yes.*

Greg's eyes were hot, as if flu was coming on, and his muscles ached like he'd just run a marathon. Giving in to fatigue was *not* an option, however; day shift was short-handed, and the records needed to be looked at during the company's business hours. Further, Greg was fully aware that Grissom expected— needed—his new graveyard team to shine.

Grissom had met Greg in Home Sure's parking lot, accompanied him inside and saw to it that the manager—one Todd Templeton—complied with the records request. Once he made sure Greg was settled, Grissom gave him a list of what to look for, then told the young CSI to call and check in, when he was ready to go.

"I know you're tired," Grissom had said. "But I need you alert. Understood, Greg?"

"Understood."

From the very start of this thankless task, Greg was ready to bail, but he knew better than to give in. Grissom wanted him to comb through these records, and Greg would sit here until hell froze over, combing away.

Gil Grissom—for all the grief Greg had given him, and all the grief Grissom had given Greg back—had really, truly gone to bat for the fledgling CSI. Getting the higher-ups to allow their best DNA technician to leave the lab, and take a pay cut, just because field work seemed "more challenging" to the upstart, was no easy task.

But Grissom had made it happen.

Of course, Greg Sanders had made a lot of things "happen" for himself, over the years.

A precocious kid who'd started matriculating a year early, he went from public school, where he regularly blew through tests, to an academy that had at least presented him a more significant challenge; then Greg had gone on to Stanford, before spending two years as a lab tech with the San Francisco PD. When he read about the amazing results the Las Vegas crime lab was racking up, he applied there, snagging a position as the DNA lab technician in this highly respected facility.

After four years of having his head buried in his work, Greg—constantly interacting with the graveyard-shift CSIs—began to crave the kind of excitement and satisfaction that these field agents seemed to meet on every case. Finally he convinced Supervisor Gil Grissom to give him a shot out in the field.

Almost everyone had told the DNA expert that he was making a mistake, including Grissom, who nonetheless had given Greg the opportunity he craved. Now, Greg owed the man for that, and much more, and silently renewed his vow to do nothing that would let Grissom down.

If that meant accepting the occasional crappy end of the stick, like today, so be it—even if it included reading meaningless reports for the duration.

As he tried to find a place to begin among the many different, unfamiliar forms, Greg considered what he'd witnessed when he and Grissom arrived at the Home Sure office.

They had been greeted at the door by a hot Latina named Tina who had immediately used her walkie-talkie to summon Templeton to meet them. She had exchanged laughing smiles with Greg, and he really hoped that that had *not* been part of her regular greeting schtick. . . .

The Home Sure honcho, in a slick gray suit, had a professional if overbearing manner; when he came out to meet them, Todd Templeton didn't offer to shake either of their hands.

"This way," Templeton said brusquely, and led them through the building.

Funny that this guy would treat them so dismissively and yet still accompany the CSIs personally, when Home Sure staff members to spare were all around. Including Tina.

They had eventually ended up back here in this fluorescent cave, where the temperature of the cool room had seemed to drop even a few degrees more, when Templeton and Grissom finally spoke to each other.

"Your wish is my command," Templeton said dryly to Grissom, pointing to the table where several piles of papers waited.

"That was fast," Grissom said. "Thank you."

Templeton's shrug was barely perceptible. "I told you we'd help any way we could."

"If you could provide some boxes, we can—"

"No. No boxes, Grissom. These records stay here. On these premises."

"You knew we wanted to take these with us," Grissom said, gesturing to the piles of paper.

The teeth-baring expression Templeton offered

was only technically a smile. "Really? Did you bring me a court order?"

"What happened to cooperating, Todd?" Grissom's face was blank, but his voice frowned.

Now the smile turned genuinely mirthful. "Why, Gil—that's exactly what I *am* doing. The records you asked for are all here; but it would be irresponsible of me to my living-breathing clients, not to mention my investors, to allow you to carry off the records of all those Los Calina residents . . . without a judge agreeing that you need them for *every* resident. It was only out of professional courtesy that I'm allowing you to make this examination here, at Home Sure."

And Templeton bowed—actually *bowed!*—and left Grissom and Greg standing there, Grissom disgusted, Greg confused.

That was when Grissom had told Greg to call when he was finished, gave him the list of things to look for, and left him in this concrete purgatory.

Initially, Greg had reread Grissom's wish list; and now the young CSI sat paralyzed by the sheer volume of paper confronting him.

Looking up in the direction of a whirring, he noticed a video camera mounted in the corner, where wall met ceiling, its snout of a lens pointed directly at him.

So, he thought, Home Sure Security thinks they need to keep an eye on CSI. . . .

He resisted the urge to idiotically wave and grin at the camera, commended himself for his maturity, and dug into the paper piles, starting with the files on the victim, Grace Salfer. He wasn't sure exactly what he was looking for and—as frequently happened since he'd moved from the womb of his lab into the harsh cold world of the field—he felt hopelessly in over his head.

Of course, this sensation was becoming such second-nature to him now that he hardly felt bothered by it.

The first form he picked up looked like a standard application: name, address, phone number. He swiftly scanned it, got nothing, blew out a breath, and read it again, this time slowly.

Through most of his life, Greg had fought the prodigy's natural urge to rush through things. A lot of school, especially high school, had been painfully easy for him. He would wait until the night (or even the morning) before class to do his homework. This habit had stayed with him, though the lab had nullified it somewhat. In the lab, things took as long as they took ("Science is not on our schedule," Grissom would say, "we are on its"); but outside the lab, Greg could still be guilty of being in a hurry.

Slow progress is real progress, he told himself. *Don't miss anything.*

Nothing new to be found in the name, address, or phone boxes.

Nearest relative was a nephew, David Arrington—was that something or nothing? He didn't know. So he made a note of it; at this rate, he should be done in about a thousand years. He also made a note of the victim's bank, where her monthly payment to Home Sure was taken by direct withdrawal. After all, Grissom might want to check her financial records to search for a motive. The rest of the form looked like fairly mundane stuff and Greg set it aside.

The next sheet was a record of the number of times the alarm had been serviced since Mrs. Salfer had moved in almost a year ago.

Greg read this carefully. Aside from normal monthly checkups, Mrs. Salfer's upstairs alarm had gone off at least half a dozen times in the first month she lived there. Motion detectors were in force except on the pathway to the client's nearest bathroom; but the alarm kept going off, anyway. A note from a Home Sure guard, Susan Gillette, stated the opinion that Mrs. Salfer herself was setting off the alarm, absentmindedly moving into motion-detector areas.

After that, Mrs. Salfer had simply started turning off the second-floor alarm, leaving the lower floor fully armed—protected by window alarms and motion-detectors. The latter, of course, did not set off the bottom-floor alarms for ninety seconds, giving the homeowner time on entering the house to key in the proper code on the pad; of course, a security guard or anyone else with that code could do the same thing.

Judging from what Greg had seen at the house, turning off the second-floor alarm seemed reasonable enough, considering the unlikelihood of somebody breaking in there—after all, the residence had no fence; and neighbors were on every side. Mrs. Salfer should have been relatively safe.

Tell it to the victim, Greg thought.

The ladder against the back of the house bothered Greg. Grissom and Sofia seemed pretty sure it had not been used, that it was some kind of ruse; but had someone used it—or even planted it—in the knowledge that the second-floor alarm was turned off?

Who was privy to that information?

Greg made a note to ask Templeton that question.

Reading on, he found out that Mrs. Salfer had no more problems with her alarm system after she stopped using the second-floor portion of it. This could mean several things—a confirmation of Gillette's theory that Mrs. Salfer was setting it off herself; that the device had finally been repaired properly by Home Sure; or that the problems of the device were limited to the second-floor.

Greg made more notes.

He went from Mrs. Salfer's records to those of her neighbors. Some of them had alarm problems, most did not, but none had problems as serious as Grace Salfer had had. The question Greg needed to answer was: Were her problems an anomaly, or was someone purposely trying to set her up? That the only Los Calina customer who was having alarm problems also was a *murder* victim seemed worth another notation. . . .

Going through the alarm records for all the houses in a three-block radius around the Salfer home, Greg discovered half-a-dozen clients who chose to leave one or more zones unprotected for one reason or another. Maybe her habit of keeping the second floor turned off wasn't that big a deal; but Greg dutifully chronicled his findings for Grissom.

Next he looked at the records listing people who

had signed in at the gate to visit the Salfer residence. These records were not the actual sign-in sheets from the gate guard's clipboard, but typed lists of names, dates, and times of Mrs. Salfer's visits. Such visits were few and far between—her nephew, Arrington, a couple of times; a woman named Elizabeth Parker stopped by at least once a month. The latter gave Greg another name to look into—Parker was a friend, perhaps, who could provide insight into Mrs. Salfer's life.

He was at it for another two hours, stopping only to go to the bathroom once, and another time to buy a bottle of soda from the vending machine in the Home Sure break room.

He did come across one other interesting piece of information: Checking alarm responses around the Los Calina community, Greg found that four overnight alarm calls had been made by that ubiquitous guard, Susan Gillette.

Could the shoe prints in the backyard have been made by the guard? Though Susan Gillette's feet were much too small to make the prints, she could've been standing in men's shoes—the shallow depth of the print created by Gillette's light weight. . . .

Gillette's employment file was not among these papers, but Greg made a fairly detailed note about his theory; and he would ask Grissom what it would take to get access to employment files.

When Greg finished, his eyes were burning, his mind fogged, with a constant pounding at his brain stem, as if somebody wanted to be let in the door to his skull. He hadn't slept for nearly twenty-four hours, and he didn't know how much longer he could hang on. He had a fleeting image of his past self in the DNA lab, lounging back in a chair as machines did the work and he read *Rolling Stone*. . . .

Smiling at himself, he thought, well, at least he had finished the records, or anyway what had been provided. Finally yanking that cell phone off his belt, he rang his boss.

"Grissom."

"It's Greg. I'm ready to go."

"Just how tired are you, by now?"

"I still seem to have a pulse."

"Catch a couple hours sleep. Then we'll meet for an early dinner and you can tell me what you found."

"Meet you . . . for dinner?"

"Yes."

"You want to eat . . . with me?"

"Why? Will that be a problem?"

"No, it's . . . sure. Cool. Where?"

Grissom told Greg, then ended the call.

After packing up his stuff, Greg slipped through the door into the showroomlike lobby and caught a pleasing glimpse of the young Latina he'd seen earlier. He was wondering if he was sentient enough to talk to her when he sensed someone next to him, and glanced sideways at Todd Templeton.

"Find what you wanted?" Templeton asked.

"It's a start. Thank you."

"You were back there quite a while."

"Pretty slow slog," Greg said, "all that paper—I

noticed the visitor's log books weren't among the records. Typed-up info, but not the originals. Can you tell me why that is?"

Templeton frowned. "Grissom didn't ask for them . . ."

"You asking me or telling me, Mr. Templeton?"

The security man laughed. "Telling you, son." He emphasized that last, patronizing word. "You tell your big bad boss that if he wants any more from me, he can tell it to the judge."

"You know," Greg said with a smile, "I'll bet he agrees with you."

"What?"

"I'll bet *he* thinks it's time to get a court order, too. . . . Thanks again."

Templeton was still processing that when Greg pushed through the double doors into the outside. The CSI wanted not to look back, to just keep walking to his car; but he couldn't help himself. He turned slightly and caught a glimpse of Templeton. Couldn't tell whether the security chief looked worried or not, but the guy sure didn't seem happy.

At just after nine P.M., Greg entered the nondescript Boulder Highway Diner to find Grissom already seated in a back booth, nursing a cup of coffee and reading the *Las Vegas Sun* folded flat in front of him.

Greg had been to this diner a few times before, but always with the whole team, never just him and Grissom. Actually, he couldn't think of once he'd ever done anything alone with Grissom, outside of work anyway, and the truth was (much as he told himself not to be) he was nervous.

A couple guys separated by an empty stool at the counter were having a late dinner and a few of the red-and-white booths were in use, but basically the place was heading into the slow patch that wouldn't change till the late crowd rolled in some time after midnight.

Grissom gave him half a wave and Greg let out a long, slow breath before crossing the room to join his boss. A pretty blond waitress about Greg's age angled over from behind the counter as he sat.

"Coffee?" she asked, giving him a smile that seemed genuine. Or at least, genuine enough.

"Sure," Greg said, "black," and she was gone.

"Get some sleep?" Grissom asked.

Greg nodded confidently. "That, and a shower, too, and now I'm good to go."

The waitress brought him a steaming mug, took their order and flounced off, Greg's eyes involuntarily watching the sway of her hips.

"Gathering evidence, Greg?"

He jumped a little at the sound of Grissom's voice, and looked at his boss.

"Hey," Greg said with a small embarrassed smile. He sipped the coffee, which was good and hot. "Biology. It's science, too, you know."

Grissom twitched a smile, then asked, "What do you know now that you didn't before you went through those records?"

Greg considered the question. "I know which bank Grace Salfer used to pay her Home Sure bill."

124   **Max Allan Collins**

Grissom nodded. "Check or withdrawal?"

"Withdrawal," Greg said. "I figured knowing where she did her banking would give us a leg up on going through her finances."

"You're right. But Brass'll have that information for us when we get to work tonight."

Greg felt the wind go out of his sails. *Of course* Brass would have gotten Grace Salfer's financial records. . . .

Grissom said, "It still was a good catch. We couldn't know for sure Brass would have the records. The nature of the investigative beast insures some duplication of effort."

Greg blinked, not recognizing the quote. "Who said that?"

Grissom looked at him for two seconds, then said, "Me. Just now . . .What else did you learn?"

"There was a name on the guest logs—Elizabeth Parker. She came to visit Grace Salfer at least once a month and usually more."

"Do we know who she is?"

Greg shrugged. "A friend maybe?"

"We don't deal in 'maybe,' Greg."

"I know. But—"

"When we get to the lab, see if you can track her down. . . . Good work."

The young CSI brightened. "Thanks."

Their food arrived, and they ate in silence for several minutes, before Grissom picked up the thread again.

"What did you find out about the woman's alarm?"

Greg filled Grissom in on that score.

"What about the other residents?"

"Several had sporadic alarm problems, but none seemed to be as prolonged as Mrs. Salfer's."

"Which tells us?"

"They had a really hard time fixing her system."

"Or?"

"Or someone had been setting her up for this . . . for months."

"Good," Grissom said. "Nicely reasoned."

Greg, not terribly hungry, pushed his half-eaten plate of food away, and leaned forward. "There were a couple other things that bothered me."

Grissom cocked his head. "Really? Such as?"

"The guest logs? They weren't originals, or even photocopies. They were typed lists."

"Interesting. What else?"

"They gave me the list of guards who'd worked at Los Calina, and the shifts they worked; but no personnel files. So there wasn't any background on everyone's favorite security guard, Susan Gillette—or anyone else, for that matter."

Grissom nodded thoughtfully. "And did you ask our friend Mr. Templeton about that?"

"Actually . . . it slipped my mind. I did run into Templeton in that showroom, but he was kind of an . . . an . . ."

"An asshole?"

Greg was astonished at this word emanating from Grissom—a man who could drop an anvil on his foot and not swear.

"Pretty much. He made it clear we'd need a court order for anything else we wanted out of Home Sure."

"About what I expected."

Greg finished his coffee, then said, "I did notice one other thing."

"Care to share it?" Grissom asked.

"You and Templeton—there's history there . . . isn't there?"

Grissom gave him a tight smile and turned toward the waitress across the room. "Check, please!"

6

Tuesday, January 25, 9:30 P.M.

TWENTY-FOUR HOURS REMOVED FROM THE Angela Dearborn murder, Catherine Willows sat at the large table in the layout room, which tonight seemed as icy as the blue-tinged lighting and aqua-glass walls that gave CSI HQ such a high-tech fishbowl feel. Her black short-sleeve top and black leather pants gave her the look of a stylish mourner, and she was indeed grieving, in a way . . . still feeling a keen sense of loss over this woman she had never met.

Who could say whether the poet's notion that one man's death diminished each of us—involved as we all are in mankind—was lofty nonsense or insightful truth? But Catherine certainly felt diminished by the brutal murder of Angela Dearborn. After investigating scores upon scores of homicides in well over a decade, how much capacity to absorb tragedy did Catherine have left in her?

The balance of this business was to maintain human compassion without giving in to despair while simulta-

neously avoiding any hardening toward violence and
death that might naturally build up. A CSI could be
neither optimist nor pessimist, and cynicism had no
place . . . or sentimentality, either.

Still, early on, Grissom had told her, "Distance is
necessary in this discipline—but don't stand so far
back that you can't discern the human tragedy before you."

With this in mind, she contemplated the personal
effects all but covering the mammoth worktable. Almost against her will, Catherine felt energy rising
within her. No matter how tired, no matter how
melancholy, the CSI knew she was the victim's only
hope for redress, and this gave her a jolt of combined
pride and responsibility that was like an adrenaline
rush.

She took a slow walk around the table, looking
over the possessions of the deceased, like a prospec-
tive bidder arriving before an estate auction: a green
jewelry box, three purses (which included the one
Angela been carrying most recently), cell phone,
checkbook, and laptop computer, among other
seemingly routine belongings.

A lot to go through, somewhat imposing; but not
impossible. After all, Angie Dearborn hadn't exactly
been rolling in green. The laptop, in fact, rather surprised Catherine—certainly a lot of people these
days had portable computers, but this was a fairly
high-end model.

On her cell phone she punched in the number of
freelance computer guru Tomas Nuñez, with whom
she'd worked several times. Tomas should easily be

able to tell her everything that was on Angie Dearborn's hard drive.

"*Querida*," Nuñez's baritone said with warmth and humor—his cell phone had obviously showed him her number; either that, or he now answered his phone by calling everyone "darling."

He was saying, "I suppose you're going to break my heart and say this is business."

"I certainly am . . . *querida*," she said lightly, and then soberly explained the situation.

"Strange, isn't it?" he said. "How in this technological age, we leave behind traces of ourselves, memories in a way, on the machines we use?"

"Well, from a CSI standpoint, it's certainly helpful. Thirty, even twenty years ago, crime-scene analysts would find stacks of correspondence to go through. . . . Then times changed and letter-writing fell off, and made an investigator's job harder."

"And then along came e-mail," Nuñez said. "Funny how people started writing to each other again—a lost art found."

"To which I say, huzzah. Now, when can you get to this, Tomas? We're still in an early enough stage that—"

"No prob-lay-mo," Nuñez said in mock-gringo cadence. "I can pick it up in about . . . half an hour?"

"Perfect. You're the best."

"I know."

Relishing the smile Tomas had pried out of her, Catherine clicked off and got to work.

She began with another electronic keeper of memories: Angie's cell phone, which had already been dusted for prints, giving up none but the victim's. Still, cells—whether they were phones or from fingernail scrapings—could contain a wealth of information. . . .

And this was a model she recognized, so she easily punched the menu key, scrolled through the options, and found Angie's in-box empty . . . apparently the victim had erased any voice messages. Back through the menu, and Catherine got to the call log. First she made note of all Angie's missed calls, then the received calls, finally those Angie dialed herself.

Catherine came up with a list of thirty calls, representing sixteen different phone numbers. Of those, three came up most often. She would run the frequent-callers first.

The checkbook had a balance of a little over three hundred dollars and, near as Catherine could tell, Angie's bills were paid. No checks jumped out at Catherine, either—cable company, landlord, phone company, and their typical like. No checks were for an exorbitant amount; none were to individuals.

One odd thing about the checkbook did stand out, though: Angie deposited three hundred dollars in cash every Friday . . . with the notation line for the deposit's source blank. This struck Catherine as odd. If that was a salary, for example, or maybe a regular gift from a relative, why wouldn't Angie record it?

She had just set that aside when the layout room door swung open and Tomas Nuñez strolled in. As usual, he was dressed in black from head to toe, running shoes/jeans/T-shirt. Seeing her dressed similarly, he laughed, held out his hands and said, "Great minds think alike, *querida!*"

Nearing fifty, with rough, pockmarked masculine good looks, lanky Tomas wore his straight black hair swept back and oiled, with not one strand of gray—and as long as she'd known him, Catherine had spotted no telltale roots indicated haircoloring. The black T-shirt was emblazoned with the likeness of Colombian singer Juanes; Latin music came in many forms and, Catherine knew, Nuñez was a connoisseur of most.

"*Hola*, Tomas," she said, a smile spreading. "Pull up a chair, why don't you?"

He returned the smile, revealing small and even teeth.

"Ah, I would love nothing more than to spend the day here with you, helping catalog all this evidence. . . . Okay to pick this up barehanded?"

He was reaching for the laptop.

"Sure," she said. "Everything here's been processed for prints."

"As I was saying, I'd love to keep you company . . . but you know how it is when a man runs his own business. His time is seldom his own."

"Try working for the county, sometime."

Lifting the laptop in hand, he asked, "Are we looking for anything in particular?"

"No. Well, maybe one thing . . . " She old him about the cash-deposit anomaly.

"Good to know."

He and the laptop were heading out when she said, "Come back when you can stay longer . . . *querida*."

"Don't tempt me," he said, his grin strangely shy suddenly. "You know how I feel about women in black leather."

"Actually, I don't."

"Make a wild guess."

"Tomas—you know we don't like to deal in wild guesses around here."

He laughed, rolled his eyes, and was gone.

Smiling to herself, Catherine figured they'd been flirting like this for a couple of years now; nothing had ever come of it, and she doubted it ever would. Their work relationship was too important.

But the kidding flirtation with Tomas brought to Catherine's mind another coworker, a closer one: Warrick. For a while now, she'd sensed a certain sexual tension between herself and the tall CSI. They'd shared something, not so long ago—just a . . . moment, where she'd stumbled and he'd helped her, and she wound up in his arms, briefly, eyes locked. Nothing had happened—no kiss or embrace or anything overt. . . .

Then, just when she'd been trying to sort out whether a relationship between two CSIs was even worth considering, the shake-up of the team had made her Warrick's boss.

Talk about complications.

Pushing such personal thoughts aside, Catherine got back to work. She went through the purses, and the rest of Angela's belongings, except for the green jewelry box, which she saved for last. For no rational reason, her hopes were highest for this one, like an unusually wrapped Christmas present you waited to open.

Intuition told her the jewelry box just might hold the evidence she needed. Green vinyl with gold leaf work, the object wasn't really anything all that special, seemingly the kind of doodad for which garage sales were invented; probably cost less than ten dollars, twenty years ago.

But it was just the sort of pretty little box that a woman might choose to keep a treasure in.

Catherine opened the tiny gold clasp and pushed the lid up, holding her breath in anticipation.

Inside were two sections.

The upper half held two watches, a small gold cross on a thin gold chain, and various plastic and silver bracelets and rings—nothing expensive, twenty-dollar items at most. The bottom half brimmed with a mix of necklaces and papers, including an old driver's license, a divorce decree, Angie's copy of the protection order against Taylor, a love letter from Taylor dated three and a half years ago, a drug-store receipt, and other detritus accumulated in an adult lifetime. The one thing Catherine was fairly certain she had not found was meaningful evidence.

So much for Christmas.

She was bagging up Angie's personal effects when Nick and Warrick strolled in, both in dark blue lab garb.

"Please tell me you guys have something," she said, as she stuffed the bags into a large cardboard box.

"I'd call it something," Warrick said.

Nick nodded, saying, "Yeah, we're starting to put some pieces together. I take it you're not?"

"Not yet, anyway," she said. She took a seat at the layout table, indicating with a head bob that they should do the same. "Enlighten me."

The three seated CSIs formed a triangle at one end of the worktable.

Nick said, "Blood drops on the carpeting were from the victim."

Catherine's eyes narrowed; nothing surprising about this news, but she was mentally shifting gears. "The ones we found near the body?"

"Right," Nick said. "We figure the blows got heavier and the drops came from the ends of the vic's hair."

All at once, Catherine saw it.

She saw Angela Dearborn relaxing on the couch with a magazine, wearing only the Romanov T-shirt and denim shorts, unaware of the impending end of her life.

Someone knocks at the door, and Angie rises, goes to check through the peephole. She recognizes the person and opens the door—the killer is someone she's comfortable enough with to let in. He (or possibly *she,* but in her mental reenactment *he*) *comes in, they talk, then they argue, and the more heated things become, the closer they get to violence. . . .*

. . . Then as suddenly as a match striking into flame, the two of them are really fighting, physically at each other. He's bigger, stronger, but she's tenacious and will not back down, at least not until the beer bottle crashes into her skull, blood erupting from a wound in her scalp.

Even this doesn't dissuade Angie, she only fights back harder, a cornered animal now, but then the struggle moves from the front room to the bedroom, when she finally tries to retreat behind a closed door. The killer's having none of that, though, and is into the bedroom, before she can get the door closed.

He hits her again and again, but she manages to scratch him, maybe on the arm as he delivers a blow. She's trying to use speed to outmaneuver her attacker. She clears the bedroom, but he catches her and flings her into the bathroom. They wrestle in the tiny room, but Angie manages to get free and moves back to the living room. She's going to run, but she had routinely locked the front door letting the attacker in.

She needs a weapon.

She sprints into the kitchenette. She'll get a knife, a pan, anything. Panic grips her, now; she grabs a knife and turns to find her attacker now has her trapped. She slices at his arm, he knocks the knife from her grasp and the two of them wrestle in there, eventually overturning the dining table in the small alcove and working their way back into the living room.

His blows are heavier now, he's found some blunt object to hit her with (what?) and she can't get away. She tries to fight back, but he's too strong. He hits her again and again, the blows raining down on her now. A new explosion of pain comes with each one until, finally, the pain ceases. She lies there taking it now, the punches no longer hurting, just absorbing one after the other, part of her floating above it now, watching from near the ceiling as the killer continues to brutalize her body—then merciful blackness.

Nick interrupted her thoughts. "The hair you found on the floor? Mia matched it to Taylor Dearborn."

Catherine snapped back into focus and felt buoyed a little. "Maybe this thing *is* coming together—maybe the abusive ex—"

"Slow down," Warrick said, patting the air with a palm. "The other hairs—the ones from Angie's shirt? *Not* Dearborn's."

Back to going in circles, Catherine thought. "Do we know *whose* hair it is?"

Warrick shook his head. "No. Not yet, anyway."

"What else *do* we know?"

Nick said, "We've got that fingerprint . . . Taylor's fingerprint . . . on a beer bottle that was part of the assault."

Squinting at Nick, she said, "That beer bottle can't be the murder weapon, though—surely it would've shattered, in that case. . . ."

Warrick was nodding. "Yeah, that bat I found is more like it—still waiting on blood results."

She was shaking her head. "Something isn't right. Thinking this through as an argument that gets out of hand . . . one of these typical bouts of verbal abuse that escalates into violence . . . suggests the murder weapon, the blunt object, was something the killer picked up spur-of-the-moment."

"In the kitchen, maybe," Warrick said.

She locked eyes with him. "Is anything missing from the apartment?"

"Could be—but how would we know?"

Nick offered, "Maybe the killer snatched up something in the living room—an art object like a heavy piece of sculpture."

Catherine said, "We could inventory the kitchen contents, and see what's *not* there."

Warrick remained skeptical. "I don't know, Cath—who can say *what* that might be? How can you build a meaningful inventory after the fact?"

Nick was trying to think it through. "I can't come up with anything in a kitchen . . . particularly a kitchenette like that one . . . that you could turn into an instant blunt object."

"A pan would do it," she said. "A rolling pin . . ."

"Frying pans and rolling pins," Nick said, grunting a laugh.

"Little clichéd, isn't it?" Catherine admitted.

"Could be," Warrick said with a shrug, finally buying in somewhat. Then he sat forward and his eyes were hard. "But I'll tell you one thing—if that bat, or *any* aluminum baseball bat, was responsible . . . this wasn't an argument that got out of hand."

Catherine got his point immediately. "You don't bring a bat along to ask your ex out on a date."

The three CSIs sat silently for a moment, but the same word was in all of their minds: *premeditation*.

"That makes this even weirder," Warrick said.

"How so?" she asked.

"Well, that beer bottle was definitely used to deliver at least *one* of the blows."

"With Taylor's print on it," Catherine reminded him.

"Right!" Warrick said. "Only, there's just one print of Taylor's . . . and it's right side up."

She frowned at him. "You say that as if it's significant."

"It is." Warrick mimed drinking a beer. "The print's placement is consistent with him *drinking* from the bottle."

Following this now, she began to nod. "And if he had hit her with the *bottom* of the bottle . . ."

Warrick mimed *that* action. "The print would have been going the other way—in essence, upside down on the bottle."

"Well-reasoned," she admitted.

"Thanks," he said, giving up a tiny grin.

"What about the other evidence?"

Nick said, "Nothing yet on the blood evidence under the sink."

Warrick put in, "The bloody shirt from the bedroom hasn't come back yet, either."

These things take time, Catherine could hear Grissom saying. *Impatience doesn't help.*

She asked, "How about the scrapings from under Angie's nails?"

"Still in the lab," Nick said.

Warrick said, "DNA keeps its own time schedule, as we all know too well . . . and we dumped a ton of it on Mia. She's doing the best she can."

Catherine nodded again. "What does Doc Robbins have for us?"

"Morgue's been backed up," Nick said. "He's doing the autopsy now."

"*Right* now?"

"Right now."

To Warrick, she said, "You were with Larkin when he took Dearborn into custody—did the suspect have any scratches or cuts?"

Shaking his head, Warrick said, "Not that I could see. I even pushed up the sleeves of his shirt. Forearms were clean."

"Hands?"

"Nope—no bruising or scrapes on his knuckles."

"But there wouldn't be," she said, "if he was using that baseball bat."

They sat in silence for a few moments.

Finally she asked, "Am I the only one who feels like the evidence is leading us around in circles?"

Nick grinned. "You are definitely not alone on *that* ride."

"Definitely not," Warrick affirmed.

"Well, something is not right here. So . . . let's take a step back to basics."

Warrick shrugged. "Never a bad idea."

"Why," she asked, "do people murder each other?"

"We can rule out serial killing," Warrick said, adding dryly, "even though Vegas is the current U.S. capital of that particular sport. . . . Angela Dearborn's murder is brutal enough for that, but otherwise, bears none of the earmarks."

"I agree," Nick said. "So we're back to the four biggies . . ."

"Drugs, sex, money, love. All right," Catherine said, ticking them off on her fingers. "Drugs?"

"None on the premises," Warrick said. "Of course, tox screen isn't back yet."

"She wasn't raped or sexually violated."

Nick shook his head. "Not from what we could see. We'll know more after the autopsy, but I would say—not raped."

"How about money?" Catherine asked, raising a third finger. "She only had about three hundred in her checkbook, and another forty or so in cash in her wallet."

"Which the killer left behind," Nick reminded them.

"Yeah," Warrick said, "and I checked her financial records. Besides the checking account, Angie had a savings account with around a grand. Not exactly independently wealthy."

She waggled the last finger. "That brings us back to love."

"Consensual sex the spark, you think?" Nick asked. "Back in the sack with the ex, then when the reconciliation proves momentary, old arguments flare back up?"

"Happens every day," Warrick said.

"*Nothing* feels right," Catherine said, and stood. "Let's go check on Dr. Robbins's progress—maybe he can point us somewhere."

The autopsy room was cool, almost cold, only one of its several steel tables in use. Angela Dearborn lay under a fluorescent light that made her nude unnaturally pale body seem even more washed-out.

Wearing light blue scrubs, a clear plastic shield over his face, Dr. Albert Robbins seemed engrossed with something inside Angie's mouth.

As they approached, Catherine took care to not disturb the man who had served as Clark County's medical examiner since 1995. Steel crutch leaned in its usual place in the corner, he had not acknowledged hearing them come in.

Without looking up, he said, "Something broke her teeth off. Something hard."

Catherine was at his side but a step behind. "Could a beer bottle have done the damage?"

He considered that for a moment, then shook his head. "Something harder—more mass. She had good teeth, and good teeth don't break off that easily. The best of teeth can be knocked out, of course, but *these* teeth . . . " He drew back the victim's upper lip so the three CSIs could see the mangled mess that had been Angie Dearborn's mouth. ". . . these teeth were shattered."

Catherine, distancing herself from the brutality,

asked, "Can you think of anything that might have done that?"

Warrick asked, "A baseball bat?"

Robbins said, "If it were an aluminum bat, yes."

Catherine asked, "Can you really narrow it down to that one possibility?"

He shook his head. "No. But I may find something later."

At his side now, Catherine pressed. "What else can you tell us about her?"

Robbins glanced at the CSI, his eyes thoughtful. "She was in good health . . . before this beating. Tox screen is clean."

"No drugs?"

"A small amount of alcohol. One beer, maybe."

Catherine frowned. *"Nothing?"*

Robbins shook his head again. "She was on birth control pills, Loestrin, but nothing else. Not even an aspirin."

"Sexual violation?"

And again he shook his head. "No evidence of sex at all, at least not the day she died." He gestured with a latex-gloved hand to numerous bruises, red and purple blotches. "But she did have these contusions on her arms, legs, and ribs."

Catherine winced. "Recent injuries?"

"Yes."

"All from this attack?"

Robbins nodded.

"What about time of death?"

"Core temperature had dropped significantly, when she was brought in." He paused; his head raised and the eyes behind the plastic shield tightened. ". . . I'd say she died sometime between eight and ten, the evening of the attack."

Catherine did some fast math. "When we got there, she'd been dead almost twenty-four hours. . . ."

"I'll have more for you later," Robbins said, not quite shooing them out of his workplace.

They nonetheless took the hint. In the hall, they were about to separate and take care of their individual tasks when Catherine's cell phone chirped and everyone froze.

"Catherine Willows."

"Hey, it's Larkin. I'm getting ready to take a crack at interrogating Taylor Dearborn."

"We call it 'interviewing' in Vegas."

"Call it whatever you like—if you want to be in on it, you or one of your people oughta get over to the jail."

"I appreciate the invitation. We could use some context."

"How so?"

"We're gathering puzzle pieces and can't quite grasp the picture. Has he lawyered up?"

"Yeah, on the restraining order beef. But he volunteered to talk to us about his ex-wife, without an attorney present."

"Cool." Catherine covered the phone and said to Warrick, "Larkin's about to interview Taylor Dearborn. One of us needs to at least watch that go down. You were in on the arrest, so—"

"On my way," Warrick said, and was off.

Catherine informed Larkin and broke the connection. Then she turned to Nick. "See if you can get the

DNA lab to put a rush on the scrapings from under Angie's nails."

"Do what I can. What about you?"

"I'm going back to her cell phone records, and see if there's something there."

Nick gave her his patented lopsided grin. "A CSI's exciting work is never done."

Catherine laughed lightly, but her expression was humorless as she said, "The exciting part will be nailing this sadistic killer. Maybe Warrick'll come back with the answer."

And, despite their common goal, they headed in opposite directions.

Warrick Brown caught up with Larkin just outside the interview room. He fell in alongside the detective, but before they'd even exchanged greetings, their attention went to Taylor Dearborn, hands cuffed behind him, wearing the orange Clark County jail jumpsuit. He was escorted with a hand on the arm by a uniformed guard, delivering him for interrogation.

The prisoner appeared to have deteriorated emotionally since Warrick last saw him, eyes red and puffy, hair uncombed, his skin a pasty white. His complexion was about the same as his ex-wife's had been when Warrick had seen the woman's corpse on Dr. Robbins's lab tray.

The guard led Dearborn into the room. Larkin and Warrick lingered in the corridor.

"You got anything new?" the detective asked.

Warrick said, "Doc Robbins thinks Angela wasn't killed until between eight and ten that night."

Larkin nodded, smiling slightly. "You know, that just might be helpful."

"Yeah?"

"Turns out Taylor's alibi checks out and—"

"He really *was* having dinner with Mayor Harrison?" Warrick couldn't hold back the grin.

Even Larkin had to chuckle—it had been a hell of an alibi. "He was indeed. His Honor even remembered Taylor by name and described him to me."

"Did the mayor remember what time he and Taylor were hangin' together?"

Larkin's eyes tightened and so did his smile. "The mayor didn't meet Taylor until they gave out the awards—around seven-thirty. Mayor Harrison said he spoke to Taylor for a couple of minutes after the ceremony, then didn't see him again. Both the mayor and his aide confirm that Harrison was out of there by eight, though."

"Ah," Warrick said. "That means Taylor might've had time to get from the dinner at City Hall back to Angie's and do his thing. Little less traffic at that hour. Coulda happened like that."

"Yes it could," Larkin said. "Let's go have a talk with our reformed wife-beating doper."

"Hey now . . . guy's innocent till proven guilty."

"I'm keepin' an open mind, Warrick—including to the possibility that this guy's the scumbag we're after."

They entered the interview room to find Dearborn seated at the table, cuffs removed, the guard hovering over him. Then Larkin gave the guard the high sign and the man stepped out.

Warrick and Larkin took the two chairs opposite

Dearborn, putting the detective directly across from the suspect. Dearborn hadn't looked at Warrick once—guy was keeping his eyes glued on the detective, as if he knew who his enemy was.

"So," Dearborn said, "I was where I said I was, right? The mayor himself confirmed that. Right?"

Larkin folded his hands and smiled coldly. "Well, I've got good news and bad news on that score, Mr. Dearborn."

"I *was* there!" Dearborn said. He was trembling just a little; maybe he craved a smoke.

"Mayor Harrison confirmed your alibi, all right."

A deep, relieved sigh heaved out of Dearborn.

"Hell, Taylor—you mind if I call you 'Taylor'? His Honor went so far as to say he remembered you."

Dearborn seemed more relaxed now; the trembling had disappeared.

Larkin smiled blandly. "That was the good news, by the way."

The prisoner sat back, stiffening.

"The bad news, Taylor? Bad news is Mayor Harrison said he didn't see you after he gave you your pin . . . and he left around eight."

Mildly indignant, Dearborn said, "So what? That sounds about right. Why is that a problem?"

"Well, that depends. What did you do after the banquet, the ceremony?"

Dearborn began to fool with the zipper of his jumpsuit. "Listen, uh . . . I'm dyin' for a cigarette. Either of you guys got—"

Larkin put on a blatantly phony expression of sympathy. "Sorry, Taylor—this is a smoke-free environment. And that doesn't mean free smokes."

Face screwed up with frustration, the suspect asked, "Why do you assume I'm dirty in this, Detective? I mean, here I am talkin' to you in good faith, no lawyer around . . ."

Larkin sat forward. "I'm not making that assumption, Taylor. I'm really not. But I do see you as a good suspect—I'd be lying to say otherwise. And I've read your jacket. You beat up on Angie when you were married, and you broke the restraining order the night she was killed. I'd be irresponsible not to look hard at you—don't you agree?"

With a dejected shake of the head, Dearborn said, "Yeah. Yeah, I can see that. So what do you want from me? I really did *not* do this; I *loved* her."

Warrick remembered Catherine's four motives for murder: *sex, drugs, money . . . and love.*

The detective said, "Then level with us."

Dearborn swallowed thickly. "After the awards dinner, I . . . I started to drive back over to Angie's."

"Started?"

Still fiddling with the zipper, Dearborn said, "Yeah, I was gonna stick that medal I earned in her face, and . . . then about halfway there, I thought, *screw* this, she doesn't want to see me, she's already pissed at me for coming by earlier. I felt enough resentment toward her . . . that she hadn't appreciated how I cleaned myself up. That I thought I might lose my temper or something. I figured, I'd just call her tomorrow. Then I went home. Only . . . *this* is tomorrow, isn't it? And I can't call her. Ever again."

The suspect seemed on the verge of tears, but the detective didn't give him a chance to let emotion take over, asking, "What time did you get home?"

Dearborn shrugged. "Hell, I don't know . . . I wasn't paying attention. It's not like I knew I needed a damn alibi! . . . Sometime between eight-thirty and nine, I suppose."

"Anyone see you?" Larkin asked.

Dearborn shook his head glumly. "Besides my dog? Nobody—not as far as I know. I just drove straight home."

"What did you do once you got there?"

"I don't know."

"Stop and think. Give us every step."

"Well, I parked in the drive. Went in the front door. Used my key, of course. *This* detailed?"

"Did you turn on the TV?"

"No, I read."

Warrick knew Larkin had been trying to help the suspect—if Dearborn had watched a television show, that could provide a sort of alibi in itself: name of the program, description thereof. . . .

"Back it up a step, Taylor. Were the lights on in any of your neighbors' houses?"

"I don't remember."

Larkin was getting frustrated, but Warrick's attention was drawn to the top of Dearborn's jumpsuit, the suspect nervously pulling the zipper up, lowering it, up, lower, so on and so on.

And then Warrick thought he saw something within the shadows at the top of the jumpsuit.

For the first time since the interview began, Warrick spoke.

"Stop," he said, and the other two men both froze and sent their eyes his way. "Mr. Dearborn, unzip your jumpsuit."

Warrick's hair might have been on fire, the way Dearborn looked at him. "What the hell?"

"Unzip your jumpsuit."

"I don't think I have to do that," Dearborn said. "I have certain rights—"

"Just unzip it to the waist."

His eyes wide, Dearborn finally did as he was told. The zipper slowly peeled down and revealed four red, nasty scratches on the man's chest.

"What happened there, Trav?" Warrick asked.

Dearborn looked down at himself in surprise, as if the wounds were stigmata that had just magically appeared. "Oh, these!"

"Those."

"Coda! My dog? We were wrestling, and it got a little rowdy. That's all."

Larkin's expression was openly scornful. "Your *dog*?"

Warrick rose and came around the table to face the suspect.

Still talking to the detective, Dearborn said, "You said level, and I'm leveling. I was rolling around with my mutt and got scratched—playin' with a dog's not against the goddamn law now, is it?"

"May I?" Warrick asked, leaning down to get a closer look.

Dearborn frowned, nervous. "Maybe my lawyer *should* be present . . ."

"You want us to get your lawyer in here?"

In the meantime Warrick was inspecting the wounds: a long, jagged scratch about three inches long running down the middle of Dearborn's chest; another nearly as deep to its left; then two outside scratches that hadn't even broken the skin. The wounds did look more the work of an animal than a human; but with her life in the balance, might not the victim have been clawing like an animal?

Warrick looked more closely and thought he spotted something.

"Hold still," he said, and brought out a tiny magnifying glass on a key chain.

"What kind of toy is that?" Dearborn asked.

"Don't knock it," Warrick said. "It works, and I don't have a full crime-scene kit in my pocket."

"Why the hell should I allow you to—"

"Because if you're really innocent, Mr. Dearborn, the evidence can only clear you."

While Dearborn thought about that, Warrick bent over the suspect, inspecting the deepest scratch again, this time with the tiny magnifying glass. He returned to where he thought he'd seen a tiny discoloration.

Yes, there it was—a bit of something hard and white. . . .

Warrick straightened and looked down at the suspect, who reflexively moved to wipe off his front; but Warrick caught his hand. "Really hold still now."

"What the hell are you up to?" Dearborn asked, a measure of fear in his voice now.

"Something's in there, and I want to get it out."

Dearborn peered down, trying to see whatever Warrick saw. *"Hell* no!"

Warrick cast a glance toward Larkin, who sat back, seemingly enjoying the show.

To Dearborn, Warrick said, "Look, whatever scratched you left something behind. If it was Angie, you're going to jail . . . but if you're telling the truth, and Coda did this . . . well, then, my friend, that dog of yours might just be man's best friend, for real—as in, Coda might be the one to clear you of this murder."

The glance Dearborn gave his chest now seemed less terrified, almost hopeful. "All right! Go ahead."

After getting out tweezers and a tiny plastic evidence bag from his pocket, Warrick leaned in one more time. He found what he was looking for, closed the tweezers around it and pulled it free even as Dearborn yelped a little.

"Sorry," Warrick said, putting the sliver—which now appeared more translucent than white—into the bag and sealing it. "I'll take this back to the lab."

Dearborn asked, "And then what?"

"Then we'll see."

And he left the suspect with Detective Larkin.

Less than half an hour to go in the shift and Catherine couldn't wait.

No overtime for her tonight: She was going home to see her daughter. Of course, "seeing" the girl would amount to kissing the sleeping child on the forehead; but that was better than most days of late. With no overtime tonight, Catherine could get to bed early and at least be around to have breakfast with Lindsey and even drive her to school.

The guilt and frustration welled up inside her, then instantly subsided as David Hodges strode through her office door.

"I've got the records for that phone dump you asked for," he said. Slight of build with dark hair and the dark beady eyes of a carrion feeder, he tossed the file folder on her desk. He wore his usual light-blue lab coat over a white shirt and dark slacks.

"Why do *you* have this, David?" she asked. "Aren't you working in the trace lab?"

"Yeah," he said with a perky nod. "I was up in the break room, talking to Conrad, and he asked me to drop those off with you on my way back."

Conrad as in Conrad Ecklie—what was their boss doing at the lab at this hour?

"Oh it's 'Conrad' now? You two're getting pretty close."

Hodges shrugged noncommittally. "We're friends. It's not against the law, Catherine. I find I get more with honey than salt."

"Do you?" she said, thinking how gratuitously unpleasant Hodges could be. "I'll remember that."

"Yeah, you might take that to heart."

"Well, David—thanks."

He stood there for a long second, as if expecting more out of her, whether gratitude or sarcasm; then retreated.

Catherine turned to the matter at hand.

Angela Dearborn's phone records told an interesting story.

The young woman had spoken to her mother out of town, and her nextdoor neighbor, but only regularly placed calls to one other number, which belonged to a party who also called Angie regularly—more regularly even than ex-husband Taylor, who called awfully frequently for somebody with a restraining order against him.

The number meant nothing to Catherine—why should it?—but the name was familiar. She didn't

immediately make the connection, just felt the reso-
nance and paused and thought about it.

Then something went cold inside her.

Glancing at her watch and knowing that overtime
was inevitable now, Catherine discarded the thought
of kissing the slumbering Lindsey, gathered up the
phone records, and went off in search of Gil Grissom.

7

Tuesday, January 25, 11:00 P.M.

GIL GRISSOM HAD NO REGRETS.

If he had his life at the crime lab to live over again, he could think of few things—other than a tiny personal lapse here and there, where he'd inadvertently hurt a feeling or two—that he would do differently.

Certainly he would not go back and become a political animal and doubted himself capable of that, even if he wanted to. Like the scorpion who talked the frog into ferrying him across the river, only to fatally sting the frog halfway and condemn them both to death—Grissom's character was too firmly set.

He did miss his team—losing colleagues as trusted, as valued as Nick, Warrick and Catherine, cost him dearly; their friendship, the chemistry of that little group, had enabled the graveyard shift to achieve remarkable results. The praise and attention they'd inevitably received had just as inevitably led to jealousy, political infighting, and break-up.

On the other hand, Catherine had earned the right to head up her own team. He considered himself in part a teacher, and a teacher who held onto a gifted student too long could wind up smothering that student. He had recommended her for promotion, and he wished her well. This feeling was as genuine within him as the slightly bewildering sense of loss he was experiencing, not having her at his side.

Right now, the saving grace of all this was a sense of relief.

Relief that the night shift still protected him, somewhat, from the presence of politicians and bureaucrats who only came out by day, retreating to the cool underside of their respective rocks at nightfall.

Relief that everyone was coming together so well. Yes, they lacked the experience of Catherine, Warrick, and Nick; his one holdover, Sara, was of course excellent at her job, even if her emotions seemed slightly askew of late. And Sofia had proven to be a talented crime-scene analyst in her own right, with Greg doing exceptionally well for a rookie.

Still, they had been together for such a short time that sometimes the right hand didn't know what the left was doing, requiring him to stand guard over them. Suddenly he realized that the precision teamwork of the old players had come to spoil him—he hadn't been a babysitter for a long, long time.

Even so, he was taking pleasure and even a little pride at the way Greg was (allowing himself a pun) blossoming in the field.

Feeling fairly good about himself, considering,

Grissom went into the break room to find Conrad Ecklie sitting there. Ecklie lingering into night shift was never a good sign. That the deputy director had not availed himself of any refreshment—appeared instead to be waiting for someone—was also not an omen of delight.

"Conrad," he said with a polite nod.

"Gil," Ecklie said in that liquid, pseudo-friendly manner that made Grissom's teeth hurt. "I was hoping to run into you. . . . Sit down, would you?"

"Mind if I get some coffee first?" Grissom asked.

"No. Go right ahead. . . . We need to talk."

Grissom poured himself a cup of the break room's black liquid that the CSIs had agreed to call coffee; Ecklie of course was aware that Grissom's ritual upon arriving at CSI was to do this—meaning Ecklie indeed had been waiting for him.

Sitting across from Ecklie, Grissom managed a smile and said, " 'Need to talk?' Sounds ominous, Conrad. Has a certain . . . principal's office ring."

"I don't mean it to. But we do have a problem."

"Do we? Should I . . . guess?"

Now Ecklie managed his own smile. "I wouldn't ask that of you—I know how you feel about guesswork. I admire that about you."

"Thanks," Grissom said, thinking, *Could we just skip the patronizing twaddle?*

Looking down at hands tented before him, the balding bureaucrat said, "Gil, I got a call today . . . from Todd Templeton."

Grissom maintained a bland front. "Over at Home Sure. Really."

His unblinking eyes meeting Grissom's now, Ecklie said, "Really . . . and he's quite . . . " Ecklie searched for the right word. All he could come up with was ". . . unhappy. Templeton claims you've been harassing him."

Grissom shook his head. "Blatantly untrue," he said. "I know he resents me, so I've been painstaking about maintaining a polite, professional manner."

"That's not *his* story."

"Well, his 'story' is just that. And he's a known liar, so I don't really see what there is to discuss."

Ecklie's eyes remained on the CSI. "Templeton claims he's been cooperating with the Los Calina investigation."

Grissom gestured with an open hand. "That much is true. Although earlier today, he refused further help to Greg Sanders, and was suggesting we'd need a court order to get any *more* cooperation."

Ecklie considered that. Then he said, "Templeton's version is a little different—he told me that no matter how much he tries to cooperate, you keep asking for more."

"Conrad, he volunteered the records. One of his security company's clients was murdered. It's in his interest to cooperate. . . . Why are we talking about this?"

"I'm just trying to make sure the right protocols are being followed. It's clear you have a history with this individual. Tell me why I shouldn't demand that you recuse yourself from this case?"

"Conrad, you can do that if you wish. I can only assure you that we're strictly following protocol, and I'm limiting my contact with the man."

"Gil, I'm going on record, giving you the opportunity to make this decision yourself—you'll receive a memo to that effect."

Ah, yes—the politician's paper trail. . . .

"But," Ecklie continued, "you know it's not my way to interfere with a supervisor. I'm not going to second-guess you. But I am giving you the opportunity to stand down."

Before the conversation could move a syllable ahead, Catherine burst into the room, out of breath, a sheaf of papers in one hand.

"Excuse me, Conrad," she said. "Are you in a meeting, or is this . . . social?"

"It's a meeting," Ecklie said. "But we're winding down."

"Well, I need to talk to Gil," she said. "An urgent matter—a development in two murder cases."

Grissom asked, "What kind of development?"

She gave him a narrow-eyed look. "The kind where we need coordination between night shift and the other shifts," a vague answer that sounded specific.

Grissom immediately knew that—whatever this was about—she preferred to talk to him *without* Ecklie listening in.

Possibly Ecklie sensed that, too, and had respect enough for them to stand and say, "I'll get out of your way, then."

Grissom said, "Let's go to my office, Catherine." He turned to the bureaucrat, nodded. "Conrad. Thank you for the advice."

"That's what I'm here for, Gil. To guide you toward making your own, correct administrative decisions. . . . Watch for that memo."

Soon, in Grissom's office, an uncharacteristically frantic Catherine was seated across from his desk, on the edge of her chair, the papers clutched in her hands like an actor with script pages that had been presented last-minute.

"What is it?" he asked, leaning forward, hands folded. Around the room, on a number of shelves, various jarred critters and science projects all seemed primed to listen as well.

"Gil, have you heard of a woman named Angela Dearborn? Have you run across that name in any way, the last twenty-four hours or so?"

Grissom thought about it, shrugged, shook his head.

Finally she put the papers on his desk, smoothing them out. "She was murdered Sunday night. My team drew the case when her body was found Monday afternoon."

"Okay," Grissom said, wondering where this was going.

Verbally Catherine laid out the entire Angie Dearborn case, and all the evidence she, Warrick, and Nick had collected and processed to date.

Unsure why she was sharing this, Grissom said, "Sounds like you're heading in the right direction—doing your typically thorough job."

"I have to say, yeah, I thought we were doing all right—the evidence was making me dizzy, turning around on itself, but the ex was looking good for it."

"Scratches Warrick found on the guy's chest," Grissom said, nodding. "I can see that."

"Then just now—everything changed."

"How so?" he asked, sitting forward, interested.

Catherine flicked at one of the sheets of paper on the desk—her own notations. "I got the phone dump for the Dearborn woman's cell . . . everybody she'd been talking to lately. And one name came up more frequently than all the others."

"All right . . ."

"Gil, the name that came up—the person Angie Dearborn spoke to the most—is a woman *also* recently deceased . . ."

Finally Grissom caught up with her, and snatched up Catherine's cell-phone notes, but even before he saw the name on the sheet, he'd said, "Grace Salfer."

"The murder victim *your* team is investigating," Catherine said.

"You've confirmed it's the same Grace Salfer? It's a fairly unusual name, but—"

Catherine read the Los Calina address from one of the pages.

Grissom sat back, interlacing his fingers behind his head, considering this new information. "How did they know each other? How old was Angela Dearborn?"

"Thirty-three."

"Grace Salfer was eighty. That they were friends is possible, but . . . were they related?"

Catherine shook her head, blond locks bouncing. "Apparently not. Angie's mom lives out of state, and the closest thing to family she has here is that abusive ex-husband. We'll dig further, obviously, but—if so—she doesn't appear to be a *close* relative of Salfer's."

"Our victim seems to have only had one close relation, a nephew—David Arrington, a show-biz booker out at the Platinum King."

Catherine cocked her head. "It's possible an eighty-year-old and a thirty-three-year-old can be friends, but . . . I don't know. So—do we have two murders, and one case?"

"Too early to tell." He mulled a moment. Then: "How about the rest of swing shift? Nick and Warrick still here?"

"They are."

"Gather them, would you?" Grissom stood. "I'll get my team together. Then let's meet in the layout room—ten minutes? And let's compare information, and see how we can help each other."

Forty-five minutes later, both teams were scattered around the layout room, and up to speed on each other's cases.

Catherine and Grissom stood at either side of a blackboard at front. Sara, Greg, and Sofia had pulled up chairs, with the big layout table to their backs. Warrick was perched on a counter nearby, Nick leaning against a wall.

"Okay," Grissom said. "We have two seemingly unrelated murders with one very big anomaly— these two, apparently disparate women spoke to each other by phone almost daily. Is it possible this fact is *not* related to either of our cases? That it is indeed an anomaly?"

Sofia, the other person here with supervisory experience, said, "Possible but doubtful. It'd represent an incredible coincidence—two murder victims, killed on the same night, who knew each other well? I don't think you'd have to work hard to convince *any* of us of the unlikelihood of that."

"We have two very different women," Grissom

said. "An old, wealthy woman, and a young, poor one. . . .What could they have in common?"

The silence grew until it felt like another presence in the room.

Finally, Greg said, "Went to the same church, maybe?"

Catherine and Grissom traded pleased looks.

"Definitely worth looking into," Catherine said, as Grissom wrote it on the board.

Warrick asked, "Did they ever visit each other?"

Confident now, Greg chimed in, "The list from the Los Calina guest log did *not* show any Angie Dearborn."

Nick said, "Let's get Detective Larkin to have another go at Angie's nextdoor neighbor—maybe she saw the Salfer woman stop by Angie's apartment."

Grissom made another chalkboard note.

Sara asked, "Who did Angie work for?"

Catherine shrugged facially. "We haven't been able to track down an employer yet."

Sofia asked, "Did Angie pay her bills regularly?"

"Yes."

"Then the young woman had income."

Catherine nodded. "Indeed she did—a weekly cash deposit of three hundred dollars; but we haven't been able to find the source yet. No notations in her checkbook or other financial records."

"Blackmail payments from Grace Salfer?" Greg asked.

Warrick and Nick seemed to be processing whether that was likely when Grissom jumped in. "Would Angela Dearborn record blackmail proceeds as deposits in her checkbook?"

Greg answered that himself, deflated a little. "No—unlikely Angie would've even put cash like that in the bank."

"Wait," Nick said, eyes narrowing as he sat forward. "What if Angie wanted to *look* legit? Own up to three hundred a week, when she's really collecting five or six?"

"That would be a stretch," Sofia said.

"Only if we're talking blackmail," Nick said. "What if Angie did something else for Grace? And like a lot of people floating under the income-tax code, preferred being paid in cash?"

Warrick asked, "Paid for *what*, though?"

Nick was on a roll. "Maybe Angie worked for the Salfer woman—cleaning maybe. What shape was the Salfer house in?"

"Tidy," Grissom said. "Very."

Warrick was shaking his head. "But if Angie was Grace's housekeeper, coming by weekly or even more often, wouldn't she show up on the Los Calina sign-in sheet at the gate?"

They all considered that, and Grissom recalled Catherine's comment about evidence going in circles.

Sofia said, "Hey, we're just brainstorming here. What kind of work could Angie have done for Grace, or involving Grace, where they would talk on the phone but Angie would never visit the woman?"

They explored that for a while, not really getting anywhere, but Grissom nonetheless felt the tug of a smile.

"Okay," he said at last. "There's still plenty for both teams to do on their respective cases. Let's plan on meeting here again tomorrow night, and see where we're at."

Catherine nodded her agreement. "Angie's financial records are incomplete at best. Warrick, I want you to see what else you can find. First thing tomorrow."

He nodded.

"Nick, when you come in, keep tracking the evidence and see where we're at with the labs."

"You got it."

Catherine turned to Grissom, passing the ball.

He said, "Greg, you found this other friend of Grace Salfer's, who was on the list of visitors from the Los Calina gate—Elizabeth Parker, I believe?"

"That's right."

"Well, I want you to find Brass, go over Grace Salfer's finances, and then at the end of the shift, interview the Parker woman."

"Speaking of Brass," Greg said, "I looked all over for him when I got here. Couldn't find him."

"Have you paged him?"

"Well, I wouldn't want to bother him. . . ."

Everybody just looked at Greg, who shrugged sheepishly.

With patience so exaggerated it was unconvincing, Grissom said to the young CSI, "Call his cell and page him if necessary—he's probably working something else; but we all have a right to contact him about our case. Cases, now."

"Will do," Greg said.

Turning to Sara, Grissom asked, "What do we know about the ladder we found leaning against the Salfer house?"

Without referring to notes, Sara said, "Standard aluminum extension ladder, sold in any one of a hundred hardware stores. We got one partial print, but nothing that matched up in AFIS. Still making its merry way through the other databases."

"But that print did *not* belong to Salfer?"

"It did not."

"All right," Grissom said. "See if you can track down its origin. Let's check it against the prints of Home Sure's staffers."

Greg said, "If Templeton won't give *that* info up willingly, it's court-order time."

"Don't need one, Greg," Sara said. "We already have a database that includes all Las Vegas security-industry employees."

Grissom added for Greg's benefit, "They have to be fingerprinted as part of the licensing requirements and their individual background checks."

Sofia asked Grissom, "What should I focus on?"

"If there's a connection between these two murders, the two people who seem to have the most to gain are Taylor Dearborn and David Arrington. I want you to see if there's a connection between those two."

Sofia nodded, and jotted in her small notebook.

"If you come up with something significant," Grissom said, "and you can't reach Catherine, call me."

"And vice versa," Catherine said. "*Any* time—shift be damned."

Grissom continued, "But—I think it's safe to assume this is one case now. Keep that in your mind, always."

And everybody went off to work their aspect of the new case: the Angela Dearborn/Grace Salfer investigation.

Knowing Captain Brass often stopped by the lab to personally check on the progress of evidence processing, Greg Sanders made the rounds checking on him. After almost twenty minutes of this, Greg slipped into the break room, opened a bottle of juice, sat at a table, and took a long pull.

Greg couldn't help feeling funny about calling a captain of homicide. He was so new at this, and about as unseasoned as a CSI could get. Somehow it didn't seem his place. Silly, really, considering how long he'd known Brass, and how supportive the captain had been in Greg's efforts to move from the lab to the field.

So finally he took a deep breath and punched Brass's number into the cell phone (it wasn't even on the speed dial yet). He heard it ring on the other end, then jumped a little as someone's cell phone went off in the hall nearby.

"Brass," a voice said behind him, *and* in his ear, making Greg start, his juice bottle teetering on the table. He just grabbed it before it could fall over and spill.

The young CSI turned and saw Brass in the doorway, smiling puckishly as he put away his cell phone.

"Jeez!" Greg said, and sucked in a breath, and put his cell away, too. "You scared the hell out of me!"

Brass chuckled as he came over to sit with Greg. "You're just the guy I was looking for."

"*You're* looking for *me?* Captain, I've been trying

to find you since I got here. You been working on the Grace Salfer case?"

Brass nodded. "But I haven't checked with Grissom for a while. Anything to update?"

"Quite a bit, actually."

Greg brought Brass up to speed.

The detective shook his head. "It's only happened a handful of times—two cases converging into one—but it can really throw you."

"I don't know," Greg said with a shrug. "To me, it's a major break—if all these pieces we were trying to fit together belong to one big puzzle, we now have a real chance of putting the picture together."

"Good point." But Brass seemed preoccupied. "You, uh, went out to the Home Sure office with Grissom early today, right?"

"Yeah. He took me out there, set me up in a back room to go through files and records."

"Was Todd Templeton there?"

"The head guy? Sure."

"Did he and Grissom interact at all?"

"Interact?"

"Come on, Greg, this is important."

"Grissom was with me when Templeton provided the space and records and everything, yeah."

"How did they get along?"

Greg had the odd feeling he was about to betray Grissom; and yet his supervisor was a stickler for the truth, so . . .

"They *didn't*," Greg said. "It wasn't really Grissom's fault—he was polite, didn't needle the guy or anything. But Templeton was sort of a . . . a . . ."

"Prick?" Brass smirked humorlessly.

"Anyway, I'd say there was no love lost between those two."

Brass was studying Greg. "How's your memory?"

"Good. Okay. Fine. Why?"

"Tell me what they said."

Greg did his best.

Then: "All right, Captain—now tell me what this is about. And why do I think your disappearing act has something to do with it?"

Brass was eyeing Greg with new respect. "Because it does, Greg. I've been on the phone tonight—at home. I didn't want to call from my office."

Greg knew there'd be a good reason for that, but did Brass the courtesy of not asking for it.

The detective was saying, "Mostly I talked to a guy I know on the Reno P.D."

"Why Reno?"

"That's where Templeton worked," Brass said. "When he and Grissom had their run in."

"What run in?"

The detective rose and got himself some coffee, and explained to Greg how hostilely Templeton reacted when Brass first showed up at Home Sure Security with Gil Grissom in tow.

"Tell you the truth, Greg, Templeton was more forthcoming than Gil about their little feud. Our peerless night-shift supervisor doesn't seem to think what happened between him and that slick security guru is worth talking about."

Greg lifted an eyebrow. "It does explain why Templeton was such an asshole today, grousing about cooperating . . . saying next time we'd need a court order."

Brass sighed. "Well, if Gil wasn't going to share this with me, I wanted a point of view other than Templeton's. So I thought I better check in with my Reno buddy."

"And what did you learn? If you don't mind sharing."

Brass leaned forward; he spoke softly, even though he and Greg were otherwise alone. "Turns out Templeton was a dectective, a crime lab supervisor who tampered with evidence against a suspected cop killer."

Both Greg's eyebrows went up this time. "*What?* Holy—"

"Seems Templeton thought he had the right guy and, rather than depend on the sketchy evidence they had, the lab boss helped science along—used the results of a DNA test to implicate his suspect."

"How?"

"Templeton didn't have a match until he met the suspect and got a sample from him; then, suddenly, the suspect's DNA shows up at the crime scene. It was like that detective who took a blood sample from O.J., then stopped by the crime scene on his way to the lab—looks lousy even if the detective *didn't* do anything. Templeton claimed he was clean, but an outside expert proved him dirty."

". . . An outside expert named Gil Grissom."

"Exactly."

Greg gestured with open hands. "Then the hostility is all on Templeton's side. Why should Grissom recuse himself from this case? He has no real ax to grind."

But Brass was shaking his head. "This was a cop

killer case, remember. Emotions run deep; hatred takes root."

"And Grissom ruined their case?"

"Not at all. In fact, he pointed out the real evidence that nailed the perp. Still, to this day, certain cops in Reno feel it was Grissom who railroaded their guy—Templeton."

"I don't follow that."

"Well, there's not much to follow, Greg. Suffice to say, some police in Reno believe Grissom was trying to make himself look good, really earn his paycheck; and apparently he and Templeton had words during the inquiry."

"That's stupid. Gil Grissom would never cook the evidence. Not *ever*, for *any* reason, let alone something as frivolous as—"

"Greg, you know that, and I know it—and for that matter, you can bet Todd Templeton does, too." Brass shrugged elaborately. "But there's a group of angry cops in Reno who still believe that Grissom got Templeton fired."

Greg was shaking his head. "I still don't see how that bears on anything, Captain."

Brass leaned forward, his eyes hard. "Greg—Grissom having worked on a case where Templeton's involved? That could come back to bite us at trial."

"But Templeton's not even a suspect."

"He doesn't *have* to be. The victim was his company's client, which puts him in the middle of things, including as keeper of the keys of a good deal of evidence."

"I disagree." Any nervousness about dealing directly with a seasoned cop like Brass had evaporated now; Greg was standing up for his mentor. "Templeton and Grissom's history has no bearing on Grace Salfer's murder—strictly peripheral."

"I wish that were the case," Brass said glumly. "We've already received records from Templeton without a court order, as you well know."

"So what?"

"So—when we arrest a suspect who goes to trial, the defense attorney could say that Templeton caved because of the previous conflict with Grissom."

"Oh, come on."

"Greg, that's what defense lawyers do—create doubt. And a good defender will raise doubt as to whether Templeton cooperated willingly or whether Grissom threatened to ruin him again, like he did in Reno. And there are still people up there, cops, who would swear Gil did it before."

The young CSI considered that. "Well, then, we'll just have to go through the financial records and find evidence that they can't tie to Grissom. If he's got nothing to do with it, they can't use him to create doubt."

"If I've got nothing to do with what?" Grissom asked from the doorway.

Brass spun in his chair and Greg had a sick, sinking feeling.

Not ducking it, Brass said, "I've been talking to some people in Reno."

"Really," Grissom said, his voice neutral. He strolled over and sat down, his manner striking Greg as too casual. "About what, Jim?"

"You know 'about what,' Gil—you and Templeton."

"Oh, are we back to that?"

Greg sat mute witness to this taut exchange between the two men he most respected here at CSI . . . or anywhere, perhaps. He was fascinated, and terrified.

Brass was saying, "We needed to know exactly what went down between you and Templeton in Reno, once upon a time. Because, frankly, Gil, you haven't been anxious to tell me."

" 'We' need to know, Jim? Or *you* needed to know?"

Brass shifted in the seat, clearly uncomfortable with this conversation. "I take no delight in this. All I know is, we have a murder case that could conceivably be compromised by existing hostility between the lead CSI and a key witness."

Watching Grissom told Greg nothing; the man seemed as cool as Brass did uncomfortable.

The CSI supervisor finally said, "I suppose you're right, Jim. And what did you find out?"

"That some cops in Reno still blame you for losing one of their own."

A tiny tightness manifested at a corner of Grissom's mouth. "You know that's not even worthy of discussion."

"*I* know it—only you and I aren't the ones deciding whether it's worthy of discussion or not. What matters is what a smooth lawyer can do to a jury with information like that."

"Templeton was the one who tampered with evidence," Grissom said. "That makes him the one who almost let a cop killer walk."

Brass swallowed. "I think you should recuse yourself."

Greg was wishing he were anywhere but here; he felt like an intruder, an eavesdropper. . . .

"Todd Templeton was a sloppy, lazy detective," Grissom said. "He always took the path of least resistance, Jim. Dig some more. You'll learn that this wasn't the first case Templeton botched, taking the easy road instead of the right road. Why do you think an outside consultant was brought in, anyway?"

"I see your side of it. I agree with you. And you still need to recuse yourself."

Grissom leaned forward, his eyes intense, his voice cool. "This was just the first Templeton botch that happened to involve a cop killer. Jim, I reviewed numerous cases of his. The man fudged lab results, 'misplaced' evidence that didn't fit with his theory of a crime. Guys like this give crime labs everywhere a black eye."

Brass said, "Are you doing the same thing right now, by not standing down?"

Grissom blinked.

Somehow, Greg knew that his mentor had been deeply hurt by this remark. But Grissom said nothing.

Brass, also sensing what his words had done, leaned in and said, "Gil—sometimes being right isn't enough. Look around you—consider this political climate. Do you *really* want to deal certain people *this* hand of cards?"

Grissom stood. "I have work to do."

And he was gone.

Feeling he'd been coldcocked, Greg sat with his eyes and mouth wide open.

Brass chuckled dryly. "Yeah, kid—he *is* human. Sometimes I think it's his best quality. I only wish I could've got through to him."

"Maybe you did," Greg said, but wasn't sure.

Brass rose, stretched. "I've got work to do, too. Grace Salfer's financial records are singing their siren song. I could use some help."

Greg was on his feet, too. "I can give it to you."

Hours later—about thirty minutes before the scheduled end of shift—both the detective and the nascent CSI Greg Sanders were in the layout room, still poring over documents from Grace Salfer's financial records, when Grissom strolled in as if the night's earlier exchange had never occurred.

"You two having any luck?" he asked.

Greg looked to Brass who looked back at him, signaling the young man to take the lead.

"Actually, yes," Greg said. "A couple of interesting things."

"Good," Grissom said. "We're meeting in my office. Five minutes?"

Both Greg and Brass nodded.

And Grissom was gone again.

"The guy does bounce back," Brass said, with a laugh.

About five minutes later, when Greg and Brass arrived, Grissom was already behind his desk. Extra chairs had been brought in, so that when Sofia entered, followed closely by Sara, they were all soon seated.

"All right," Grissom said. "Who made progress?"

Sara said, "The ladder will have to be tracked down during the day." She arched an eyebrow. "Just aren't a lot of twenty-four hour ladder stores, even in Vegas. We did get a hit on the partial print, though."

"Where?"

"A Home Sure Security employee."

Brass asked, "Who?"

Though Sara was poised to speak, Grissom answered: "Susan Gillette."

Agape, Sara stared at him. "I've said it before—you *are* a witch."

"Warlock," Grissom corrected wryly. "Where was the print?"

"Left side, maybe four rungs from the bottom."

Grissom nodded. "What does that tell you?"

Nodding back, Sara said, "That's right about where Gillette would have touched it, if she came around the house like she said."

Greg said, "She didn't *mention* touching it. In fact, she made a big deal about not disturbing the crime scene."

Grissom considered that. "Any number of reasons why she may not have mentioned she touched the ladder—she didn't remember doing it, or was embarrassed about it."

"Or," Sara said, "just an oversight."

Grissom raised a finger. "It's also possible she was setting up an alibi."

Sofia asked, "Even if we explain away Gillette touching the ladder, what about her being at that AA dinner Taylor Dearborn attended?"

They all swung toward her.

"How did you find that out?" Grissom asked, impressed.

"I've been looking for any sort of connection between Taylor and Grace Salfer's nephew. At first I couldn't find anything. Only thing they seemed to have in common is they're both residents of the Vegas valley."

"Not exactly narrowing the field much there," Sara said.

Sofia nodded. "So—once it seemed I wasn't going to find a tie between Taylor and Arrington, I widened the search. That was when I, frankly, stumbled onto Susan Gillette."

"Stumbled onto her how?" Sara asked.

"Well, it was thanks to Captain Brass."

Brass grinned. "You're welcome—what did I do?"

"You got a court order and a guest list from the AA dinner. I just went through it and bang, there our perky little security gal was."

"She's everywhere," Greg said dryly.

"Oh," Sofia said, "and I also found out that Home Sure guard, who called in sick the night of the murder, was at the hospital with food poisoning. His alibi checks."

Sara asked, "Why didn't Home Sure just send somebody else out to cover?"

"Short staffed. That flu going around?"

"All right," Grissom said. "We've got a direction to go in now. Anything else?"

Brass gave Greg a nod, prompting him.

"Couple things," Greg said, "both interesting. First, according to Grace Salfer's banking records, she withdrew three thousand dollars cash every month. You might assume that was everyday living expenses, only . . ."

Brass said, "Only for a woman of eighty, that's high. Maybe some of that—all of that, even—went to Angela Dearborn."

"That accounts for the three hundred a week cash deposit," Grissom said, eyes narrowed.

Frowning, Sara said, "We still don't know why Angie was on the payroll."

Brass said, "Actually we do. Greg?"

The young CSI, if pressed, would've had to admit he enjoyed the rapt attention he was commanding from his fellow CSIs right now, including his boss.

Greg said, "May come as no surprise that we learned the beneficiary of Grace's life insurance is her nephew, David Arrington."

"How much is the policy worth?" Grissom asked.

"A quarter of a million dollars."

Sara was nodding, chin crinkling in consideration. "Sounds like a motive for murder."

Greg said, "The major heir of Grace's will is *not* Arrington, however—David gets the insurance, and some other smaller parts of the estate, but the lion's share goes to . . ." Greg opened the folder containing the will and read a passage he'd marked earlier. " '. . . *my housekeeper, companion, and best friend, Angela Dearborn.*' "

The room remained silent long enough for Greg to count to ten in his head. What a great moment this was, and right now Greg knew he'd made the right decision, turning CSI.

"Housekeeper," Sara said, nodding. "*There's* the three hundred a week."

Sofia asked, "Best friend? How did we not know any of this?"

"It's easily explainable," Grissom said. When they all turned to him, he granted them all a tiny beatific smile. "Isn't that right, Greg?"

Greg tried to think of why it was easily explainable.

And his joyful moment fizzled: He had nothing.

He could feel their eyes on him, *Grissom's* eyes on him. This was a test . . . and he was about to fail it. He was just about to admit as much to Grissom when the right piece of evidence popped into his mind.

He knew the answer.

"Because," Greg said, "Home Sure took her name off the visitor's list."

Grissom's smile widened.

"What?" Sara blurted.

"When Grissom asked for all the records," Greg said, "Todd Templeton did *not* give us the original visitor's log sheets. I never found out why, for sure. Oh, I asked, but Templeton claimed that Grissom never asked for the originals, saying it was a privacy issue, you know—us seeing the list of visitors of other residents. All I saw was a typed list that supposedly contained the names of all of Mrs. Salfer's visitors."

Sara said, "And Angela Dearborn's name wasn't on it."

Greg nodded. "Angela Dearborn's name was not on it."

Grissom sighed, clapped once, and said, "All right. . . . We need to question Susan Gillette about the ladder, and about her possible connection to Taylor Dearborn through AA. We also want to talk to

Todd Templeton about this 'oversight' with Mrs. Salfer's visitor list, and to track down the origin of that ladder if we can. Anything else?"

Sofia said, "Don't you think it would be helpful knowing if David Arrington was aware his aunt's will left her estate to her housekeeper?"

Grissom nodded. "Very helpful. Do it, Sofia. Greg, I still want you to talk to Mrs. Salfer's friend, Elizabeth Parker."

"Will do."

Grissom's guests all rose to leave and, as they ambled out, he called to the last in line—Brass. "Jim, can we talk a minute?"

"Sure."

"Alone?"

"Sure."

Brass waited for Greg to exit, then closed the door and turned to Grissom. "Shall I sit back down?"

"Why don't you?" Grissom picked his glasses up off the desk and fingered the frame absently. "I've considered what you said about my recusing myself from this case."

As he sat, the detective said, "And?"

"I can't."

Brass frowned. "Gil, I think—"

"It's not that I don't respect your judgment. In retrospect, you're probably right. But I'm in this too deep now for recusing myself to do any good."

Brass did not think this was a particularly compelling rationale; but the thought *had* crossed his mind. Still, he thought it was the wrong decision and said so.

"I understand," Grissom said. "But you've convinced me to take a back seat on this. I'm going to keep a low profile."

"That's a start," Brass said.

"When you go talk to Todd Templeton, I won't be along."

"Good call," Brass said.

"Don't take Greg either—he and Todd tangled, a bit. Maybe Sofia or Sara can have better luck with him."

Nodding, Brass said, "Okay. I'll try that."

Grissom sat back, ran a hand over his eyes. "You know, Templeton's already gone to Ecklie about this."

Brass nodded. "I do know."

"Oh?"

Another nod. "Conrad asked for my opinion."

"So he knows where you stand."

"Yes, but it's not where you think. Gil, I told Ecklie that you did nothing out of line, and that Templeton cooperated voluntarily."

This seemed to confuse Grissom. "You didn't tell him you thought I should recuse myself?"

"No, Gil," Brass said, and rose. "I told *you*. Remember?"

And Brass left Grissom alone to ponder that.

8

THAT SWING SHIFT AND NIGHT shift were now working as one big team pleased and gratified Catherine Willows.

Any misgivings, any niggling guilt, over her position as shift supervisor were assuaged by the collaboration, even the synergy, of the two teams becoming one.

And, despite his tenure, Grissom did not seem to be angling for overall leadership. Gil had, in fact, called earlier in the day saying he was taking a step back, explaining briefly about the Reno investigation that had cost Templeton his job.

"Frankly, Catherine," he'd said, "minimizing my participation would be a plus."

If anything, Grissom seemed to be indirectly indicating he wanted her to step forward. She liked that.

And she liked not having to worry about dealing with Ecklie about all this overtime. Now that these two murder cases had become one, she'd have considerably less explaining to do to the deputy director. Ecklie would have no choice but to approve all of both shifts' efforts in solving the intertwined murders.

When the local media got wind of this convoluted double murder case, national TV—particularly the hungry eye of cable's 24-7 news outlets—would not be far behind. And that would make solving the case a top priority for the politically minded.

Murders didn't attract tourists to Sin City; but if murders there were, please God, let them be solved ones—tourists liked solved murders. And that meant the sheriff, and the mayor, liked solved murders, too.

"*Querida,*" Tomas Nuñez said, leaning in Catherine's open office door.

Looking up from her work, Catherine smiled. While she was in a rust-orange sweater and matching leather slacks, Nuñez stood before her in his usual black jeans, boots, and black T-shirt—the human billboard today touting a band called Ozomatli. Under his arm, he carried a laptop computer—Angie Dearborn's—and a folder that, presumably, held his report.

"Tell me you found something," she said.

His black mustache drooped over a similarly downcast mouth. " 'Have a seat, Tomas,' " he mocked, a pretend edge of irritation in his voice. " 'Make yourself at home, Tomas. Tell me how you have been—we never get to talk anymore, Tomas,' " and "—he drew up a chair and sat, the laptop (fittingly) on his lap—". . . I *do* have something for you."

"I'm glad to hear that—this case is getting complicated."

"How so?"

"Angie Dearborn's murder has been linked to an-other recent murder. I really can't tell you any more than that."

"Need-to-know basis? Well, here's what *you* need to know—Angie Dearborn's accounting program in-dicates she's been putting three hundred dollars in her checking account, every week."

"That tallies with what we already know, but thanks."

"Maybe so, . . . but did you know Angie was mak-ing five hundred a week, cash—living on two hun-dred and banking the rest?"

"No," Catherine admitted. "But that confirms a theory we floated yesterday. And we have another theory about who was *paying* her . . ."

"If your theory's that a Grace Salfer was paying her, you can move that over into the fact column."

"That's very helpful, Tomas. Thank you."

"Ah, but I have saved the best for last—Angie was maintaining a semi-regular e-mail correspondence with her ex-husband."

"Really? She had a restraining order on him."

Nuñez shrugged. "Well, she may have wanted to keep the guy so-many-yards-away, but it didn't in-clude her e-mail in-box."

"Could you print those out and—"

"Ahead of you, *querida*. You can read them your-self, but they're pretty innocent—friendly but not romantic."

He handed her the folder and she shuffled through the pages printing out a dozen or so e-mails between Taylor and Angie Dearborn.

"You did good, Tomas," she said.

"You never know in my game," Nuñez said. "I can't promise results, because who's to say *what* winds up on somebody's computer? But nowadays, more lingers than anyone cares to think about."

"I trust you have a bill for me."

"Dinner and a movie?"

"Shoot me an e-mail," she said with a grin.

He laughed, gave her the bill, wished her *buena suerte* and left her to read through the various e-mails, which proved to make interesting, even enlightening reading.

Taylor seemed to be working hard at getting Angie to take him back via the indirect route of sharing with her his progress, cleaning himself up, and endlessly apologizing for the past. She was friendly and supportive but stopped short of opening any real door on a renewed relationship.

And Taylor avoided anything sexual, at all—a perfect (if sadly desperate) gentleman.

A knock at the door announced Marty Larkin standing framed there—another man in black, or anyway black and gray; black sportcoat with charcoal slacks, gray shirt and (not that surprisingly, to Catherine) a darker gray tie. She waved him in and he strolled to a chair and sat down, resting an ankle atop a knee.

Catherine asked him if he was up to speed on the now joint murder investigation.

"Yeah, Warrick's been keeping me in the loop. Curiouser and curiouser, somebody said once."

"Lewis Carroll."

"If you say so. Are *you* curious 'bout what I found out from Nellie Pacquino?"

"Nellie Pacquino—that's Angie's nextdoor neighbor, right?"

Larkin nodded. "She knew that Angie worked for some older woman, and that Angie and the older gal'd become friends. That's roughly it."

"Give me the full, smoothed-out version."

"Well, Nellie had no idea that Angie was named in the old woman's will. The only thing along those lines was Angie saying, one time, that she felt a little guilty, the old lady paying her so much."

"Is that right?"

"Yeah, apparently the old gal took a real interest in Angie, and they'd sit and talk, and of course Angie's various working-class financial woes came up, and Grace gave her a raise, to make her life easier."

"Five hundred cash, off the books, for periodic housecleaning—that's pretty darn good money. . . . Marty, do you think it's possible Angie didn't even *know* she was due to inherit that money from Grace?"

Larkin shrugged. "I knew a guy who got a substantial surprise bequest from a distant relative he'd been nice to, second cousin or something. Just outta the blue."

Catherine considered that. Then she said, "If money isn't the motive—and Taylor didn't kill her out of obsessive love—then why was Angie killed?"

"Not sure I'm following," Larkin admitted, sitting forward, gray tie dangling.

"Well, killing Angie for money she hadn't inherited yet makes no sense."

"Granted."

"And Warrick's not convinced that Taylor is guilty."

"I gotta say, *I* still like him for it."

A wry smile carved itself in Catherine's cheek. "I don't think you're right, Marty—no matter how attractive it is to assume a wife-beating ex is responsible. Take a look at these."

She handed him the e-mail printouts, and he read them for a while.

Then he shrugged and says, "Doesn't prove anything. Psycho killers are 'nice' to their vics online all the time."

"Well, surely you have to admit the evidence against Taylor keeps hopping the fence. And if these murders are interwoven, why the hell would Taylor want *Grace Salfer* dead?"

"Stop, Cath—you're givin' me a migraine."

But she didn't stop. Leaning back in her chair a little, Catherine thought out loud: "If we take Taylor out of the equation, we're back to money, sex, love, or drugs. Angie didn't do drugs, hadn't had sex recently, and—other than Taylor—seems to've been unattached. That leaves money—and she was set to inherit a sizable quantity of that, if anything happened to Grace Salfer."

"Okay," Larkin said, sitting forward again, eyes lively. "I'm with you . . . keep goin'. . . ."

"That means if the motive was money, and Angie didn't know about the inheritance, the *killer* somehow found out about Angie being in the will."

"Who could find *that* out?" Larkin asked.

"How about Grace's next of kin—the person who otherwise would inherit? The nephew?"

"David Arrington," they said at the same time.

"Well," Larkin said, "there's a guy we need to talk to, ten seconds from now."

"Who?" Warrick asked, appearing in the doorway.

Catherine waved him in, sat him down, and filled him in on the budding Arrington theory.

"Makes sense," Warrick said, hunching over, hands interlaced. "I was just coming to tell you—and it's good to find you both here—that our friend Taylor Dearborn looks to be in the clear. The blood on that bat is rodent's blood—he really was killing the little critters."

"Slam dunk my ass," Larkin muttered. He seemed miffed—at himself.

"What about the scratches to Dearborn's chest?" Catherine asked.

"Mia just showed me the DNA report—that fragment I tweezed from the wound was a piece of canine claw. Taylor seems to have been telling the truth about his dog scratching him."

"That's what I get," Larkin said bitterly, "jumping to goddamn conclusions."

Nick wandered in with a frown, reading from a sheaf of papers and shaking his head.

"Who ruined *your* day?" Catherine asked.

"We've got a problem," Nick said, planting himself near the door. "The skin under Angie's fingernails? It does *not* belong to her ex-husband."

Warrick squinted. "*Mia* gave you that?"

"Yeah. Just now."

Looking in the direction of the DNA lab, as if trying to see around the corner and through the wall to Mia at her desk, Warrick said, "I was just in there, and she didn't give *me* those results!"

Nick gave him a sly grin. "Maybe you've lost your touch."

"Oh-kay boys," Catherine said. "Save that for recess. Back up and give us more detail, Nick . . ."

He held up the report. "The skin under Angie's fingernails isn't Taylor's."

"All right, all right, I get it, "Larkin said, holding up his hands in surrender. "The abusive ex is *not* the killer—we are officially shopping for a new suspect."

Nick turned to Warrick. "How much of this movie did I miss?"

Warrick told Nick about the canine scratches and the rat-blood baseball bat.

"Now this," Nick said, with a flip of the lab-report sheet. "We've lost our favorite suspect. . . . Or is that *only* suspect?"

"Not necessarily," Catherine said, and shared her thoughts about the inheritance and Grace Salfer's will.

Warrick said, "What do we know about David Arrington?"

"Not much I'm afraid," Catherine said, opening a file folder. "Brass is the only one to have spoken with him thus far. The guy appears to make good money; he's Doug Clennon's righthand man at the Platinum King."

Larkin said, "Do you know what people with lots of money want?"

"Lots more money?" Nick asked innocently.

"Bingo," the detective said.

"Maybe it's time we found out some more about this guy," Warrick said. "Brass only made a next-of-kin death notification—looking at Arrington like a suspect is a whole other deal."

"I'll talk to the bereaved nephew," Larkin said, getting up, "gladly."

Warrick said, "What was that you were saying before, Marty? About jumping to conclusions?"

Larkin laughed and said, "I never said I was a quick learner."

Catherine gestured with a gently lecturing forefinger. "Marty, make sure you touch base with Brass before you talk to Arrington. We are two teams working one case, now. No need in duplicating efforts."

"Or," Nick said, "stepping on toes."

Catherine nodded. "Exactly."

Warrick said, "If we're through with Taylor, is there any point holding him, on this restraining order thing? I mean, really—he's not exactly gonna go around and bother Angie at this point."

Larkin looked at Catherine, but she shook her head. "That's not a CSI call, Marty. You decide."

Larkin asked Warrick, "You think I was out of line with that guy?"

"Not really my place to say," Warrick said. "But we've put the poor bastard through a lot and, if he's been leveling from the start, think about it: He just lost the woman he loves, and instead of dealing with it, gets to dance around with us."

"If you think I'm gonna cry over some wife-beating son of a . . . " Larkin shook his head. "Hell. Yeah, yeah . . . cut his ass loose."

Warrick grinned at him. "I dunno . . . seems to me you learn pretty quick."

Larkin grinned back and told him to go to hell.

Catherine patted the desk with two hands. "Okay, we've all got work to do—let's get to it."

They did.

Warrick found Mia in the lab, where she was bending over the gas chromatograph/mass spectrometer. The attractive young DNA expert wore a white blouse that peeked out from under a light-blue lab coat. Her black hair was straight, parted left of center, ends flipping up above her shoulders. She had a symmetrical face with a straight nose, evenly set wide eyes and full, lightly rouged lips.

A small CD player on the counter softly played Nina Simone, an alternative Warrick had suggested when he caught Mia listening to Avril Lavigne.

She looked up as he entered. "Don't even *start* with me! Those results came out *after* you left. Nick just happened to walk in and I gave them to him. . . ."

"Means a lot," Warrick said with a little smile, "knowing you're that sensitive about my feelings."

Mia glared at him, eyebrows pinched. "Sensitive? Don't even *go* there! I just did not wanna hear any of your b.s., Warrick Brown."

His face fell.

But his hurt expression had hardly formed when Mia cracked up. "Ohmigod, if you could *see* the look on your face!"

He managed to laugh. "Okay, okay—you got me. But I *will* get even—better not let that guard down."

"Around you? Not likely."

"What about the dress shirt from the Dearborn apartment?"

Mia went to a counter and retrieved the plastic evidence bag, and brought it over to him. "Blood doesn't belong to Taylor Dearborn, but it does match the DNA samples from under the vic's nails . . . *and* the hair you removed from her shirt."

"Good work," he said, already forgiving her for sucker-punching him. "Mia, you've been a big help."

The wattage of her smile nearly blinded him. "You have your moments." She nodded toward the CD player.

He grinned. "I told you Nina was the real deal."

"I hate to admit you were right, but she is way cool."

Mia's perfume lingering in his nostrils, Warrick made his way to the lock-up. Before long, a uniformed guard was leading Taylor Dearborn—still in his orange jumpsuit—into the interview room, where Warrick already sat, the bag with the shirt on the table before him like a meal.

"Uncuff him, please," Warrick said.

"You sure?" the guard asked. He was a portly guy, near forty, and looked just a little tougher than your average junkyard dog. "Normally there's a detective with you CSIs."

"Just do it."

"Oooh-kay."

The guard slipped the cuffs off Dearborn, who immediately rubbed at his wrists, as he practically almost fell into the chair across from Warrick.

"You want me to stay?" the wary guard asked.

Warrick shook his head and did not speak again until the guard had given him a raised-brow "you're on your own" look and was outside.

Warrick reached into his jacket pocket and withdrew a pack of cigarettes and book of matches. He tossed them across the table.

The prisoner looked far worse than when they first brought him in—haggard, eyes bloodshot, beard a wispy black haze; Taylor Dearborn might have been locked up for weeks. He eyed the cigarettes suspiciously.

Finally, Warrick said, "Those are for you."

"What happened to no smoking?"

Shrugging one shoulder, Warrick said, "Detective Larkin's not here today."

"Yeah, and what a fuckin' shame *that* is."

Then Dearborn snatched up the cigarettes, tore away the cellophane, the foil, and shook one free. Soon the prisoner was inhaling like a drowning man coming up for the third time.

"Taylor," Warrick said, "we know you didn't kill Angie."

Dearborn's eyes tightened; his expression was skeptical, as he blew out a smoky cloud in a way that seemed somehow derisive.

"It doesn't do anybody any good keeping you in jail over that restraining order, now."

Dearborn's eyes widened, his head went back. "You're . . . shaking me loose?"

"That's right."

"Yeah, well . . . thanks."

"You don't seem thrilled."

Staring at the orange tip of the cigarette in his right hand, Dearborn said, "My job's probably screwed."

Warrick nodded. "Raw Shanks Diner."

"Yeah. They make a 'mean burger'—remember?"

"I do remember. You want me to put a word in with your boss?"

Hope dared to dance in the prisoner's eyes. "You . . . really think it would do any good?"

"You said yourself, it's a good place to work."

"It is—but he can be a hardass, if you screw up too often . . ."

"I won't tell him about the restraining order. I'll let him know your wife was murdered, and in addition to being broken up, you had to suffer this indignity. I'll say we cleared you, and that you cooperated with us."

Dearborn studied Warrick. "You'd do all that?"

"You got my word."

"Why?"

"Because it's the right thing to do."

Dearborn thought about that. "You aren't in AA, are you?"

"No . . . but I went to Gambler's Anonymous a couple times. Nobody in this life is perfect, Taylor."

"If they were," he said without irony, "you'd be outta business."

"True. But I do need to ask you one more question."

Dearborn dropped his cigarette to the floor, ground it out, and lit up a fresh one. Then he sat back. "Go ahead. If I know the answer, it's yours. Owe you that much."

Warrick shoved the evidence bag across to Dearborn—so the prisoner could see the light blue dress shirt within . . . and its blood stains. "That yours?"

Dearborn stared at the shirt for a long moment. Finally he said, "Have you been screwing with me?"

"No."

"Has this all been talk? Shaking me loose, vouching for me with my boss . . . ?"

"No."

"Because . . . because I don't know if I should answer you."

"It's your shirt, isn't it?"

". . . Yeah. Yeah it is. But that's not my blood. I never got hurt or bled or anything, or . . . oh hell." Dearborn dropped the evidence onto the table, as if the plastic bag were a red-hot stone. "Is . . . is that *Angie's* blood?"

"No. We're fairly sure it's the killer's."

Dearborn grunted, sneered, took an angry drag at the cigarette. "Good." He shoved the evidence bag back across to Warrick. "I hope the son of a bitch bled to death. I hope it took all night."

Warrick said, "I know this is difficult, Taylor . . . but we need to know what your shirt was doing at Angie's, when she didn't seem to want anything to do with you."

"I thought you said *one* more question."

"It's the same question. You know it's the same question. *What* was your *shirt* doing there?"

Dearborn sat and smoked and stared at nothing. Then he dropped the second cigarette to the floor, ground it out, and lay his head on the table, arms folded like a schoolkid taking a nap at his desk.

"Taylor?"

The man's voice was muffled, his lips against his orange-jumpsuited sleeve. "It's old, that shirt. . . ."

"Old?"

"From before . . . before we split up. She didn't like pajamas. Some girls like sleeping in guy's shirts. She always slept in my shirts, old shirts. Back when we were together? But . . . but she musta kept sleeping in them." His eyes were bright, trails of tears shining on his face.

"Okay, Taylor," Warrick said, satisfied.

"Was she . . . wearing my shirt when she was killed?"

"No."

"I don't get it—why was it bloody, then?"

"We don't know yet."

"Mr. Brown—Detective Brown?"

"Make it 'Warrick.' "

"Warrick—are you going to catch this bastard?"

Warrick met Dearborn's eyes and nodded. "Count on it."

The CSI rose.

"Warrick?"

"Yeah?"

"Funny thing is . . . you guys did me a big favor, locking me up."

"How's that?"

"I think, Angie getting killed like that?"

"Yeah?"

"If I hadn't been locked up in here . . . I'd have fallen off the wagon, big-time."

At the door now, Warrick drew a deep breath, let it out. "I believe that. . . . But you stay sober now, Taylor."

"Did you beat gambling, Warrick?"

"Taylor—I beat it every day."

"I hear you."

The two men nodded at each other, and Warrick and his evidence bag slipped out.

While Brass accompanied Sofia and Sara to call on Todd Templeton at Home Sure, Greg Sanders wound up in the company of his night-shift supervisor, going to check on Grace Salfer's friend, Elizabeth Parker. On their way to the city's northwest side, Grissom made it clear that this was Greg's interview—he was just along to supervise, and fill in, since neither detective on the joint case was available.

The Parker woman's small nondescript framed house on Danaides Court was typical of the neighborhood, cookie-cutter homes that reminded Greg of black-and-white photos of suburbia he'd seen in old magazines from the fifties.

On the second ring of the bell, the door cracked open and a sliver of a well-wrinkled face peeked out at them through one lens of metal-frame glasses.

As instructed, Greg took the lead. "Mrs. Parker?" he asked. "We're with the Las Vegas Police." He held up his CSI laminate on its necklace.

The door opened wider, and the woman used both lenses now to have a closer look at the identification badge.

Everything about her was small—she was a head shorter than Greg and likely weighed in at around one hundred pounds. Her silver hair was swept back and her features were birdlike from tiny eyes to a hawkish nose; she wore blue jeans and a long-sleeve flowered blouse with a white cardigan.

"I'm Elizabeth Parker. But I haven't had a problem."

"Ma'am?"

"I didn't call the police, young man."

"Uh, no—I'm Greg Sanders and this is my super-visor, Gil Grissom. We're from the Las Vegas Crime Lab."

"Oh!" Her expression turned grave. "Oh, yes, of course you are. You're here to talk about Grace. Come in, please."

She stepped out of the way to allow them in, then shut the door and led them into a living room that seemed built to scale for someone her size. Despite her sweater, the thermostat was set just south of eighty.

A love seat and two chairs made a U in the middle of the room, bookshelves lining two side walls, a picture window on another wall allowing afternoon sunlight to filter through sheer curtains.

She asked if they'd like something to drink and the CSIs declined with thanks; then she gestured for them to take the love seat, which they did, while she perched on the edge of a chair, ever birdlike.

"Were you and Grace Salfer friends?" Greg asked.

"Oh yes," she said, drawing a tissue from inside her sleeve—she was not crying, she was just pre-pared. "We were very good friends. I can't imagine . . . Well, I'd say the world has become a ter-rible place, but there's always been unpleasantness, hasn't there?"

With a world-weary smile, Grissom said, "Unfor-tunately, yes."

Greg asked her, "What can you tell us about Mrs. Salfer?"

"Grace," she said wistfully. "Well, her name said it all, didn't it? Carried herself with such dignity, such effortless grace . . ."

"How did you come to know her?"

"Grace and her husband lived just across the street," she said, "for, oh . . . fifteen years, anyway. Then Pete, her husband, was promoted, got a handsome pay raise. Well, it wasn't long before they moved out of this little neighborhood with its crackerboxes. Pete got kind of full of himself. But coming up in the world didn't change Grace any— she and I kept in close touch."

"Do you know of anyone who might have wanted to harm her?"

She shook her head. "No, I'm sorry. Not a one."

Thinking she'd responded a little too quickly, Greg asked, "Could you stop and think about it? Someone must have—"

"Young man, it's just about all I *have* been thinking of, since I learned of this tragedy. The idea of someone . . . someone murdering a person like Grace . . . I can't think of a solitary soul who even disliked Grace, let alone do something as . . . something as senselessly cruel as this."

"Yes, ma'am. . . . Did you know her housekeeper— Angela Dearborn?"

"Angie? Oh my yes. She was Grace's guardian angel after Pete died. She came in, took care of Grace, became her friend. Like a daughter to Grace—they would sit and talk and listen to each other's problems and opinions. . . . I feel terrible!"

"Why?"

"I should have thought to call Angie. And express

my condolences—Grace and that girl were like family to each other. Poor thing must be crushed over
this."

The awful irony of those words stunned Greg, and
it was left to Grissom to say, "I'm sorry to have to tell
you this, Mrs. Parker . . . but Angela Dearborn is
dead, too."

The woman's hand shot to her mouth and tears
pooled and overflowed, and the tissue finally came
in handy. "Don't tell me, she . . . Angie . . . was in
the house at the same time, when this—"

"No, ma'am," Greg said, reasserting himself. "She
was a murder victim, as well—but it happened in
her own place. We're trying to figure out if there's a
conn—"

Grissom cut him off. "Would you happen to know
anything about Mrs. Salfer's estate?"

Mrs. Parker, swallowing, her composure returning, shrugged. "Grace was well-off—Pete made a lot
of money, and invested well. I believe I already
made that clear."

"What about her will?"

"Her . . . will?"

"Yes, ma'am."

Mrs. Parker shifted uncomfortably on the chair,
and Greg and Grissom traded glances—the word had
struck a nerve.

"I shouldn't talk about such things," Mrs. Parker
said, primly. "It's not my place."

"I understand how you feel," Grissom said. "But it
may well have a bearing on her murder."

That last word made her shudder. She was shaking her head now, withdrawing into some invisible shell.

Greg forced the woman to meet his gaze. "Please, Mrs. Parker—you may have information that could help us catch this killer."

Mrs. Parker had a deer-in-the-headlights expression, but clearly she was mulling what Greg had said.

He pressed: "The same killer may be responsible for Angie's death, as well. If he's killed twice . . ."

Grissom's expression indicated the young CSI had said enough.

Meanwhile, Mrs. Parker sat. And stewed. They let her.

Finally, dabbing at her eyes with her tissue, she made her decision. "The will was set up to give the bulk of Grace's estate to Angie. She was such a godsend for Grace."

Greg asked, "What about her nephew—David?"

"Well . . . David *was* in the will. . . ."

"Was?"

"They had . . . a . . . what you might call a falling out. A sort of difference of opinion about . . . really, this isn't my place, I feel very awkward about—"

"Mrs. Parker," Grissom said, his voice soft but with a sternness. "You need to tell us what you know. Decorum does not enter in."

She nodded and sighed. "I do understand. . . . Grace and David did not agree on a certain aspect of David's lifestyle. Grace thought his behavior was wrong, but correctable, and that he was merely willful not to even try to change; and she would not leave him her estate while they had that conflict. I'm not saying she was right or wrong, just that, well . . . that's how she felt. And after all it *was* her money."

"David was gay," Grissom said flatly.

Greg looked sharply at his supervisor, who'd been ahead of him.

"He is a homosexual, yes," she said. "Personally, I have a live-and-let-live attitude about such things— for Grace, it was in part a religious issue. I told her my understanding, everything I've read, indicates that sexual orientation is not a matter of choice. I felt it was unfair of her to expect David to change, since he likely was born that way."

Greg said, "But she didn't agree."

"She wouldn't hear of it, and I valued our friendship too much to bring the subject up again. And, as I say, she was free to leave her money to whomever she chose, and David was financially well-off already, himself, with a very good job I understand . . . and, of course, I understand her feelings about her 'daughter'—Angie, who could really *use* the help."

In the SUV, on the way back to the office, with Greg at the wheel, dealing with heavy traffic on Elkhorn Road, Grissom called Brass on the cell.

"Did my friend Todd Templeton cooperate, Jim?"

"What do you think? Templeton says he won't give up those sign-in logs without a court order, and if any mistakes or omissions were made in the transcriptions of Grace's visitors, it has to be a simple keyboarding error."

"So we need a court order."

"I've got a call in to a judge now. Meantime, we're

picking up Susan Gillette so we can have a conversation with our favorite 'fellow law enforcement professional.' "

Grissom filled the detective in on Mrs. Parker's interview.

"Nephew left out of the will," Brass said, "as punishment for being gay—wow. Sounds like a murder motive to me."

Call waiting clicked in Grissom's ear—he checked the caller ID: Catherine.

"Gotta take this, Jim."

"Okay."

Grissom took Cath's call, and asked, "What's up?"

"Gil—how would like some test results?"

"Tell me what they are first, and then I'll tell you if I like them."

"Fair enough. Carpet fibers in Grace Salfer's hair are from her living room."

"So that's where she died."

"Would seem so," Catherine said. "And Doc Robbins says the liver temperature puts the time of death around midnight. That Los Calina guard—what's her name, Gillette?"

"Susan Gillette, yes."

"Wouldn't she have been on duty by then?"

"Yes," Grissom said. "And her *next* tour of duty is in a CSI interview room, very shortly. . . . Brass is bringing her in now."

"Sweet," Catherine said. "What's she like?"

"Perky."

"Ah."

"I hate perky."

Catherine laughed in his ear; then she said, "One

more thing—prints on the dresser in Grace's bedroom were her own."

Grissom would have preferred an illuminating surprise; but the evidence was the evidence. He asked, "Is Larkin working on David Arrington?"

Catherine's voice was frustration-tinged. "Yes and no. Marty's doing background on him now. He was going to interview Arrington, but the guy wasn't home and didn't answer his cell. A call to his office at the Platinum King got a secretary, who said 'Mr. A' is taking a few days off. Supposedly he's out of town."

"I hate it when a good suspect is out of town."

"Don't we all."

When Grissom and Greg got to HQ, they arrived just ahead of Brass, Sofia, and Sara, who entered the blue-tinged, glass-walled world of CSI with a disheartened Susan Gillette in tow.

The young woman—today in black turtleneck sweater and jeans with Rockport walking shoes, lugging a black purse only slightly smaller than a duffel bag—was not handcuffed; no arrest had been made. But the bounce was clearly out of her step, the eager puppy quality of Los Calina replaced by a foot-dragging weariness indicating she carried a heavy weight on her slim shoulders.

Brass led her into an interview room, Sara joining him. Grissom, Sofia, and Greg entered the observation booth next door.

"Have a seat, Ms. Gillette," Brass said pleasantly.

Susan Gillette plopped into one, her hands resting on the table, her eyes downcast.

Brass and Sara sat opposite.

"All right," Brass said. "Let's get started."

The diminutive security guard raised her head as if it took a real effort. "Started with what? I don't understand this at all. I mean, I want to cooperate, but . . ."

"How well do you know Taylor Dearborn?"

The security guard seemed baffled, eyes popping as if for comic effect. "What?"

"Not 'what,' Ms. Gillette. 'Who?' "

"Taylor something? Taylor *what?*"

"Dearborn."

She shook her head, hair flouncing. "Uh-uh. No. Never heard of him."

Behind the one-way mirror, Grissom cast a glance toward Sofia and Greg, who seemed unmoved by the guard's response.

"You've never heard of Taylor Dearborn?" Brass asked.

She put on a smirky *"duh!"* expression, and said, "No," turning it into three syllables. But behind this, she was obviously afraid.

"That's funny, Ms. Gillette—both of you were at the AA dinner the other night."

Susan Gillette's smirk disappeared and now embarrassment colored her features. "Oh. That? You mean, the dinner with the mayor?"

"Yes. *That* AA dinner the other night."

She leaned forward, suddenly earnest. "Captain Brass, there were a lot of people there. You think being in AA means you know every alcoholic in Vegas? Please."

"*This* alcoholic is named Taylor Dearborn. Skinny guy, dark hair, big eyes . . ."

"Oh, *Tay*-lor!" she said, as if Brass had been mispronouncing it.

"Taylor Dearborn," Brass said; the name was becoming the detective's mantra.

"We don't use last names in AA, and actually, I do know a Taylor from meetings I attended . . . who fits that description, yes."

"And?"

"And what? Seems like a guy getting it together."

"So, then—you *do* know him."

"No!" Gillette said, and shook her head vigorously. "I've never *even* spoken to the guy. I don't socialize or date or anything with other . . . other alcoholics."

"Will Taylor back up your story?"

"How would I know? He may or may not know who you're even *talking* about. I'm not exactly the only 'Susan' in AA."

Abruptly, Brass changed the line of questioning. "Did you touch the ladder leaning against Grace Salfer's house?"

Gillette's eyes narrowed. "Touch . . . the . . . *ladder*?"

"Repeating the question," Brass said, a little testy now, "is not answering the question. Did you—"

"I did *not* touch the damn ladder!" She pounded a small fist on the table.

The detective said, "That's better—now let's just bring the volume down a bit. You say you did not touch the ladder when you walked around the house?"

"No!"

"Ms. Gillette, if you did touch it—accidentally, when you came around the house—just say so. I know you're concerned about being accused of tainting the crime scene, but—"

"No, no, no—I did not touch that goddamned ladder!"

"Okay. Okay. Nonetheless, your fingerprint is on there—do you have some other explanation for how—"

"No."

Sara entered in for the first time, withdrawing from a folder a photo of the fingerprint on the ladder. "The ladder print matches yours—from your security industry application? Are you sure you don't know how it got there?"

Gillette turned her hands palms up. "I have no idea unless . . . unless *you* made a mistake, honey."

Sara's eyebrows rose and Brass said, "If she says it's a match, it's a match."

The woman spoke through her teeth; a vein next to her left eye was standing out. "I did *not* touch that ladder."

"Look, look, look," Brass said, "here's the deal. We've got your fingerprint on the ladder. The footprints in the flower bed were made by someone applying about the same amount of pressure you might have, standing in men's shoes. You had opportunity, you had a key, you had the alarm code."

Gillette looked stricken; they all saw the blood drain out of her face until it was pale as a blister.

"We *know* you had difficulties with Mrs. Salfer. You have displayed a certain volatility, at the crime scene and, for that matter, in this interview room. Tell me why we *shouldn't* be looking at you—hard— for the Salfer murder?"

She had begun shaking her head halfway through Brass's speech, but she waited till he was through before saying, "I'm telling you, I swear to you, you are looking at the wrong person. I never *touched* the ladder, or any *other* damned . . . "

They all watched as her expression turned distant, and color returned to her face.

"What is it?" Brass asked.

"I . . . I may have touched that ladder."

"Tell us."

"About two weeks ago, I bought some supplies for Home Sure. Wire, alarm stuff . . . and an aluminum extension ladder."

"You bought the ladder for Home Sure?"

She nodded. "Yeah. Mr. Templeton gave me the money himself, and shooed me over to a Home Depot on Maryland Parkway."

"Do you usually run errands like that?"

"No. But he's the boss, and if he asks . . . you know how it is."

Brass and Sara were staring at her.

"*What?*" Gillette said. "You asked how I could have touched that ladder, and, well, if that's the ladder I bought, then that explains it . . . right?"

Brass said, "Not really. You've just admitted to buying the ladder found at the crime scene—a ladder that seems to be part of the murder itself."

Again she looked stricken. "Oh . . . my . . . *Gawd* . . ."

"And at Home Depot," Sara said, "the security cameras most likely caught you buying that ladder."

"All I did was buy the stupid thing for Home

Sure—as an employee!" She leaned forward, smiling. "I'm not worried."

"Not worried?" Brass said.

"Naw! Mr. Templeton'll back me up."

Behind the glass, Grissom said, "Don't count on it, Susan."

Wednesday, January 26, 3:30 P.M.

A STOKED NICK STOKES, feeling on top of the case, stopped by the break room for a bottle of water only to find a glum Detective Marty Larkin at a table, staring at his cell phone like it was a particularly baffling piece of evidence.

"This looks like a Zen moment," Nick said.

Larkin looked up, as if not sure whether to be irritated or just start weeping. "Damn thing doesn't wanna ring."

"Heard about the watched pot never boiling?" Nick asked, getting a bottled water out of the fridge. "Same principle holds true for—"

"Could you keep your good mood to yourself?" Larkin asked, only half-kidding.

Nick screwed off the Evian cap. "Get you something? Water? Cyanide? Decaf?"

That got a grim chuckle from the detective. "Any of those will do. When they plant me tomorrow, or the next day, make sure the headstone says, 'Killed by a slam dunk.' "

"Maybe you guys in North Las Vegas get slam dunks once in a while. Over here in the big town—"

"I think I will have some decaf."

Nick went over and poured him some, asking, "Whose call you waiting on, anyway?"

"Judge Scott. Trying to get a search warrant for David Arrington's house."

Nick handed him a Styrofoam cup of steaming liquid. "Yeah? Why didn't you say so. I know where that guy is."

Larkin's eyes widened. "Judge Scott?"

Sighing, Nick asked, "Bro—when was the last time you slept?"

Larkin shrugged. "Last week sometime?"

"Arrington," Nick said slowly. "I know where David *Arrington* is."

The detective perked up. "Where?"

"Also I know where Judge Scott probably is—or at least I can narrow it to half a dozen golf courses. . . ."

"Throw a drowning man a rope, Stokes! Where the hell is David Arrington?"

Nick shrugged, glugged a gulp of water. "Reno."

"Reno? Why the hell—"

"He's at the Platinum King Casino in Reno. He books oldies acts into both of Clennon's resorts— here *and* Reno."

"His secretary said he was taking time off! You got this how?"

Taking another pull from the bottle, Nick eased

back in his chair. "Knowing people in high places is almost as overrated as knowing people in low places—I have contacts in-between, including a young lady who works at the PK. She says he's supposed to be out of the office until tomorrow or the next day."

"Why'd his secretary say he was taking time off?"

"I don't know. Maybe he doesn't like to be bothered with Vegas business when he's doing Reno work." Nick smiled pleasantly. "You should ask Arrington."

"I don't know whether to slug you or hug you, Stokes."

"A simple written thank-you note will suffice."

Catherine strolled in, got a cup of coffee and joined them at the table. "Any breaking news, gentlemen?"

Larkin explained about the warrant, after which Nick brought her up to speed about Arrington's whereabouts.

"Have we learned any more about Arrington?" she asked.

Nick said, "He was with Clennon's casino in Reno before moving here a year-and-a-half ago or so. He's been working out of both casinos for about the last five years, but he used to live there."

"Do we know why he moved?"

Nick shrugged. "Maybe to be closer to his aunt. She's the only family he has. *Was* the only family."

Catherine considered that, then asked, "Do we know anything about his personal life?"

Nick shook his head. "Not really. Brass said he got the impression the guy was a swinging bachelor of sorts, taking advantage of his position as a booker, to date showgirls and the like. . . . Why?"

Catherine raised an eyebrow. "Swinging bachelor maybe, but probably not pursuing showgirls—Grissom and Greg interviewed Grace Salfer's friend, Elizabeth Parker. The two women go way back, to before Salfer's late husband started earning major bucks. Anyway, Mrs. Parker says her friend Grace's nephew, David, is gay—Grace disapproved, apparently due to conservative religious beliefs, and it seems ultimately that's why Grace kept the lion's share of the inheritance out of his hands."

Larkin was nodding. "And earmarked Angie Dearborn, instead."

Nick was squinting, apparently not quite buying this. "My contacts talk about the guy like he's a real ladies' man."

Larkin said, "Maybe he's still in the closet. Platinum King has an older, baby boomer constituency."

"There are plenty of reasons in today's society," Catherine said, "for gays to conceal their personal lives."

Larkin's eyebrows went up. "Maybe so, but it seems our friend David couldn't conceal it from his aunt."

Catherine looked from the detective to the CSI. "Can we look into this discreetly? If Arrington is innocent in this, I don't want to inadvertently 'out' him—if he chooses the closet, that's his business."

"Don't ask," Larkin said, "don't murder?"

Catherine didn't smile.

"Don't worry, Cath," Nick said. "I know just who to talk to."

Before Nick could rise, Larkin's cell phone finally trilled.

"See," Nick said to the detective, who chuckled, though the reference was lost on Catherine.

"Martin Larkin."

Nick watched as the detective's grin spread and he gave them a thumbs-up.

"*Thank* you, Judge Scott," Larkin said. "Sorry to bother you on the links." Then he broke the connection and told his colleagues, "The warrant'll be in the fax machine any minute now."

"I love it when a plan comes together," Nick said.

"Maybe so," Catherine said with a grin, "but leave it to Marty and me to use that warrant. You go dig further into Arrington's background. Carefully."

"Kid gloves, Cath," Nick said.

"Any developments, don't be a stranger."

Moments later, at his desk, Nick dialed a number he knew by heart.

"Good afternoon, thank you for calling the Platinum King Casino—this is Jennifer; how may I direct your call?"

"Don't direct it anywhere," Nick said. "Hold onto it."

The cool professional voice morphed into something warm and personal. "Nicky, two calls in one day? You're a bad influence."

"I can but try. Listen, Jen—you gave me good info before, but I need you to dig a little deeper."

"I can but try," she mimicked.

Nick could almost see the dazzling smile of this lovely twenty-four-year-old brunette, who looked more suited to a chorus line than a switchboard chair. He and Jen had gone out several times, always had fun, and neither put pressure on the other to take it to any other level.

"We need to talk a little more about David Arrington."

Her voice lowered to a near-whisper. "Nicky, I told you this morning—sharing information about other PK employees is frowned upon. Bad *enough* I told you where Mr. A *really* went. . . ."

"Jen, just a couple questions is all."

"If you want background on Mr. A., why aren't you going through Human Resources?"

"What I need isn't official background, Jen—I don't care where he worked last or went to school."

An awkward silence followed.

Finally, she broke it, still whispering: "What do you want to know, Nicky? Make it quick."

"This one isn't easy to ask, Jen."

"Nicky, you're a big boy. Ask. I have work to do!"

". . . Your 'Mr. A'—his Casanova reputation. Is it on the level?"

"I . . . I'm not sure I follow."

But suddenly he knew she did. "Is he straight?"

"He's always been a stand-up boss, and—"

"That's not what I mean, Jen, and you know it."

Another long silence.

She seemed hurt. "Why would you ask something personal like that?"

"I'm sorry, Jen—it's come up in the course of an investigation. I wouldn't bother you with this if it weren't important. Is David Arrington gay?"

In the next patch of silence, Nick pictured Jennifer sitting at her switchboard, looking around to make sure no one was listening in.

She said, "Well . . . there has been talk."

"What's the general consensus?"

"No one knows for sure. He goes out with show-girls, and other female entertainers, singers from the lounge for example, the occasional waitress . . . takes them out to dinner."

"Where he can be seen?"

"I didn't say that. But people do speculate about it sometimes. How he never seems to have a relationship—any female he goes out with, no matter how nice a time they have, never gets asked out again."

"So he might be feeding a reputation as a guy dating a lot of good-looking women, when really he's putting up a kind of front?"

"You're the detective, Nicky."

"When this subject comes up, with your girl-friends, what do they—"

"Everybody kind of assumes he has some long-term relationship in Reno. That's where he was from, and he still spends a lot of time there."

"A male or female relationship?"

"No one knows, and we probably shouldn't care. Listen, Nicky, I don't feel good about this conversa-tion. It makes me feel . . ."

"Icky?" he asked.

"Icky, Nicky?" she asked, and laughed, and so did he.

She said, "I think that word *does* describe what you've put me through. . . . You owe me, and you're gonna pay."

"I'm off Saturday. I'll call you at home, and we'll negotiate terms."

"Okay. . . . Nicky? Mr. A's always been very nice."

"I'll keep that in mind."

His next call was to Catherine, to report his findings. "Brass has connections in Reno," she said. "Call him and fill him in, and ask him to check up on Arrington's past and present there."

"Mark it off done," Nick said.

In the passenger seat of Marty Larkin's Taurus, Catherine ended the call, then turned to the detective and shared what Nick had told her.

"Maybe the answer's in Reno," Larkin said, turning the car onto Coronado Drive.

Soon the NLVPD detective wheeled to a stop in front of Arrington's house. They sat in the car and studied the spacious pastel-green Mission-style stucco with the expensive Xeriscaped yard.

"We don't know that Arrington has really done anything wrong," Catherine said. "Meaning no reflection on your work, Marty—already in this case, we've put one innocent family member of a murder victim through hell. I'd just as soon not use a ram on that place, if we can avoid it."

"Can you pick locks?"

"Not really."

Larkin shrugged and put on an innocent smile. "Gee. Then it looks like the ram."

"Let's just take a minute to walk around the house, Dirty Harry—maybe there's another way in."

Larkin frowned. "Come on, Cath. You know this case has given me some residual anger. The ram would help me work that out."

"How about a compromise? Open the front door by banging your head on it."

With a good-natured laugh, Larkin said, "You win. Let's take a look 'round back."

The front offered no easy access. They circled around the garage, Catherine leading, and came up against a six-foot wooden fence with a locked gate.

Larkin asked, "*Now* can I go back to the car and get the ram?"

"Hang on, Marty. Just give me a boost so I can get over this thing."

Larkin made a step out of his interlaced hands and bent his knees slightly.

Most days Catherine wore flats to work, and luckily this was one, as heels would have made this little maneuver next to impossible, while landing on the other side barefooted did not exactly appeal, either.

She set her right foot on his offered hands. "On three?"

"Yeah. One, two . . ."

". . . three," they said together, Catherine jumping as Larkin straightened and lifted. A second later, the rounded top of the fence was within her grasp, Catherine grabbed hold and pulled herself up with the ease and grace of the former dancer she was. She had just a moment to check the ground before she let go of the fence and dropped on the other side to the grass.

The yard was empty—no Xeriscape back here, rather a lush lawn, small immaculately trimmed bushes here and there around a huge deck which surrounded a pool and separate hot tub.

Climbing the two steps up the deck, she went to the nearest window and found the curtains drawn and the window locked.

"You okay?" Larkin called from beyond the fence.

"I'm cool," she called back. "I'll find a way in, and meet you at the front door. Just be patient!"

"Sure, whatever."

She passed two more locked windows before reaching sliding glass doors looking onto a tile-floored dining area with an oak table and six chairs.

After slipping on latex gloves, Catherine tried the handle and found it unlocked. She had figured as much—people with high-fenced-in yards often didn't bother locking their back doors, figuring no one would have the audacity or the ability to climb a six-foot wooden privacy barrier.

Letting out a slow breath, she slid open the door. No dog came running, no sound emanated from within, other than the whisper of the air condi-tioner.

"Mr. Arrington!" she called. "LVPD! Are you home, sir? We have a warrant to search the prem-ises! Mr. Arrington?"

The room—indeed the house—remained silent.

Not taking any chances, she unholstered her weapon and brought the revolver up. With the sun starting to set, shadows shrouded the dining room. She found the light switch and flipped it on. Moving through the house, she kept her eyes open for movement and continued to call out for Arrington with no response.

Returning her pistol to her holster, she opened the front door and found Larkin waiting on the stoop, hands on hips, foot tapping.

"House seems clear," she said.

"That's not a CSI job," he said, frowning.

"I was first in. I cleared it. Get over it, Marty."

He stepped into the entryway, which was just off the living room, both areas covered with rich gray carpet.

Adjacent to the living room—essentially an entertainment center decorated with show-biz photos—was a smaller chamber, a restful space with a sofa under a picture window, a coffee table with a few magazines, and a small rock garden. Asian art lined most of a walls, but low-slung bookcases with massive art-oriented volumes nestled here and there.

"Shall we get to it?" Catherine asked.

"Now *this*," Larkin said, "is where I should follow the CSI's lead. . . ."

Sofia Curtis appeared in the doorway of Sara Sidle's office, blond hair flowing free today, unfettered from its occasional ponytail.

Sitting at her computer monitor, Sara had finally removed the last layer from the pile of footprints they found in Grace Salfer's entryway.

"Where's Grissom?" Sofia asked.

"Don't know."

Looking around, obviously a little uncomfortable, Sofia asked, "What are you working on?"

Sara told her about the footprints.

"Any luck?"

"I've weeded out *our* shoes, the EMTs, the patrolmen, and Brass. I've still got a couple prints I haven't IDed. One is almost certainly Grace Salfer's. The other is a man's shoe. Looks like the print from the flower bed."

"You've eliminated a lot, though—that's good."

Sara looked from the screen to the blond CSI. "Why do you need to see Grissom?"

Sofia frowned. "Think I've found something . . . but I'm not sure."

"What?" Sara asked, swinging in her chair toward the visitor, suddenly interested.

Sofia leaned against the doorjamb. "I kept digging into David Arrington's background. If he *did* kill his aunt for her money . . . and eliminated Angie Dearborn because she stood in the way of him inheriting . . . it's going to be important that we have a handle on his motive."

"Well, the motive seems to be his aunt disinheriting him, because he's gay."

"Which means finding proof of his lifestyle becomes crucial."

"Think that'll be difficult?"

With a shrug, Sofia said, "If Arrington *is* gay, he's buried deep in the closet. But while I was looking through employment records from the PK in Reno, I found an odd, *maybe* connection."

"Connection to what?"

Before Sofia could respond, Nick popped up behind her in the doorway. "Anybody seen Grissom?"

"No," Sofia said, glancing back at him, "I'm looking for Gil, too."

"Come in and sit down, you two," Sara said, and they did.

"Now," Sara said to Nick, "what have you come up with? Share it with the rest of the class. . . ."

Nick shrugged and said, "Catherine wanted me to find Brass, to have him look into something in Reno.

I couldn't find him, so I started poking around myself, via Internet and phone. I think I've got a couple of interesting wrinkles."

Sofia arched an eyebrow at Nick. "A connection to the case back in Reno, by any chance?"

"Yeah—concerning David Arrington."

"Me, too."

They looked at each other curiously now.

"You first," Nick said.

Sofia leaned forward. "I was just starting to tell Sara—I went through the employment records of the Platinum King Casino. Turns out, while Arrington lived in Reno, Todd Templeton—"

"Worked in the PK security office," Nick said. "I just found the same thing."

Agape, Sara said, "You got to be kidding! When was this?"

"Right up until Arrington moved to Vegas," Sofia said. "Apparently after Grissom exposed Templeton as untrustworthy, the guy managed to land a top security position at Reno's Platinum King."

Nick raised a finger. "Ah, but did you also discover that Templeton moved to Vegas only *three weeks* after Arrington?"

Both women looked at him.

Sara said, "*That's* interesting. . . ."

"Nice catch, Nick," Sofia said, shaking her head in admiration.

"One other thing," Nick said. "And this may be the biggest of all—I did some digging into Arrington's finances. I didn't get as far as I'd like, but what I did find . . . well."

"Spill, Nicky," Sara said.

"Arrington is a major investor in a certain local business. Seems to have put everything he has into that business."

Sara laughed. "Don't tell me!"

Sofia asked, "Not Home Sure Security?"

"He's the principal investor—Templeton's own share of 'his' company is significantly smaller than David's."

"They're in business together," Sara said.

"At least," Nick said.

The three CSIs sat and smiled at each other; they were basking in a satisfying mutual moment: This case had just come together.

But plenty was left to be done.

Sara shooed them out. "You guys need to find both Grissom and Catherine, and share all this. Meantime, I'll see what I can do with these prints and catch up with you."

Then Sara got back to work on matching the prints from the entryway to the ones in the flower bed. The question was, would the prints match? And if they did, whose shoes *were* they?

Brass and Grissom entered the latter's office. Grissom got behind his desk, Brass sitting opposite the CSI supervisor, the detective's head pounding after the difficult interview with Susan Gillette.

"What do you think?" Grissom asked.

"I think I can use a drink."

"This is a dry office . . . at least mine is."

"It would be. . . . I also think Susan Gillette has the IQ of one of these pickled specimens of yours."

The glassed-in critters seemed to take no offense.

"So let's say the height requirement isn't the only standard she didn't meet," Grissom said, "when she tried to get on the Vegas PD, and wound up in private security work instead."

"Yeah. Let's say that."

"Can we also say, she's innocent?"

Brass considered the question as it hung in the air between them. Finally, reluctantly, he said, "Yeah, godammit—I think she may be innocent."

"Can we prove someone's trying to frame her?"

"Jesus, Gil, that's *your* job! *I* can just theorize—*you* find evidence that supports it."

"If that were true," Grissom said, "we at CSI would be the worst kind of scientists. And we aren't. What we do is find the evidence, develop it, *then*—when we have proof—we interpret."

Brass frowned. "Are you *sure* this is a dry office?"

Grissom, smiling but not responding, looked over as Nick and Sofia came through the door without so much as a knock.

"Gris," Nick said, "you know where Catherine is?"

The CSI supervisor shook his head.

"With Larkin," Brass said. "They're serving a search warrant at Arrington's house on Coronado Drive. They called me a little while ago—doesn't sound promising."

Turning back to Grissom, Nick said, "Sofia and I have a theory."

Brass laughed, and said, "Well by all means! We're all *about* theories around here!"

Grissom laughed, once, and Nick asked, "What did I miss? What's funny?"

"Please say your theory," Grissom said, turning

his chair toward where Nick and Sofia stood, just inside the door, "has some new facts behind it."

"It does," Sofia said.

Nick said, "I believe we know who David Arrington's longtime companion might be. His partner in business . . . and in life."

Grissom's eyes narrowed; Brass sat forward.

"Another male employee left the Platinum King in Reno and moved to Vegas around the same time as Arrington." Nick smiled, just a little. "This employee had a top security job at the PK, and it's just possible that Arrington got his friend that job, considering how otherwise difficult it might've been for this individual . . . who'd been recently disgraced . . . to land a such a cherry position."

"Don't tell me . . ." Grissom began.

Brass said, "Todd Templeton."

Sofia nodded. "Nick found proof that he moved to Vegas less than a month after Arrington."

"That doesn't prove anything," Grissom said.

"How about Arrington being the chief investor in Home Sure Security?"

"The hell!" Brass, who would fall off his chair if he sat any farther forward, said, "Never mind whether they have a romantic connection—that's a hell of a business connection, right there."

"It's good, Nick," Grissom said. "Very good. But we have a stronger case if the relationship between Arrington and Templeton is also a personal . . . frankly, sexual . . . one. *If* what we're saying is, Templeton and Arrington together took out both Angie Dearborn and Grace Salfer, so that David could inherit and he and Todd share the wealth . . ."

"That's what we're saying," Nick said.

". . . then it makes more sense if the two men are lovers. Partners in more ways than simply business."

"There's another aspect," Nick said. "Gris, you know better than anyone that Templeton tampered with evidence. Doesn't it appear he may have been framing people right and left, here?"

Brass said, "His employee, Susan Gillette for one."

"Abusive ex-husband Taylor Dearborn," Sofia said, "for another?"

Grissom said, "I'm convinced. Can we convince anyone else? A judge and a jury, say?"

"Let me make a call," Brass said.

"To whom?"

"A guy I know in Reno."

After excusing himself, Brass went down the hall, found an empty office and closed himself inside to use his cell. Ten minutes later, he was back in Grissom's office.

The other two had taken the chairs now, so Brass just leaned against a shelving unit, the eyes in bottles staring at him. "Proving the lover issue may not be easy. Maybe not even possible."

"You're not saying we're wrong about this," Nick said.

"No—not at all." Brass shrugged. "What I am saying is . . . well. I talked to a friend who's a detective in Reno. He said it was fairly common knowledge, on the force, that Templeton played for the other team."

"*How* common?" Grissom asked.

"Sort of a workplace open secret. But cops are a funny breed, I don't have to tell you that. They deal every day in the secrets of other people, of vics, of suspects, even witnesses. And the truth is, everybody's got something in their closet—sure doesn't have to be gayness. So cops at work, they give their brother cops plenty of space."

They all knew this was true.

Brass went on: "Nobody cared what Dectective Templeton did behind his bedroom door, or who he did it with . . . as long as he didn't bring it to the office. And kept helping them win cases."

"And he did that, all right," Grissom said. "Faking and manipulating evidence."

Sofia asked, "What about at the Platinum King?"

"At the Reno PK," Brass said, "Templeton just did his job. It's not an intimate workplace like a cop shop—hotel has hundreds of security employees, including part-timers, and a lot of turnover."

Sara poked her head in. "Who died?"

"Actually," Nick said, "we've broken this case—we're just not sure we can do anything about it."

He filled her in.

"Well, I don't know if it helps," Sara said, "but I've got a match to the shoes in the flower bed. Whoever wore them was definitely inside the house—and in there *before* going outside."

Grissom asked, "How do we know that?"

"There's no dirt from the flower bed in the entryway. Something weird on the shoes, too—didn't show up much in the flower bed, but in the dust lift? Obvious blemish on the sole—almost like a wad of gum on the bottom of his shoe. Our killer committed the crime, then did the outdoor set up—phonying it up as a botched robbery."

"We need more evidence," Grissom said sternly. "Templeton has nothing to tie him to this crime except that his company provided the security for the Salfer home."

"He knows Arrington," Nick said. "And Arrington's a partner in Home Sure."

"Which proves what?" Grissom asked. "That perhaps Arrington's aunt helped Home Sure get the Los Calina gig?"

Brass sighed darkly and said, with obvious reluctance, "Can we really say Arrington and Templeton are better suspects than Susan Gillette? She had motive, opportunity and her fingerprint was found at the crime scene."

Sara was shaking her head. "What motive did that ditsy security guard have?"

"Here's a possibility," Grissom said.

Susan Gillette is called to the Salfer home on a false alarm for what seems the thousandth time. She's a high-strung young woman, and she and the old lady begin to argue; it turns into a screaming match, and it gets physical. . . .

Suddenly Susan has strangled the woman.

What can she do?

She quickly fakes a robbery attempt, using a ladder still in her car—she'd bought it earlier, for her own purposes, home fix-up. But she clumsily leaves a print behind. (Later, she will blame her boss Todd Templeton, saying he asked her to buy the ladder, and that's why the print is there.) She finds men's shoes in the house—belonging to the late husband—and puts them on and leaves a convenient print in the flower bed, to further fake a burglar having committed the crime.

Brass frowned. "I liked it better," he said to Grissom, "when you once were claiming *not* to do theories. . . ."

From the expressions on the faces around him, Brass decided even Grissom seemed to agree.

Arrington's house had not given up a thing.

Catherine and Larkin had been through the living room, the sitting room, dining room, kitchen, two bathrooms, three bedrooms, the laundry room, and the garage . . . without finding so much as a bloody tissue.

The sun had long since gone down.

"Bupkus," Larkin said. "Damn it, anyway. You had enough fun for one day?"

Catherine shook her head. "I want to go back to the laundry room. There's one more place to look."

"Where?" Larkin asked, falling in behind her as she walked through the kitchen.

"Just a stray thought."

"Well here's another, Cath—maybe we need to have the Reno boys pick up Arrington."

"We had enough for a warrant to search the house—but we're not even *close* to an arrest warrant yet. . . ."

In the laundry room, Catherine turned on the overhead light, revealing a washer and dryer to her left. Next to them was an old Formica-covered chrome-legged dinner table whose latterday use was to fold laundry on.

The opposite wall was home to shelves of detergents, soaps, and other cleaners. On the wall at the other end was a door to the double-garage.

"Under the table," she said, pointing a latexed finger, "there's a removable panel—I noticed it before. Might be a crawlspace under the house."

"Doesn't *that* sound like fun . . . no wonder you didn't mention it till last. . . ."

She got out her Mini Maglite and shone its beam into the shadows, like a tiny searchlight on a miniature prison yard during a breakout.

Larkin's eyes followed. "Yeah, there it is. Probably a CSI job, going down there, don't you think?"

She smirked at him. "Not till I get some coveralls on, it isn't."

Those coveralls, and other of her equipment, had been packed in the trunk of Larkin's Taurus, before making the trip out here. After retrieving the workclothes, she returned to Arrington's bathroom in the hallway, between the bedrooms, and changed into them.

When she came back, she found Larkin leaning on the washer. He looked like he was about to fall asleep.

"Am I keeping you up?" she asked.

He shrugged, smiled. "Long week."

"Marty—it's only Wednesday."

"Who asked you?"

She pried up the panel, shimmied under the table, and slipped feet first to the dirt floor of the crawlspace, and got down in there. . . .

No bugs, thankfully—though Grissom would no doubt have been disappointed; but no bugs meant no cobwebs. Also, no light—she switched on her mini Mag. With no room to stand, and barely enough room for her to crawl, the only compensation was how huge the space was, apparently the full size of the house, though her flash could only see a few feet at a time.

She went to work, crawling, like the time.

She didn't know how long she had been down there, but she could feel sweat turning the coveralls damp, and they were dirty, too, of course, and she couldn't wait to get out of this vast grave and get to a shower. Still, she pressed on.

Must be under one of the back bedrooms now, she thought, far away from the laundry room.

She swept the light back and forth until she finally lit the farthest corner. When her light hit it, the beam returned to her, glinted off something.

Something metal.

Something silver.

Scrabbling forward, she closed the gap until she could clearly see the object under the beam: *an aluminum baseball bat.*

She reached the object and examined it closely, carefully—dark spots, dried blood, maybe, on the shaft. Kneeling close, she even saw what appeared to be an auburn hair or two, encrusted in blood.

Not moving the bat, she photographed it with a disposable camera, which she then stuffed back in a coverall pocket. Carefully and with a little difficultly, she took a large evidence bag from another pocket, unfolded it and she placed the bat within; then started the long, slow crawl back toward the laundry-room portal.

It had been a long dirty night, but they had their prize. *But whatever had possessed this idiot to keep the weapon? Why hadn't it been discarded, not hidden?*

As she neared the hole, she called to Larkin, but he didn't respond. Probably outside, getting some air or catching a smoke or something. She lifted the bat up and a hand took it from her.

"Thanks, Marty—didn't think you could hear me."

She popped her head up through the hole and found herself staring at the unseeing eye of a gun barrel, which stared unblinkingly back. Beyond the weapon, a man she assumed to be David Arrington wielded what looked very much like Marty Larkin's Glock.

"He can't hear you," said the small pale dark-haired man. His eyes were dark and glittering behind tortoise-shell glasses, and his sick smile was centered within a wispy mustache and goatee.

"Mr. Arrington," Catherine said.

"Out now, slowly . . ." His voice seemed cool and quiet. ". . . keep your hands on the edge as you pull yourself up."

She did as she was told, and then he practically hauled her the last foot or so, like yanking up something stored down there; he groped down the side of her body until he found her sidearm.

He wrested it from the holster, then waved Larkin's gun at her as a signal to stand up.

She did.

He was a careful one, though, backing up to the laundry-room doorway, stuffing her gun in the waistband of his tan slacks, butt nestling against his charcoal, long-sleeve dress shirt. His short-cut hair looked unkempt—maybe he'd driven back from Reno with the top down . . .

. . . or, more likely, had just tangled with a tough cop.

Out in the kitchen, she could now see Larkin on the floor in a heap, unconscious or dead. Either way, he was no help.

Arrington leveled the gun at her head. "Who the hell are you? What are you doing crawling around underneath my house?"

"Catherine Willows," she said, keeping her voice controlled. "Las Vegas Crime Lab."

Suddenly rage colored the previously controlled voice. "Which entitles you to break into my *home*?"

"The back door was open. And we have a search warrant."

He pulled a wadded piece of paper from his pocket. "So I saw. Do I seem impressed?"

Catherine said nothing.

"You people broke into my house," Arrington said, a little wild-eyed now. "Pretty good chance, don't you think, of a jury acquitting me? And that evidence you found, it'll just disappear."

"You look smarter than that, Mr. Arrington."

"I came home, discovered two home invaders, I panicked . . . and protected myself. Not a bad defense; workable. Fair to even, I'd say. Pretty good odds, for Vegas."

Catherine said nothing.

Arrington's eyes behind the glasses tightened to slits. "What *else* do you people know? What *else* do you have?"

"Plenty. Killing us will only make your lethal injection a certainty."

Eyes and nostrils flared. "Shut up!"

On the floor, behind Arrington, Larkin was starting to move. Alive. At least for now.

Taking a step closer to her, Arrington aimed between her eyes. "I like my odds better with you dead, lady."

Larkin, coming to, groaned.

Arrington spun toward the sound . . .

. . . and Catherine struck.

As Arrington lowered the gun to aim at Larkin, Catherine grabbed the man from behind, locking her arms around his.

Arrington must have had some training, though, because he immediately bent at the waist, using her momentum against her.

Even as her feet lifted off the ground, Catherine clawed for her pistol in Arrington's belt.

Her fingers found the gun butt as she started over. With Arrington bent, she could not wrench the weapon free; but as she came down over the top of him, she squeezed the trigger.

The gun's discharge was a thunderous explosion in the confined space.

Catherine went flying, crashing into the kitchen and practically landing on top of Larkin.

A howling Arrington fell to the floor, gun clattering away from a hand clawing the air in distress. He held his thigh near his crotch as he screamed.

Catherine rolled, came up, pivoted and sprinted toward her attacker.

Arrington tried to get the gun out of his belt, but Catherine dove over him and snatched up Larkin's pistol, then swung back to Arrington just as he pulled her gun free from his waistband. He began to raise the weapon, but she was faster, taking one quick step and laying the cold barrel of Larkin's pistol against Arrington's temple.

"How do you feel about the odds now?" she asked.

"You . . . you shot me!" Hurt, bewildered, his face free of glasses that had fallen off in the melee, he was clutching his thigh, blood squeezing through his fingers.

Her upper lip curled back. "You're lucky I missed," she said.

10

WITH THE PERP IN CUFFS, Catherine Willows took the liberty of getting out of the dirty coveralls and back into her sweater and slacks. Because this had been an officer-involved shooting, she bagged the coveralls in plastic.

Then she gave Grissom a quick call on the cell, to inform him of the arrest—and the baseball bat she'd taken into evidence; he congratulated her, and brought her up to speed on the Arrington/Templeton connection.

"From where I stand," she told Grissom, "we look good for Arrington—but what do we have on Templeton?"

"Not much," Grissom admitted.

"Guy was a detective who played games with evidence, right? You think he's arranged for his partner to take the fall, if the scheme collapses?"

"You asking for a guess, Catherine?"

"Go wild, Gil—make an educated guess."

"Yes."

They broke the connection.

When she returned, Larkin's radio call for an ambulance had brought quick results, the vehicle pulling up just as the NLVPD detective was finally getting around to Mirandizing the suspect.

The paramedics informed Catherine that Arrington's wound was minor enough that it could be dressed here. While the ambulance crew dealt with the suspect, who was seated at a kitchen table in his boxer shorts, his tortoise-shell glasses back on, Catherine corralled Larkin for an explanation.

The detective pointed to a kitchen counter, past where the paramedic activity was going on: a taser gun lay there next to Mr. Coffee.

"Son of a bitch crept up behind me," Larkin said, in a flustered manner that showed he couldn't quite choose between embarrassment and anger, "and tasered my ass!"

Catherine covered her mouth with a hand.

"You think that's funny, Cath?" he asked, frowning, then began to laugh and shake his head.

A smiling Catherine said, "You're to be congratulated not throttling that creep, when you took him into custody."

"Come on—we both know who took him into custody. Catherine Willows, if you ever get tired of the CSI racket, we got a spot for you in plainclothes in North Las Vegas."

She chuckled and touched his sleeve. "Marty—that's one of the nicest things anybody's ever said to me."

Soon, Arrington's superficial wound cleaned and dressed, the paramedics departed, their reluctant host remained seated at the kitchen table, cuffed hands in the lap of his boxers.

Although he had the right to remain silent, Arrington did not choose that option.

"I am going to sue your goddamn asses off," he said, trembling, near tears. "Once I'm done with you, you'll never work in Vegas or law enforcement again. I have a friend who's forgotten more about your profession than you'll ever know! And he'll help me put you people right where you belong—on the street, out of work!"

Catherine, arms folded, stood nearby. Pleasantly, she said, "That friend wouldn't be a certain disgraced former detective from Reno, by any chance?"

Arrington's shocked look was immensely satisfying to Catherine.

"You're gonna love this next part," Larkin said to the seated suspect. "You're a bigshot booker for Doug Clennon, right? Guess what—this time *you're* gettin' booked."

"Hilarious," Arrington said. "Remind me to schedule you at the Platinum King—we need a new men's room attendant."

Larkin growled and helped Arrington up, the suspect wriggling and wrenching.

"Hey!" Arrington said. "Take it easy! Police brutality!"

Catherine rolled her eyes. "Oh, please."

"Listen, lady! I can't walk! You *shot* me!"

"I remember. It's what they call in the movies a flesh wound. You'll live—at least until the needle."

Larkin started to escort Arrington out of the kitchen and the guy howled like a werewolf.

Steadying the suspect, Larkin said, "Stop fighting and walk. I hurt myself worse shaving."

Arrington moaned as he trundled melodramatically along, but at least he did comply, and they got him to the car, and put him in the backseat. Catherine stowed the bat, her bagged coveralls, the bagged taser gun and her other gear in the trunk, and they made the trip to CSI HQ.

Immediately Catherine dropped the bat off at the lab. Nick and Warrick would supervise the evidence gathering and testing of the probable murder weapon while she sat in on the interview with Arrington.

When she approached the interview room, she found Larkin, Brass, and Grissom waiting in the corridor.

Brass said, "Gil says you've got this guy cold for the Angie Dearborn killing."

"We will if the blood and hair on the bat I found under his house match the victim's."

Grissom said, "I'm troubled that he'd hang onto the murder weapon."

Catherine shrugged. "Same thing occurred to me—it was well-hidden, though."

"But a CSI would know to look there," Grissom said.

Brass frowned. "You think Templeton is framing his own partner?"

Grissom said, "Usually the evidence tells its own story—but in this case, you have to wonder whose story is being told."

"What about his aunt?" Catherine asked. "Do we have anything linking this guy to her murder?"

"Nothing," Grissom said, "beyond theories of conspiracy."

They just stood there for several long moments.

Then Catherine asked, "Where does Susan Gillette figure into this?"

"Templeton seems to have framed her," Grissom said. "He was aware of the Gillette woman's run-ins with Mrs. Salfer, and arranged for Gillette to buy and handle the ladder left at the scene. And at the very least, Templeton knew the ex-husband would get the brunt of the investigation into Angela's murder."

Catherine frowned at Grissom. "Do we have anything on Templeton beyond his business partnership with Arrington?"

Brass said, "Well, there's the Home Sure aspect of the Grace Salfer murder—that ladder with Gillette's fingerprint, a Home Sure employee."

"Anything else?"

The detective shook his head. "We haven't even really confirmed that these men are lovers."

"But we're getting there," Grissom said, obviously concerned that a pall had fallen over the investigators. "Sara matched the shoe prints in the flower bed to prints she found in Mrs. Salfer's entryway with the electromagnetic printlifter. They may well be Templeton's shoes."

Catherine frowned thoughtfully at her former supervisor. "How do you see this going down, Gil?"

Arrington is distraught that his aunt is disinheriting him. He had counted on coming into the old woman's money, having put all his savings into Templeton's business.

Templeton convinces his lover that the old woman must

go. But Aunt Grace dying and leaving her money to Angie Dearborn simply won't do—and just killing the Dearborn woman doesn't guarantee the aunt would restore David to her will—perhaps she'd leave her estate to her church, for example. Taking both women out almost simultaneously— but the aunt dying after *Angie—means that the old woman's estate will revert to her next of kin . . . David.*

But David can't face killing his own aunt—he still has some feeling for the woman; so Templeton takes care of Grace Salfer, while David takes his frustrations out on the "bitch" who (from his point of view) cynically wheedled her way into his aunt's good nature and supplanted David in her heart . . . and will.

Catherine said, "So Templeton murdered Grace, Arrington killed Angie, and they even had two patsies, Susan Gillette and Taylor Dearborn, lined up to take the fall."

"That's how I see it," Grissom said. "Nonetheless, we don't have enough probable cause yet to get a judge to issue us a search warrant on Templeton. That makes this Arrington interview crucial."

Grissom followed Brass into the observation booth—where Sara, Sofia, and Greg were already assembled—and Catherine and Larkin went into the interview room.

In his rumpled charcoal dress shirt, David Arrington sat, leaning an elbow on the table and cradling his forehead in his head. He looked sick. *As well he should,* Catherine thought.

She sat across from their suspect, while Larkin remained on his feet, but leaning in with his hands on the tabletop.

Before Larkin could speak, however, Arrington

straightened and seemed suddenly at ease, as he
said, "Why should I talk to you without a lawyer
present?"

Larkin's eyes flared. "Well, then let's send for your
lawyer—sooner he gets here, sooner we can get to
trial, sooner you'll be found guilty."

Arrington just smiled at him. "You're just miffed
over that taser."

Larkin sneered. "You think assaulting an officer is
amusing, David?"

"Is that the worst you people can do? Assault?
You entered my home; I didn't know you had a warrant. You two are lucky to be alive. . . . You, Detective . . . Larkin, is it? That taser wasn't even set that
high. Coulda been set much higher. I could have
killed you, and trust me—I wouldn't lose any sleep."

Catherine asked, "Have you lost any sleep over
Angie Dearborn?"

Arrington turned toward her and couldn't conceal
his distress. ". . . Who?"

Larkin sat.

Catherine said, "Angie Dearborn. The young
woman you brutalized with a baseball bat to get
your aunt's inheritance."

"I didn't 'brutalize' anybody! I, uh, do know that
name. She was my aunt's housekeeper. I don't know
anything about this, uh, Dearborn woman being remembered in Aunt Grace's will."

"Have you lost any sleep over your aunt's murder?"

"I don't even have to dignify that with—"

Catherine shrugged. "You must have had some
attachment left for her, because you couldn't do it
yourself. Your friend Todd did it for you."

"You know, I do want my lawyer. Get me a lawyer."

Catherine looked at Larkin, whose eyes were drooping; they had booted it, he clearly thought.

She didn't.

"Mr. Arrington," she said. "We'll get you a lawyer. But since you almost killed me, have I earned the right to ask you one question, first?"

"I don't know. Have you?"

"Why did you hold onto that bat? Why isn't it in Lake Mead or some landfill right now?"

"That . . . that bat under my house. . . you put it there. You crawled under my house and you framed me."

"We didn't. Maybe your ex-detective friend did."

"Todd didn't put it there!"

"How do you know that? Because *you* did? And if you did, your fingerprints are probably on that bat. Now, I realize you certainly thought to wear gloves, killing Angie Dearborn—but did you think to wear gloves when you hid the bat in that crawlspace?"

The suspect's eyes widened; his mouth dropped open. But he said nothing.

"Perhaps I'm wrong," Catherine said. "Perhaps when the lab reports come back, the blood and hair on that bat won't belong to Angie Dearborn."

He put his elbow on the table again, hand on his head.

"And perhaps the DNA evidence will clear you," Catherine said reasonably.

Arrington frowned at her. "What DNA evidence?"

Larkin suddenly lurched forward, grabbed Arrington's sleeve, and jerked it up to show three long ragged red streaks on his forearm.

Through his teeth, the detective said, "DNA from these scratches—in the skin we scraped from under the dead Dearborn woman's nails."

Arrington jerked his arm away and pulled down the sleeve of his shirt. "You can't manhandle me like that! My . . . my cat did this."

Catherine gave Larkin a sharp look and the detective sat back down.

She leaned toward Arrington. "David—please. You're not stupid and neither are we. You don't even own a cat. I searched your house, remember— no litter box, no water bowl."

Arrington just shrugged.

"Again," Catherine said, "we may be wrong about you. You tell me—the blood on the shirt in Angie's bedroom—maybe that isn't your blood. Maybe it isn't your blood in the kitchen sink and drain trap."

Arrington's shoulders slumped; he was staring toward Catherine, but not at her, his eyes fixed on the table right before her.

"If so," Catherine said, "I apologize. When all that evidence turns out to clear you, well . . . you *may* need a lawyer, just to sue the county. And will our collective face be red."

Arrington sat so still he might have been dead, himself.

"On the other hand, if your prints are on the bat, if Angie's blood and hair are on it, too . . . and if it was your skin under her nails, and your blood on the shirt and in the sink and . . . well, you might want to consider cooperating. You might find that the district attorney would view cooperation favorably—it's been known for someone in your position to trade death row for a prison sentence."

"What . . . what kind of cooperation?"

"I have the idea that you weren't the instigator, here. That someone you loved manipulated you and used you and talked you into participating in a murder scheme that really wasn't your style. You've never even been arrested before, have you, Mr. Arrington?"

"No . . . that's true. I've never been arrested."

Catherine's eyebrows went up. "Of course, I could be wrong. You may have killed Angie in the evening, and then in the middle of that same night, murdered your aunt."

"I did no such thing!"

"I may be wrong, and this was all your idea, *only* your idea. After all, you probably knew your aunt's security code, or perhaps you knocked on the door and she just turned off the alarm and let you in. No reason for her not to open the door to her only living relative on a rainy night."

Larkin said, "Motive and means and opportunity. The big three, David."

Arrington's face contorted; was he scowling or about to weep?

Catherine asked, "Mr. Arrington, I would just like to know . . . did you hate your aunt? Or did you love her?"

He swallowed. "Yes."

Then he began to cry.

Catherine came around and sat beside the suspect. She gave Arrington several tissues and waited. Finally . . .

"Tell me," she said.

"Aunt Grace . . . she'd always been so kind to me. Supportive. My mother was kind of a . . . cold fish, but Grace, she encouraged me, my interest in the arts, if I had a performance . . . or in sports, if I had a game, she'd be there. She was my biggest cheerleader."

"She didn't know you were gay."

He shook his head. "No. I think my parents did, but we never discussed it, and they both died, fairly young, and Grace . . . she was a little unsophisticated, as I guess, in such things. When I moved back to town . . . maybe I was a little self-serving in wanting to get close to her again, since I'd invested so heavily with Home Sure . . ."

Behind the glass, Grissom raised a fist in "Yes" fashion.

". . . and when we sat down and talked one afternoon, she said, 'David, I'm leaving everything to you, on one condition.' I asked what condition that was, and she said, 'You've been a bachelor too long—you've sown your wild oats, you and I are all that's left of the Salfer family line . . . I want you to settle down and get married. I'll never have grandchildren, but I can have grandnieces and grandnephews.' I suppose . . . I suppose I could have played some kind of game with her, and if I'd taken time to think about it, only . . . what she said kind of blindsided me, and I blurted the truth out. I told her, 'For Christ sake, Aunt Grace—can you be so blind? I'm gay! I'm a gay man, and I'm in a serious, committed relationship, and . . .'"

He began to cry again.

More tissues, then he said: "We talked several times after that. She said it was a sin, and I could be forgiven, and change. It was a choice and I could be the other way, the 'natural' way. She said she still loved me—'love the sinner, hate the sin'—but she wouldn't listen to any rational argument."

"*Were* there arguments, David?"

He nodded. "We fell out . . . completely. I did continue to call her, but it was strained. She told me I'd chosen my life, and that I seemed to be financially successful without her anyway, and she was leaving everything to her 'little angel,' that housekeeper. It's criminal how these leeches worm their way into gullible old people's lives! Still, Aunt Grace always said . . . always said she loved me."

Catherine allowed him to cry again, then asked, "Why keep the bat, David?"

"It was a . . . memento."

Catherine winced. "Of the crime?"

"No! No . . . nothing so . . . so grotesque. It was from middle school."

"Middle . . . ?"

"I was on the baseball team. I hit the winning homer. Everybody crowded around, I was up on the team's shoulders. I really felt accepted. I really felt . . . felt like a real man."

He leaned forward, covering his face, but the tears were over; he was out of them. "My aunt was there. She saw me hit that home run."

"Why . . . why use it in a murder, David?"

"I didn't use it! Todd used it! Well . . . no . . . he went and got it from my study and he gave it to me and said it was perfect for . . . 'doing the deed.' I think he . . . think he thought it was . . . funny. I'd told him about hitting the home run, and he thought I was a silly, ridiculous fool, cherishing a moment like that. We argued about it, a long time ago . . . but I'm sure that's why he talked me into using it. He said he'd researched Taylor Dearborn, and that before the guy became a doper, he'd been involved in sports, played a lot of baseball . . . something like that."

"If you will give us a full statement," Catherine said, "and detail Todd's role in these murders . . . and testify against him . . . your prospects for having a future will be greatly improved."

He eyed her suspiciously. "You're not really this nice. You're not really concerned about me. You're just manipulating me."

She gave him a sad smile. "Not the first time someone's done that to you, is it, David?"

He drew in a deep breath. "I'll make a statement. I'll make a full statement. But you have to promise me one thing."

"Yes?"

"You've got to protect me—or he'll kill me, too."

"Who?"

"Todd. Todd Templeton. We've been together for over ten years—I know how he thinks. And it isn't pretty."

In the observation booth, Grissom had his cell phone out, punching in Judge Scott's home number. It was late, but that could not be helped.

As the phone trilled in his ear, Grissom turned to Sara and Sofia. "We've still got that search warrant for Arrington's house. Get out there and find any evidence of Templeton's presence in that place. They're not living together, but if they've had a long-term relationship, there's got to be something."

Both women nodded and left.

In the interview room, Arrington was answering Larkin's questions, the detective low-key and all business now.

"How did you get into Angie Dearborn's apartment, David?"

"That was easy. I had an old badge Todd gave me. He told me one badge looks pretty much like another, so it wouldn't matter that it said Reno on it. All I had to do was flash it in the peephole, Todd said, and tell the Dearborn girl I wanted to ask her some questions about one of her neighbors. Way it worked out was actually a little different. . . . I was hiding in the back stairs when her ex stormed out; I'd heard them fighting, which was perfect. I just knocked on the door, held up the badge, said one of the neighbors had called and that I just wanted to make sure she was okay. She opened right up, let me in. But I didn't anticipate she'd be such a fighter—it's a good thing I had a lot of resentment built up, because she had a lot of fight in her—wildcat. Nearly scratched my arm off."

Catherine asked, "Why would Todd want to frame two innocent people, like Taylor Dearborn and Susan Gillette?"

"Partly to deflect attention away from us, partly because . . . there's some guy who works here named Grissle or something that Todd wanted to get back at. Busybody who got Todd fired in Reno. Outsmarting this character was to Todd some sort of . . .

I dunno, sick game. Plus, Todd figured if things did get hairy, he could always claim that this Grissle was harassing him just like he did in Reno."

"Could the name have been Grissom?" Catherine asked. "I'm not trying to prompt you, David, but—"

"*That's* the name. *Grissom.*"

Catherine glanced toward the mirror . . .

. . . behind which Grissom's cell phone rang, and he answered.

Judge Scott approved his search warrant, promised to fax it over immediately, and Grissom broke the connection.

"Let's go," he said to Brass.

In the car, the detective drove while Grissom stared straight ahead.

"You were right about this guy," Brass said.

"But you were right I should've recused myself," Grissom said. "I hope my presence doesn't screw up the prosecution."

"How could it," Brass said, "with his boyfriend singing chapter and verse back there like that."

"If you're uncomfortable with me helping make this bust," Grissom said, not looking at his friend, "drop me off somewhere and I'll find my way home."

"Shut up," Brass said.

The drive was a long one, and they rode in silence until Grissom's cell rang again.

"Grissom."

"It's Sara."

"Find anything?"

"The ALS showed several stains on the sheets of Arrington's bed. We're getting them to the DNA lab now, along with some hairs we found on the pillows. The hairs appear to be from two different sources. If Arrington and Templeton have been sleeping together in that bed, we'll know it."

"Fast track," he said, and broke the connection as they were getting off Highway 93 in Boulder City.

Templeton lived in an apartment on Avenue G, just off Adams Boulevard, in a complex maybe a ten-minute drive from David Arrington's house. They walked up the concrete outside stairs to the second floor, the place reminding Grissom more of a sixties-era motel than an apartment house.

Brass knocked and they got no answer.

Behind the curtains of the picture window, Grissom could see no light.

Brass pounded on the door again and this time, after a moment, illumination leaked out around the curtain border.

"Who is it?" Templeton's voice bellowed from behind the closed door.

Before Brass could speak, Grissom called, "Gil Grissom, Todd."

"Always a pleasure, Gil! *More* proof of your goddamn harassment!"

"We have a search warrant, Todd."

"Bend over and file it, Gil!"

Brass glanced Grissom's way. "Such vulgarity—I don't think he likes you."

"You can open the door, Todd," the CSI said, "or we can kick it in. Want to skip that step?"

A lock clicked, then another and finally a chain slid as the door opened slowly.

"Let's see your damn paper," Templeton growled,

hair askew, looking half-awake in a UNLV T-shirt and sweatpants with leather slippers. The slippers reminded Grissom of Grace Salfer's, a little. *Hell to be disturbed in the middle of the night . . .*

Brass handed Templeton the faxed search warrant and the Home Sure honcho sighed and moved aside for them.

The tall, sharp-featured suspect stood reading the warrant as the detective and CSI appraised the living room, done in tasteful Asian art and furniture, a space Grissom guessed had been feng shuied within an inch of its life. Next to the door sat a small wooden rack with four different pairs of shoes—two the wingtip variety the CSI sought.

Astounded, Templeton looked up from the warrant. "You wanna look at my *shoes*?"

"Yeah, Todd," Grissom said, smiling. "Since we can't look into your soul."

"Oh, you're a fuckin' riot, Grissom. You two heels cool *your* heels while I call my lawyer!"

"That's your right," Brass said casually. "As is remaining silent, and having a lawyer appointed for you if you cannot afford one."

Templeton frowned. "What the hell . . . ?"

Brass added, "But from what your partner in life and love, David Arrington, is telling us, about your double-homicide inheritance scheme, you probably do want to call some top-end criminal lawyer. Legal aid may not cut this."

"I don't believe David told you a damned thing," Templeton said. "And what's this 'love' bullshit? He's an investor in Home Sure, and a friend. We're both straight men who've dated plenty of women. End of story."

Bagging the first pair of shoes, Grissom interrupted. "Just the beginning of the 'story,' really, according to David, who's shared everything about you two for the last ten years . . . including your pact to kill Grace Salfer and Angela Dearborn, and frame a pair of innocent bystanders."

"David is an emotional individual," Templeton blustered. "I like him, but he goes off on wild emotional tangents, and clearly his aunt's death has, hell, unhinged him somehow."

"Work on that," Brass said, hauling out the cuffs. "Maybe there's something in there for you. . . . Hands behind your back, please."

"And anyway, you'll make new friends inside," Grissom said. "Of course interaction is limited on death row."

The look of hatred in Templeton's eyes was not one Grissom would soon . . . *would ever* . . . forget.

"You . . . have . . . *nothing*."

Grissom inspected the soles of the second pair of shoes and saw the old chewing gum on one, just as Sara had predicted. "Turns out I *can* look into your soul. My God, Todd . . . you are still sloppy."

"Go to hell, Grissom. Your presence here taints this whole case!"

"Does it? Or does it merely point up that you were always a short-cut guy—that was your flaw as a detective and crime lab supervisor, and it's your downfall as a criminal 'mastermind.' "

"This isn't over, Grissom."

"It's over. From the start, you made sure only the worst of your Home Sure crew were assigned to Los Calina when your game got played. But you were in such a rush to frame Susan Gillette, to make the crime scene look like she was the one trying to fool us, that you used your own damn shoes! Probably put your hands inside them and pressed down, to imitate the lighter weight of a small woman. You were a detective, Todd—what do you think? What's your expert opinion? When I get these back in the lab, am I going to find evidence from that flower bed on them?"

"I want my lawyer."

Brass said, "We'll get you one at HQ."

Grissom got right in the suspect's face. "We've already got your prints in Salfer's house . . . and I'll bet we can trace directly to you the failure of Home Sure replacing that sick guard at the gate the murder night."

Templeton spat in Grissom's face.

Grissom brushed it off with his latex-gloved hand, and said, "I'm not ready for a DNA sample just yet, but thanks, Todd. . . .You really should have thrown the shoes away. Of course, maybe you were waiting for that inheritance to come through, to buy a spiffy new pair."

"You planted this evidence," Templeton said. "And all you've got besides that is David. I told you he's unstable. He did this, and is trying to pin it on me."

"Hey," Brass said lightly, "there's another way to go. Work on that one, too."

Templeton lurched forward, but Brass held him

back as the suspect said to Grissom, "My lawyer will blow David out of the water, and your planted evidence, too!"

"He'll try," Grissom said. "And maybe your attorney *will* be able to make David look unstable—stable people don't generally murder their own aunts, much less the aunt's housekeeper. But what I heard David say had the ring of truth."

"Subjective crap," Templeton snarled. "Some CSI you are!"

Grissom held up the shoe again. "I'm a pretty fair CSI, Todd. See, when you don't fudge evidence, when you gather it properly, and test it properly, you can trust it. People lie all the time; but the evidence doesn't know how, even when a sad case like you tries to manipulate it."

"I'll beat this, Grissom. And I'll beat you!"

Brass dragged Templeton toward the door, but Grissom stopped them, with a hand on the detective's arm.

"Just don't get it, do you, Todd? This isn't about me, it never was. It's not even about you—I never had anything against you, personally. It's about the evidence, the science. It's always been about the science."

Templeton looked back at the CSI blankly. Maybe he would never understand.

Brass took the killer out, Grissom trailing after, pulling the apartment door closed behind him. *Well, if Templeton landed a life sentence and not death row, at least the man would have plenty of time to ponder it. . . .*

Brass loaded Templeton into the backseat, then he and Grissom climbed in front. As the car pulled away from the apartment, Grissom kept an eye on Templeton in the rearview mirror.

"You're so goddamn full of yourself," Templeton said, sitting forward with his hands cuffed behind, chin crinkled like a hurt child. "Gil Grissom—the perfect CSI!"

"Never claimed to be," Grissom said. "It's an imperfect world; always will be, as long as human beings are around. And only a fool thinks there's such a thing as a perfect crime."

A TIP OF THE TEST TUBE

My assistant Matthew Clemens helped me develop the plot of *Killing Game*, and worked up a lengthy story treatment, which included all of his considerable forensic research, from which I could work. Matthew—an accomplished true-crime writer, who has collaborated with me on numerous published short stories—does most of the on-site Vegas research, and is largely responsible for any sense of the real city that might be found herein.

We would once again like to acknowledge criminalist Lieutenant Chris Kauffman CLPE—the Gil Grissom of the Bettendorf Iowa Police Department—who provided comments, insights, and information; Chris has been an important member of our CSI team since the first novel, *Double Dealer*, and remains vital to our efforts. Thank you, too, to another major contributor to our research, Lieutenant Paul Van Steenhuyse, Scott County Sheriff's Office; and also Sergeant Jeff Swanson, Scott County Sheriff's Office (for autopsy and crime-scene assistance).

Books consulted include two works by Vernon J. Gerberth: *Practical Homicide Investigation Checklist and Field Guide* (1997) and *Practical Homicide Investigation: Tactics, Procedures and Forensic Investigation* (1996).

Also helpful were *Crime Scene: The Ultimate Guide to Forensic Science*, Richard Platt; and *Scene of the Crime: A Writer's Guide to Crime-Scene Investigations* (1992), Anne Wingate, Ph.D. Any inaccuracies, however, are my own.

At Pocket Books, Ed Schlesinger, our gracious editor, provided a keen eye and solid support. The producers of *C.S.I.: Crime Scene Investigation* sent along scripts, background material (including show bibles) and episode tapes. Thanks especially to Corinne Marrinan, the coauthor (with Mike Flaherty) of the indispensible Pocket Books publication, *CSI: Crime Scene Investigation Companion*.

Anthony E. Zuiker is gratefully acknowledged as the creator of this concept and these characters; and the cast must be applauded for vivid, memorable characterizations. Our thanks, too, to various *C.S.I.* writers for their inventive and well-documented scripts, which we draw upon for backstory—particularly true in this novel, which attempts to deal with the volatile period following the break-up of the original CSI team.

Finally, thanks to the fans of the show who have extended their enthusiasm into following these novels.

ABOUT THE AUTHOR

MAX ALLAN COLLINS, a Mystery Writers of America "Edgar" nominee in both fiction and nonfiction categories, was hailed in 2004 by *Publishers Weekly* as "a new breed of writer." He has earned an unprecedented fourteen Private Eye Writers of America "Shamus" nominations for his historical thrillers, winning twice for his Nathan Heller novels, *True Detective* (1983) and *Stolen Away* (1991).

His other credits include film criticism, short fiction, songwriting, trading-card sets, and movie/TV tie-in novels, including *Air Force One*, *In the Line of Fire*, and the *New York Times*-bestselling *Saving Private Ryan*.

His graphic novel *Road to Perdition* is the basis of the Academy Award–winning DreamWorks 2002 feature film starring Tom Hanks, Paul Newman, and Jude Law, directed by Sam Mendes. His many comics credits include the *Dick Tracy* syndicated strip; his own *Ms. Tree*; *Batman*; and *CSI: Crime Scene Investigation*, based on the hit TV series for which he has also written three video games, two jigsaw puzzles, and a *USA Today*–bestselling series of novels.

An independent filmmaker in his native Iowa, he wrote and directed *Mommy*, premiering on Lifetime in 1996, as well as a 1997 sequel, *Mommy's Day*. The screenwriter of *The Expert*, a 1995 HBO World Premiere, he wrote and directed the innovative made-for-DVD feature, *Real Time: Siege at Lucas Street Market* (2000). His latest indie feature, *Shades of Noir* (2004), is an anthology of his short films, including his award-winning documentary, *Mike Hammer's Mickey Spillane*. He recently completed a documentary, *CAVEMAN: V.T. Hamlin and Alley Oop*, and a DVD boxed set of his films will appear next year.

Collins lives in Muscatine, Iowa, with his wife, writer Barbara Collins; their son Nathan is a recent graduate in computer science and Japanese at the University of Iowa in nearby Iowa City.

Join top authors for the ultimate cruise experience. Spend 7 days in the Mexican Riviera aboard the luxurious Carnival Pride™. Start in Los Angeles/Long Beach, CA, and visit Puerto Vallarta, Mazatlan, and Cabo San Lucas. Enjoy all this with a ship full of authors, entertainers, and book lovers on the

"Authors at Sea" Cruise

April 2–9, 2006.

Mail in this coupon with proof of purchase* for the book *CSI: Killing Game* to receive $250 per person off the regular **"Authors at Sea"** Cruise price. One coupon per person required to receive $250 discount. Coupon must be redeemed by April 1, 2006. For complete details call **1-877-ADV-NTGE** or visit **www.authorsatsea.com**.

PRICES
STARTING AT
$749
PER PERSON
WITH
COUPON!

If you enjoyed *CSI: Killing Game*, be sure to look for other *CSI* titles from Pocket Star Books!

*Proof of purchase is original sales receipt with the book purchased circled. (No copies allowed.)
**Plus applicable taxes, fees and gratuities.

Carnival
The Most Popular Cruise Line in the World.

GET $250 OFF

AUTHORS AT SEA
AuthorsatSea.com

Name (Please Print)

Address   Apt. No.

City   State   Zip

Email Address

See Following Page for Terms and Conditions.

For booking form and complete information,
go to **www.authorsatsea.com** or call **1-877-ADV-NTGE**.

12938

Carnival Pride™

April 2–9, 2006
7-Day Exotic Mexican Riviera Itinerary

DAY	PORT	ARRIVE	DEPART
Sun	Los Angeles/Long Beach, CA		4:00 P.M.
Mon	"Book Lover's Day" at Sea		
Tue	"Book Lover's Day" at Sea		
Wed	Puerto Vallarta, Mexico	8:00 A.M.	10:00 P.M.
Thu	Mazatlan, Mexico	9:00 A.M.	6:00 P.M.
Fri	Cabo San Lucas, Mexico	7:00 A.M.	4:00 P.M.
Sat	"Book Lover's Day" at Sea		
Sun	Los Angeles/Long Beach, CA	9:00 A.M.	

Ports of call subject to weather conditions.

TERMS AND CONDITIONS

Payment Schedule:
50% due upon booking
Full and final payment due by February 10, 2006
Acceptable forms of payment are Visa, MasterCard, American Express, Discover, and checks. The cardholder must be one of the passengers traveling. A fee of $25 will apply for all returned checks. Check payments must be made payable to Advantage International, LLC and sent to: Advantage International, LLC, 195 North Harbor Drive, Suite 4206, Chicago, IL 60601

CHANGE/CANCELLATION:
Notice of change/cancellation must be made in writing to Advantage International, LLC.

Change:
Changes in cabin category may be requested and can result in increased rate and penalties. A name change is permitted 60 days or more prior to departure and will incur a penalty of $50 per name change. Deviation from the group schedule and package is a cancellation.

Cancellation:

181 days or more prior to departure	$250 per person
180–121 days or more prior to departure	50% of the package price
120–61 days prior to departure	75% of the package price
60 days or less prior to departure	100% of the package price (nonrefundable)

U.S. and Canadian citizens are required to present a valid passport or original birth certificate and state issued photo ID (driver's license). All other nationalities must contact the consulate of the various ports that are visited for verification of documentation.

We strongly recommend trip cancellation insurance!

ADDITIONAL TERMS
This offer is only good on purchases made from October 25, 2005, through April 1, 2006. This offer cannot be combined with other offers or discounts. The discount can only be used for the Authors at Sea Cruise and is not valid for any other Carnival cruises. You must submit an original purchase receipt as proof of purchase in order to be eligible for the discount. Void outside of the U.S. and where prohibited, taxed, or restricted by law. Coupons may not be reproduced, copied, purchased or sold. Incomplete submissions or submissions in violation of these terms will not be honored. Not responsible for late, lost, incomplete, illegible, postage due or misdirected mail. Submissions will not be returned. Improper use or redemption constitutes fraud. Any fraudulent submission (including duplicate requests) will be prosecuted to the fullest extent of the law. Theft, diversion, reproduction, transfer, sale or purchase of this offer form and/or cash register receipts is prohibited and constitutes fraud. Consumer must pay sales taxes on the price of the cruise.

For further details call 1-877-ADV-NTGE or visit www.authorsatsea.com.

For booking form and complete information,
go to www.authorsatsea.com or call 1-877-ADV-NTGE.

Complete coupon and booking form and mail both to:
Advantage International, LLC
195 North Harbor Drive, Suite 4206, Chicago, IL 60601

12938